BIG JIM

by
David Lucero

For Martha and Carlo
You have always encouraged
me to do what feels right.

Big Jim
by David Lucero

Published 2015 by The Light Network
Copyright © David Lucero

Printed in the United States

Covoer Design by Javier Canez

Interior layout by Christi Koehl

Edited by Keidi Keating

ISBN: 978-0-9966403-8-1

Endorsements

"In David Lucero's gripping novel, Big Jim battles an impossibly gigantic Cape buffalo on a mystical mission to wipe out the white hunters who are decimating Africa's wildlife. Throughout this novel the reader is taken on a journey deep in the African bush for the final encounter under the watchful eye of the witchdoctor responsible for summoning the evil creature. In the climactic kill-or-be-killed battle the reader is on the edge-of-your-seat as Big Jim faces off his enemy in the long grass."

Roger L. Conlee, author of
Dare the Devil, The Hindenburg Letter, and other historical novels.

"Big Jim takes the reader on a safari where one can feel the heat and smell the dust of the hunt!"

InD'tale Magazine

"The 'you-are-there' action captures attention from opening to closing page. Big Jim presents a delightfully involving African saga for readers which explores so much more than the thrill of the hunt alone. Readers will appreciate a hunter's perspective as well as insights on wildlife management processes and challenges in a novel replete with insights on relationships and motivations."

Midwest Book Review

"Big Jim is a story of friendships and rivalries, of stunning scenery with unsurpassed beauty and the brutal reality of death that lurks—even stalks—those who don't give the land and wildlife their full respect. Lucero's book dazzles the senses of the reader with the soundtrack of safari camp activity and proves Africa is a land where the hunter can quickly become the hunted, where heroes tower over the landscape and civilized society tries its hand at the untamed bush."

Susan Colvin Brewer,
writer and safari traveler

"Big Jim *introduced me to the Africa of the 1950s. It's filled with larger-than-life characters traveling across rich, beautiful African landscapes where death can strike in the blink of an eye. Readers will be left of the edge of their seat as they travel on safari with a hunter facing his greatest challenge.*"

Matt T. Schott, award winning Sci-Fi author of
Lord Syler and the Earth Defense Force

Acknowledgments

There are two people responsible for me writing this novel. The first is my wife, Martha, for asking me to write something *she* could read. Her favorite author is none other than Stephen King. At that time I was only familiar with his fame as a writer of supernatural stories. I told her that I write action novels. She still challenged me to write a story she could read.

The only story I could come up with close enough to her choice of books was the adventure/thriller novel *Big Jim*. I'd been thinking of this type of book for some time because I've always admired the golden days of safaris from films I saw made in the 1950s. I owe my mother thanks for that, seeing how she introduced me to the movie classics I still love to this day. In *Big Jim* I figured a way of bringing a supernatural theme to an adventure/thriller I believe will meet her challenge.

My son, Carlo, also played an important part in me writing this story and encouraging me to move forward with its publication. This was his favorite story from the manuscripts I've written. So here you have it, son.

I am grateful to the authors, and professional hunters, Brian Herne and Peter Hathaway Capstick. Their books I read for my research helped me understand the unusual bond between hunters and prey.

I wish to extend thanks to Roger Conlee, Matt Schott, Susan Colvin Brewer, InD'tale Magazine, and Midwest Book Reviews for reviewing my book. Their feedback was essential to me. Once again I am grateful to Javier Canez for my cover design. He nailed it, which proves he is a true professional and has a good vision for what works.

In an odd way I am grateful to Stephen King. His book *On Writing* stated how the editor is always right. Thanks to my former human resources trainer, Susan Purcell, I learned how to look at myself through other peoples' eyes in order to better understand what they see. It is because of these two people that I am able to accept a critique of my work without feeling judged.

Lastly, I wish to extend a big thank you to my editor, Keidi Keating, for making my book come to light.

Prologue

Legends are not born in Africa. They are made.

Africa 1953

The hunter raised his heavy double rifle to shoulder level and took careful aim at his target. His concentration was disturbed momentarily when beads of perspiration rolled down his forehead, stinging his eyes. He could not help lowering his rifle, a Westley Richards .577—one of the best hunting rifles preferred by hunters on the continent—to wipe his eyes dry with a handkerchief. He always kept one in his right breast pocket for this simple piece of cloth always proved useful.

Like now. He reflected on how his English friend and business partner, Caesar Wilde, once told him, "A gentleman never travels without a handkerchief."

The hunter licked his dry lips and looked up at the sky. The sun was incredibly hot, beating down on him like a hammer. He was, however, dressed in attire to withstand the elements of the African bush. His broad-brimmed hat, long-sleeved flannel shirt, and long trousers kept him from being burnt to a crisp.

How natives tolerate this heat is something I'll never understand. He shook his head at the thought of the many privations the local tribes endured. *The perks of civilization have certainly spoiled us.*

The hunter longed for a drink. Not for water, as he preferred scotch. He wasn't a drunk, although lately most people would think him to be. His life had been turned upside down when his safari outfitting company took a crippling turn during the height of safari season.

For decades an African safari was an adventure reserved for the rich and famous. Royal families, politicians, and wealthy businessmen splurged on trips most people read about in books and magazines. For the average person, this was the closest they believed they would ever come to journey on a safari.

Then Hollywood came to Africa.

Films like *The Macomber Affair* and *King Solomon's Mines* glorified the Great White Hunter and adventures in the Dark Continent. Famous actors such as Gary Cooper, Clark Gable, Robert Stack, and more brought attention to this way of life and business boomed for most outfitters.

But not for James Peck.

His clients came far and few between. Not due to his lack of hunting prowess, but because of plain and simple bad luck.

When Hollywood film crews selected competitor outfitters other than *Peck and Wilde's African Safaris* he lost out on the publicity vacuum that followed. Everyone and his uncle wanted to hunt with the same professional white hunters who brought Africa to the silver screen.

Then author Robert Ruark wrote a book, *Horn of the Hunter*, a bestseller, which glorified Jim's friend, Harry Selby, as the epitome of the Great White Hunter. Ruark claimed Selby to be the perfect gentleman. *'He was good at playing cards, selecting good campsites, and finding plenty of game to go for a shooting. Not to forget that he kept lion, hyena, and other wildlife from eating us!'* The book not only made Ruark well-known, but brought fame and clients to Selby's doorstep.

The smug bastard even got an all expenses trip to New York, Jim reflected with envy.

Everyone wanted to hunt with Harry Selby. He grew so busy that he employed other hunters to work for his company so he could take on the extra clients. He even offered a job to Jim, which he turned down.

Maybe that wasn't such a smart move after all. Jim stuffed the handkerchief back into his breast pocket. *If I'd taken Harry up on his offer I'd be hunting with some wealthy businessman paying me through the nose to find game. Each night I'd eat roasted guineafowl with potatoes on the side, and drink champagne, beer—or both. After a game of cards and telling stories by the fire, I'd turn in and sleep comfortably in my tent.*

He shook his head in disgust. *Instead I'm here cropping elephants and buffalo.*

Jim disliked this form of killing. *Cropping* was not hunting, it was a method used to scale back over-populated herds from devastating the territory. The Game Department employed professional hunters for this task in return for lower licensing fees and privileges allowing them to take clients in selected territories teeming with game.

Jim knew it was something he could not pass. If he could not attract the rich and famous due to not being rich and famous enough himself then he could attract clients looking to hunt dirt cheap. Next to hiring the hunter himself, license fees for game were expensive. The more a client paid, the more comfortable his accommodations would be. There would be wapagazis (porters) to cook, skin game, fish, and set up camp. Comfortable tents, cots, plenty of food and drink, and the best hunters familiar enough with the territory to ensure the client made the most of his time hunting the *Big Five.*

"If I can coax clients to accept the thrill of the hunt versus the comfort of camp life, I'll do this with cheap fees," Jim boasted to his partner, Caesar Wilde.

Caesar protested lowering camp life standards would not attract paying clients, however Jim was adamant.

"If Ikram Hassan could do it and stay in business, so can we," exclaimed Jim.

Ikram Hassan was one of the few successful non-white professional hunters of his time. His company, *Poor Man's Safaris,* kept his prices lower than most outfitters. His tactic worked, and his business thrived for the rest of his life, employing family and friends who remained with him indefinitely.

"Don't worry," Jim said to Caesar. "I've no intention of being poor. It's only a means to keep our company afloat until things turn around for the better."

Caesar did not like it, but respected his partner's intentions.

Besides, Jim was the dominant partner of their outfitting company, *Peck and Wilde's African Safaris*. Having his partner's name at the head of their company disturbed Caesar.

"Americans have everything as it is," he confided in a letter to his sister. "They seem to press for more each day, despite having everything."

But Caesar dropped the matter for the time being. Everyone eventually has their day, he reasoned.

Jim moved stealthily toward the herd of elephant *(Loxodonta Africana)*. He stood downwind, which was good. They had superior sense of smell and hearing. If the herd knew he stood less than 50 yards from them, they would instantly charge.

Dense thickets and acacia trees provided the hunter with cover. Elephant eye sight was similar to humans, so as long as he remained still and out of sight he was relatively safe.

Jim recognized the lead bull elephant. It had the longest, heaviest pair of tusks he had seen in years. How this bull escaped hunters for long enough to grow such a pair was astonishing.

Just then another elephant approached the bull. It was smaller than the bull, but bigger than others in the herd. This was the master of the herd, the cow. The female sometimes proved dominant over males, picking and choosing its mate carefully. Bull elephants fought each other for mating rights, but their toughest fight proved earning the affection of the cow elephants. They remained distant and choosy over their mate. Proving oneself took more than a battle between tuskers. The bull needed to be tender and affectionate.

They have more in common with us than eyesight, Jim thought.

Then something happened.

The herd stopped moving. Their large ears stopped flapping against their giant heads and perked up at attention. Their heads tilted slowly side to side, and their eyes scanned the thickets.

They know I'm here. What went wrong? Jim had no idea, and remained as silent as humanly possible. If he gave away his position it could spell his end.

He tapped the cotton ashbag dangling on his waist belt. A tiny cloud of wood ash floated from the bag in the direction of the herd.

I'm downwind. So how do they know I'm here?

BOOM! BOOM!

Jim recognized the sound of the blasts. It was a heavy double rifle from the type designed by gunmakers capable of bringing down the biggest, toughest beasts in Africa.

Probably a Rigby .470 or an Army and Navy .450 double rifles, he thought. Both weapons fired a 500-grain caliber bullet traveling at 2,150 feet per second. No human could survive a gunshot from one of those rifles, and it never ceased to amaze hunters how some game took two, three, and even four shots before collapsing.

The female elephant, the cow, took both rounds in the side of its head. The cow loosed a high-pitched shriek from its raised trunk, the kind of shriek which made one's skin crawl. It was not a cry of anger, but of sheer pain. The cow swayed from side to side, lowered its trunk, and crumpled to the ground.

The bull elephant ran to its mate, shoving its tusks beneath the cow in a wasteful attempt to get her to her feet. But the cow did not move. The bull lifted its head and raised its trunk high, trumpeting in defiance. It turned in the direction where Jim remained under cover of the dense thickets. The bull trumpeted again and charged.

Jim had no idea how, but the bull elephant knew he was there. Its eyes bulged with anger and determination, and its ears flapped wildly against its head, a sure sign of how angry this creature was.

Jim raised his Westley Richards .577 double rifle and took aim. Between his fingers in his left hand, the one holding the barrel steady, were two cigar-sized cartridges for reloading. The index finger of his right hand touched the trigger gently. He exhaled half his breath and held it.

The bull elephant's all-out charge would have sent most men running for dear life. Even paying clients on occasion dropped their rifles and took off like a cheetah at the sight of an African bull elephant ploughing toward them like a speeding locomotive. Indeed, the speed and agility of such a large animal amazed everyone.

Jim, however, remained unphased. He stood tall, feet shoulder-width apart, hat pushed slightly back on his forehead, rifle at shoulder level with his head resting on the stock.

"Wait," he said silently. "Wait."

He squeezed the triggers for each barrel, one after the other.

BOOM! BOOM!

With amazing speed, Jim ejected the spent shells and reloaded. He snapped the barrels shut with the stock, cocked the triggers, and raised the double rifle, all in one smooth motion.

BOOM! BOOM!

The bull elephant did not stop. It trumpeted a shriek of anger, crashing through the thickets, snapping trunks of fallen acacia trees beneath its powerful clubbed feet. The bull had determination and stamina unlike any other Jim had faced, and he had experienced many similar charges since becoming a professional hunter.

Jim backed away and pulled two more cartridges from the loops sewn over the breast pockets of his vest for holding spare ammunition. The elephant was a mere 20 yards away when he fired both barrels. This time the elephant came to an abrupt halt, kicking up red dust from the earth. It shrieked a deafening cry, and then ploughed forward.

Jim ran backwards, ejecting the spent shells and reaching for another two cartridges. This time, he was not quick enough.

The elephant reached him and swung its trunk wildly, striking Jim on the side. He flew ten feet before crashing into heavily-thorned thickets, which cut into him and tore his shirt and trousers. Jim cried out in pain from the shock of being pricked by so many thorns stinging his body. He clutched his rifle for dear life and knew it was the only thing standing between him and instant death.

Before he could pull himself free of the thickets and reload, the elephant wrapped its trunk around Jim's leg and lifted him high in the air before bringing him down and slamming him against the rock hard, rusty-colored ground.

The rifle flew from Jim's hands and the air drained from his lungs. His bronzed face turned white and his eyes bulged with fear over the sight before him. He could not recall a time when the feeling of fear had coursed through his body in such a way.

The bull elephant approached and lifted its giant hooved leg over him. He glanced to his right and saw his rifle lying a mere few feet away. Right when the bull brought his leg down with the intention of crushing his already battered body, Jim rolled clear and picked up the rifle.

The bull's hooved foot connected with the earth, kicking up dust, and then it trumpeted another defiant cry of anger and determination.

Without thinking about what to do next, Jim reflexively removed two more cartridges from the loop holes in his vest and loaded them after removing the spent shells and tossing them to the ground.

The elephant charged!

BOOM! BOOM!

The elephant dropped like a fallen giant baobab tree, kicking up more of the ever-present rusty-colored dust, which completely engulfed the elephant in a large cloud.

Something is wrong, Jim told himself.

His chest burned from pain. He felt light-headed not from the pummeling he took, but something else.

What?

Then he realized the cause of his pain.

Breathe, you fool!

Jim drew a deep breath, filling his lungs with precious air. His chest heaved with each breath, clearing his head at the same time.

The cloud of dust covering the elephant did not settle quickly. Jim waited until it did. Not taking any chances, he reloaded another two cartridges, his last pair. Spare ammunition was left in the land rover a way back, next to the *dongo*, what natives called a dry riverbed. He prayed he would not need more until he returned to the rover.

"Traipsing in the bush with an empty rifle was little different than a virgin dancing in the buff before a throng of kids well past puberty," Caesar once joked.

Right then a voice called, "Hey, you're one lucky bastard!"

Jim turned and was surprised to see who the man was. "Kowalski," he said in return. "What the devil are you doing here?"

"Same as you, I'm hunting for ivory." The man stood holding a Rigby .470 double rifle.

"So it was you that killed the female," Jim said.

Kowalski grinned maliciously.

Stanley Kowalski was a heavy-set, brutish man, who spoke in heavily accented English. His bald head glistened with perspiration and no one knew why the imbecile chose never to wear a hat. Most of his teeth were missing and those remaining in his mouth were rotting from decay. His nose looked flat, the result of too many bar room fights, which he did not always win. He stood there in dirt-grey khaki trousers, flannel shirt with sleeves rolled up to the elbow, and a pair of American-made paratrooper boots, most uncomfortable for long marches in the bush.

"I'm not poaching ivory," Jim said defensively.

Kowalski laughed his familiar hideous laugh, which reminded Jim of a hyena. "Of course you aren't," he replied, teasing. "Why else would you be in the Selous territory, the largest Game Reserve protected by the government?"

Jim would have loved nothing more than to clobber the dim-witted moron, only he was too weak and sore…for the time being.

"Not that I owe an explanation," Jim began. "I'm here on assignment from the Game Department to cull over-populated herds." He paused before adding with pride, "I never poached ivory, nor will I."

Kowalski laughed again. "With business hurting for the both of us, you may wish to rethink that."

Two natives trailed Kowalski, members of the Maasai tribe. They worked as gunbearers and trackers. They wore traditional dark-red robes, sandals, many beads around their necks, and their hair was braided in long thick knots, dangling past shoulder-length. They spoke rapidly in Swahili with each other, pointing at Jim repeatedly.

Both white hunters spoke fluent Swahili, but Jim was too exhausted to understand. "What are they saying?"

Kowalski turned sour. Whatever it was his bearers said, he clearly did not appreciate it. Turning back to face Jim, he grinned mockingly. "They're wondering how you managed to stay alive after the pummeling you took from my bull."

"What do you mean *your bull?*"

Kowalski motioned at the fallen giant elephant. "Look at the size of those," he said, pointing at the ivory. "That's the biggest tusker I've ever seen. I wager them to weigh eighty pounds each easy."

Jim agreed, but was not about to allow Kowalski to poach in the Selous Game Reserve.

"Don't look so smug," Kowalski shouted. "The Game Department takes ivory from *cropped* elephants as easily they do a legitimate hunting safari. Besides, I need the money to keep my ranch from being taken away. Selby, Ker, Downey, and other outfitters are getting all the business and not leaving us any clients. Hell, they won't even hire me as an assistant despite needing the help."

Jim was not surprised. For Kowalski to have maintained his license to hunt after all the trouble he made in past quarrels it surprised everyone that he had not been deported.

The two natives continued rambling again. Kowalski ordered them to be quiet.

"What did they say?" Jim demanded.

Kowalski laughed again. "Geez, you really did take a beating, didn't you?" He sighed with reluctance. "Very well," he started, "if you must know, they say you have the luck of *Juju* to still be alive. No broken bones, no torn ligaments, only a few cuts and scratches from the thorn bush you got tossed into." Kowalski nodded. "I have to agree, you are lucky." Then he quickly added, "But I don't think of you as a legend."

Jim looked perplexed. "Legend?"

Kowalski sighed again. "That's what these two imbeciles are calling you. They say you're bigger than life. You killed and survived when you should have been killed in place of the tusker." He paused for effect, and then said, "They're calling you *Kubwa Jim*. That's *Big Jim* in Swahili."

Jim remained confused. "What in blazes are you saying?"

Kowalski stopped laughing. "You've just been ordained. From now on your name is *Big Jim*."

Chapter 1

In early 20th Century Africa a professional hunter stood a 50-50 chance of being mauled by a lion or leopard, impaled and trampled by a bull elephant, or gored by a buffalo or rhino. These dangers shattered the romance and mystical image of going on a hunting safari, but did nothing to stop people from all over the world to venture here.

The three white men sat around the fire in the middle of camp, smoking their pipes and letting their food digest. Dinner consisted of eland, potatoes, carrots, and champagne. The Englishman would have preferred his favorite bottle of cabernet sauvignon, but wine did not fare well on safaris.

The Englishman rose from his canvas chair, admiring the view. "I never imagined such a beautiful land existed anywhere on the planet," he said, puffing his pipe.

They were somewhere in the middle of Manyara National Park in northern Tanganyika, and would remain here for the next 25 days. He had hired the hunters, and owners of *Big Jim and Wilde's African Safaris* for a month-long hunting expedition, and believed he had spent his money well.

"It's not a bad day," the Englishman said, motioning with his pipe at the two eland, wildebeest, and wart hog bagged in their afternoon shooting. "I didn't expect the hog to be so difficult to shoot," he admitted, earnestly.

Big Jim turned to look at the carcasses lying beneath the large Ficus trees common along the rivers. The trees provided good shade and the river offered fresh water and catfish to be caught.

"They're faster than people imagine," Big Jim said. "It's good you bagged it on the first shot. The damned things shout an awful cry when wounded. Enough to make you wish you were deaf."

"Your boys will skin them and preserve the heads for trophies?"

Big Jim nodded. "That's what I pay them for."

The Englishman laughed. "And that's what I pay *you* for."

The Englishman's name was Nigel Stewart, 37 years old, and born with a silver spoon. His family made their fortune in the South African diamond trade, but Nigel spent most of his time with the corporation's headquarters in London.

He stood five feet eleven inches and had an athletic build, never weighing more than 175 lbs. His face was lean, with blue eyes and high cheek bones capped off with an aquiline nose. And his skin was very white, even pinkish, thought Big Jim. This caused concern for the hunters. The sun could be unbearable in the middle of the day and they warned the Englishman to not roll his sleeves past the elbow and wear his Pith helmet when not under the shade of his tent or tree.

His hunting outfit looked out-of-date, a fashion similarly worn by Teddy Roosevelt when he went on safari in 1910, but Big Jim thought the Brit looked comfortable and kept his opinions to himself. What bothered him most were Nigel's boots. They were knee-high and weighed four pounds each.

"Are you certain you won't wear my spare boots?" Big Jim asked, puffing on his pipe. "Yours may not be practical for a long march in the bush."

Nigel shrugged. "I ordered these just for this trip," he replied. "I'll make do."

Nevertheless, Big Jim decided to have one of the wapagazis (porters) keep his spare boots on hand in case the Englishman came to his senses.

"I like the camp you chose," Nigel said. He did a complete turn, surveying the terrain.

The sound of the river was refreshing, and the Ficus trees lining the river rustled in the cool breeze. The river grass on the opposite bank appeared impenetrable and thick, but the gazelle and wildebeest managed to forge a trail in order for the herd to drink.

To the north was a wide span of open terrain, dotted with small groups of acacia trees and Leleshwa brush. The acacias were a common sight; tall, thin trees with a wide span of branches that formed an umbrella for good shade.

The Leleshwa were dense thickets of bluish-leafed bush. They grew as high as 20 feet and smelled like camphor when the dried leaves were crushed under the boot of a hunter or hooves of animals. Hunters only marched through Leleshwa brush to finish off wounded game seeking refuge here, but this was extremely dangerous for the odds of being pounced on by an angry cat were great.

"I didn't realize it gets this cold in evening," Nigel said. He put on his heavy coat and sat down. "I can see why you choose to live as you do."

Big Jim and Caesar doubted he did. Hunters were a misunderstood group. They hunted for food, not thrill. This could be belied by the trophies they kept adorned on walls of their study back on the plantation. However, they were not for show. Rather they reminded the hunter of the respect and unusual bond that grew between hunter and prey.

"This life isn't as easy as one may think," said Caesar as he sipped whisky from his tumbler. "Back in the day of Kenyon Painter and Leslie Tarlton the odds between man and beast were practically even."

"Animals like the bull elephant, leopard, lion, rhinoceros, and Cape buffalo rarely fall from a single shot," Big Jim added. "Rhinoceros have poor sight, and hunters take advantage of this. But when they charge they're more frightful than one imagines. A hunter must shoot it in the head and pray the bullet strikes the brain."

Caesar continued the lesson. "The *tembo*, Swahili for elephant, are much swifter than people believe. They run for miles, and have a keen sense of smell and sound. If you track them with the wind against you they charge to protect the herd, and rarely fall from a single shot. They come after you like a roaring train."

Not wanting to be outdone, Big Jim interjected his knowledge of the trade. "The lion is called *simba*, and leopard is *chui*. You can shoot them in the belly or shoulder and they sometimes only flinch. Other times they roll over like dead, only to jump up and strike as the hunter approaches. Clients pay handsomely to hunt the big cats in hopes of adorning their study back home with the stuffed carcass of their kill."

Now it was Caesar's turn. "Natives consider these animals a nuisance, and welcome hunters to kill them in order to keep their cattle and children safe. Indeed, it's far easier to let amateurs with rifles do their bidding than for warriors with spears."

Nigel found the two hunters amusing, trying to one-up each other. He decided to show them he was not as naïve as they thought.

"Yes, and I understand the Cape buffalo is equally dangerous, if not *the* most dangerous," he said quickly, before either could speak. "I believe they're called *nyati* in Swahili," he continued, "and considered the most feared animal to hunt because they're the most difficult to stop on charge." He had the hunters' attention and went on explaining what they already knew. "Although tame by nature, once wounded they go after their attacker until it kills the hunter or it is killed itself. And they're the only animal to lead hunters through dense bush, only to circle back and make an oblique attack, catching you by surprise."

The professional hunters tried not to show their surprise.

"You've done your research," Big Jim noted. He liked that. It meant his client would not do anything foolhardy enough to get him, or them, killed.

"I never leap into a lake before learning how deep the water to be," Nigel replied.

A hyena made its presence known with its hideous laugh.

"Fisi," said one of the wapagazis. He looked up from the chore of skinning the wart hog.

"What's that mean?" Nigel asked.

Caesar told him. "It's the name for hyena. It smells the carcasses. Those beasts have the most powerful jaws in all of Africa. If it weren't crippled by its low hind legs it'd make a formidable predator."

Nigel got the sudden itch to get his rifle. "Shall we go for a shooting?"

Caesar shook his head. "We don't go after *fisi* unless they pose a threat."

"That's right," added Big Jim. "They're scavengers, and keep the territory clean, same as the vulture." He pointed to an acacia tree where a flock of 20 vultures perched quietly on the branches, waiting for the wapagazis to leave them scraps of meat and bones from the carcasses they skinned.

"I admit they're dirty, contemptible creatures," Caesar pointed out. "In some villages they're known to enter natives' huts and carry off a small child. They infuriate ranchers by attacking their cattle, too, but for the most part we leave them alone."

Nigel sat back down. "Well, if you say so," he said with a touch of regret. He swatted another fly that landed on his hand.

"Remember to close your mosquito bier over your cot," Big Jim advised. "You'll never get a good night's sleep without a net."

"You don't have to remind me of that."

Before leaving the tranquility of the fire Nigel turned to Big Jim. "What do you know of the *Legend of the Killer Fisi?*"

Caesar let out a laugh. "You've been speaking with the natives."

"Now that I know what a *fisi* is, can you tell me about it?"

"When did you first hear of this story?"

"Yesterday afternoon your native askari, Barake, mentioned the story, but his English is poor. I couldn't understand him."

The hunters withheld their disapproval over his comment. There was nothing poor about Barake's English.

Big Jim shrugged, and motioned with a nod for Caesar to have the honor.

"Back in the thirties a village complained about a killer hyena making off with children and livestock," he started, after clearing his throat. "The natives believed the *fisi* to be a *Jabilo*, or what you'd call a Medicine Man or witch doctor. The story has it that the *Jabilo* sought revenge upon a village for settling on what he proclaimed to be his land. He carried out his vengeance by turning himself into a *fisi*, and went about attacking children and cattle.

"Bror Blixen was a famous hunter during this time and happened to be in that part of the territory while on safari. The village chiefs asked if he'd dispose of this *fisi*, and as luck would have it the creature turned up the very evening he arrived. He fired two shots from his 30.06, striking it twice in the chest before it took off. Blixen followed the *fisi* and saw the animal drop behind a large bush near a river. It bellowed one last, awful cry before dying."

Caesar paused intentionally.

"So he bagged it?" Nigel asked, pressuring him to continue.

Caesar looked at Big Jim, then back to Nigel. "Depends on your point of view," he said, like a schoolmaster speaking to one of his pupils. "When he went to where the *fisi* dropped he found it to be the mad *Jabilo*. He lay dead where Blixen was certain the *fisi* fell…and with two bullet holes in his chest."

Nigel snickered. "You don't believe such nonsense, do you?"

"Doesn't matter what we believe," Big Jim said quickly. "The natives believe it. Now let's turn in. We've got a hard day's march in the morning."

Nigel could not help letting loose a laugh. "If this is your way of providing me my money's worth for a safari," he started with a sarcastic tone, "you'll have to do better than telling me children's tales."

Big Jim shook his head. It never ceased to amaze him how people from the civilized world disregarded traditions that ran deep in Africa.

Like now. "I assure you," Big Jim said, "there's more to these tales, as you put it, than you realize."

Caesar whole-heartedly agreed. "Yes, it doesn't do to belittle native superstition. In fact, what you learn from the natives can save your life out here in the bush."

Nigel suppressed a smirk. He did not want to be rude by laughing. After all, Big Jim and Caesar had terrific reputations within the hunting community and he could see by their behavior how much they admired the Africans. He chose to be ever the gentleman.

"Very well," he began, stretching his arms in an exhaustive manner. "I defer to your good judgment."

They got up from their chairs and tapped the bottom of their pipes to clean out the tobacco. In the distance they heard the familiar hideous laugh of a hyena.

Nigel turned to the hunters. "Based on what you've said, I

suppose I should forgo the opportunity of bagging a *fisi*, yes?"

Big Jim kept his cool. He recognized sarcasm when he heard it. "I believe you're a fast learner, Mr. Stewart."

And then each hunter went off to their tent for a good night's rest.

Big Jim opened the fly to his tent, but stopped when he heard the hyena's laughing starting up again. A sudden chill ran up and down his spine, and he could not help wonder if continuing this shooting safari was a good idea.

He shrugged off the feeling. *No sense getting cold feet now,* he told himself.

Chapter 2

A Jabilo is a Medicine Man, or Witch Doctor. Natives call on the Jabilo to cure the sick, bring promise of rain and good crops, to bless their villages with good luck, and to remove evil spirits. However, this same Jabilo may bring a curse on you, followed by certain death.

The native boy awakened with a start.

There it is again! he said silently.

It was the same noise he had heard the night before. Something was in the field eating their crops. He knew it. He wanted to call for his father, but when he did the previous evening for the same reason he was ordered to be silent, and that was the end of it.

The last thing the native child wanted was a beating for waking up his family in the middle of the night, but if whatever was out there destroyed their crops the village risked starvation. It only took a moment for the boy to realize he preferred a beating to starvation.

"Papa," the boy said, anxiously.

"What is it, Tayari?" the father asked, wearily. The entire family of man, wife, three boys, and three girls shared the same dirt floor bedroom.

"I hear it again. It's in the fields."

The father pretended to listen and said, "Go to sleep."

"But, Papa…"

"Sleep, I said!"

Tayari [tah-YAH-ree] was a healthy six year old native in this Kikuyu village 50 miles north of Arusha. His father was the village chief. His name was Omel [oh-MEHL], a retired askari who had saved enough money in his 15 years of serving safari outfitters to have an actual house built of white-washed brick and mortar, with a corrugated roof and veranda stretching the entire length of the front and right side of the home.

"If this form of living is good enough for the white man we serve, it's good enough for me," Omel reasoned.

It was a definite improvement from the thatched huts made of mud and wood that most in the village of 50 families lived in. Though many looked down upon Omel straying away from their native way of life, even if it was to better himself, they were comforted by the fact that he slept on the ground like they did.

There it was again! "Papa, I hear it moving in the field!"

"Tayari!"

Tayari lay down on his blanket and stared out of the window. He identified the long stems of corn and millet stalks growing six feet high in the fields illuminated in the brilliant moonlight sweeping over the village.

Millet was a four thousand year old staple in Africa, and one of the few crops that endured the intense heat and poor soil. Its grains were turned to flour, cooked, steamed, and even eaten whole. Many villages grew the crop, and many villages had to fight off the pesky rogue bull elephants that enjoyed feeding on them.

A loud shriek pierced the night, awakening the villagers.

"I told you, Papa!"

"Stay inside," his father ordered.

Omel went to his den and reached for his .350 Rigby Mauser hanging on the wall. Holding the rifle with familiarity, he pulled back the bolt and chambered a round. This was a light-caliber rifle, unlike the heavy double rifles he used to hunt with as an askari, and it had never failed him yet.

Omel went outside where a number of men from the village ran up to him.

"I don't think this is the same bull as before," said the first man. He was a tall, skinny man with most of his teeth missing. The whites of his eyes stood out against his black face.

"Of course it is," Omel replied. There was a touch of doubt in his tone. "Do any of you have a rifle?" It was a silly question. He was the only man who could afford one.

After ordering the men to keep the women and children in their homes, he instructed the men to form a line on the outskirts of the village separating them from the millet stalk fields. They were to remain here and keep the bull elephant from entering the village. If they saw the bull approach the village they would holler at the top of their lungs, banging wood sticks against metal pots, creating as much noise possible.

"You have to keep the bull from entering the village," Omel warned. "If it does, our homes will be destroyed."

"You're going alone?" asked another.

Omel did not like the idea, but alone he would not make any noise, and elephants had a keen sense of smell and hearing. Their eyesight was not so good at night, and that was an advantage.

He stood at the edge of the field wearing a pair of dirty khaki shorts and sandals. The only other decoration was the bandoleer of .350 cartridges slung across his chest and shoulder.

Time to move.

Before entering the field he turned around and saw his family looking on from the porch of his house. He answered their stare with a single nod before disappearing in the millet field.

Whatever it was feeding on the millet stalks did not sound like the bull they were used to fighting off each season. This one seemed different. In what way, Omel was unsure.

At least the animal won't see me until I'm close enough for a brain shot, he thought. He reasoned that the corn and millet stalks would be enough concealment for him to sneak silently up to the bull and kill it.

Omel knew the surest way to kill the largest land animal on earth was to shoot a large caliber bullet through its fist-sized brain. Elephants could be knocked down with a head shot, stunned by the impact, and then quickly rise to their feet. In a stroke of luck, the bull would take off in flight to avoid further confrontation. Other times the bull would continue its charge until it killed the hunter or was killed itself.

A single shot through the brain is all I need.

Omel's plan was simple. Stealthily approach the bull through the field and get as close as possible. Bull elephants took their time grazing and the noise they made tearing up the millet stalks with their trunks, and then beating the stalks against their leg or the ground to dislodge dirt clinging to the roots would mask any sound he made.

Be silent, he reminded himself. *Their sense of hearing is great.*

He knew this from having hunted many elephant on safari with white hunters. In recent years his only time dealing with them was shooing them out of the village fields. For the most part elephants were peaceful, but the rogue bulls were extremely troublesome. They ravaged fields, destroyed homes, and were quite dangerous if threatened. Most natives had no rifles to defend themselves, only spears, which did not prove the most effective way of killing the bulls.

White hunters were endeared by many villages for their *fire sticks* that pummeled the large creatures with a single pop. On many occasions a village chief requested help from the nearest game warden to hire a white hunter to track and kill rogue bulls. This was approved in order to keep villages from starving after their fields were ravaged.

Omel did not need to hire a white hunter. He was a sure shot and was about to prove it once more.

He crept through the field slowly, taking his time before putting his full weight on each foot so that any sound was muffled against the dried vegetation crushed beneath his feet. He looked up and saw the moon illuminating the area. Were it not for the high stalks of millet he would be able to spot the bull. As it was he relied on the noise it made while feeding.

After moving 50 paces into the field he heard the bull. It was tearing up the stalks to feed on them. He recognized its noise.

Where are you?

It was nowhere in sight, but certainly close.

Another 20 paces forward he saw it.

The animal was a hundred paces to his front in clear view. The silver moonlight provided him a perfect sight. He could make out the thick dark hide covered with stubbly black hair. Its tufted tail fell short of the ground by two feet, and it made deep snorts through its nostrils as it chewed the millet. The horns adorning its head were large, dark gray, and curved upright with sharp tips. Its bulk was massive!

Wait a moment!

It was then that Omel realized he was not staring at a rogue bull elephant. This was something else. Its size was that of an elephant, but...

Elephants do not have horns, he knew. *What is this?*

Omel saw movement atop a knoll overlooking the field and village. The shape of a man appeared. He held a long wooden staff upright in his right hand, wore dark robes, and the plume of white ostrich feathers adorned on his head shone in the moonlight. He was too far away to recognize, but Omel sensed the man and beast in the field were somehow related.

What is this? Omel asked himself.

His first thought was a Cape buffalo *(Syncerus caffer)*, mistakenly referred to by foreigners as a water buffalo.

But they don't ravage fields, he knew. *They eat grass, shrub and other plants. Not corn and millet stalks.*

Whatever this beast proved to be, it had to be killed. It was destroying the village's crops!

Omel raised the Mauser repeater to shoulder level and took a bead on the creature's head. This was not the type of rifle meant for hunting buffalo. Its .350 caliber was too light to kill it. He would have preferred a .450 or .470 Army Navy double rifle.

They would do the job nicely.

All he could hope to do with the Mauser was frighten it away. Omel had hunted enough buffalo in his time to know they were extremely dangerous—and cunning! They were tame by nature, but when stirred they made you feel you were up against the devil itself.

He recalled a hunter once saying, "Hunting buffalo is like playing a game of cards with an animal whose price for failing to kill it with your first shot is your life."

Omel rested his cheek against the stock, closed his left eye slightly, and took aim with his right. He released the safety switch, which made a slight clicking noise, and balanced the 26" long barrel in his left hand. The 7lb. rifle fit comfortably in his hands, but he wished he had that double rifle.

KA-POW!

The Mauser kicked slightly in his arms and the sound of the light caliber bullet striking the buffalo with a loud *thwack* was clearly definable.

The beast shrieked a high-pitched shrill cry, which made Omel flinch instead of chambering another round. The animal stared back, its beady black eyes boring into him.

In a flash the animal charged through the field. Its heavy hooves thundered over the ground, smashing through the millet stalks and kicking up dirt in its wake.

Omel barely had time to chamber a cartridge. He raised the rifle and fired right as the beast lowered its head, slamming into him with the speed of a train. The shot had no apparent effect on the creature.

Omel was thrown 20 feet back before the beast was on him once more, goring him in the chest and stomach. It thrust its horns deep into his thighs, raised its head and shook it to and fro until the limp body of the village leader flew off like a snapped twig.

The creature shrieked another high-pitched shrill cry, slightly different in sound, rather like a cry of victory. Then it charged toward the village.

The natives had not seen what had happened to their leader, but sensed the worst and fled.

Atop the knoll on the opposite end of the field the *Jabilo* observed the scene unfolding. He smiled broadly as the beast tore through the mud huts and brick and mortar homes of the nearly demolished village. It trampled over the women and children, too slow to keep up with the men who were fast in flight.

A few men stopped, turned to face the onslaught, raised their spears, and threw them at the black devil. They might as well have thrown matchsticks, for the spears did not penetrate the thick hide of the beast. In seconds the village, having thrived for over one hundred years, was no more.

And the beast let loose another shrill cry before disappearing into the night.

Chapter 3

The tembo is Swahili for elephant. Despite its considerable bulk it can run swiftly for miles through heavy thickets and dense bush. They have a keen sense of smell and hearing, and use their tusks to impale their enemies. They are considered one of the most dangerous animals to hunt and are the true 'King of Beasts.'

Thus far, Nigel Stewart was pleased with his African hunting adventure. In the first five days he had bagged a lion, leopard, and rhino, and was now on the prowl for a bull elephant, *Loxodonta Africana*. The escarpment along the southern edge of the Serengeti had game aplenty, but their licenses did not permit them to hunt here.

"Why not?" Nigel asked.

The great herds of wildebeest, elephant, zebra, Grant gazelle, and buffalo migrating across the wide open, grassy plain looked too generous to pass.

How many times am I going to have to tell this arrogant bastard? "The government is turning the Serengeti into a safe reserve," Big Jim explained. "It means no hunting." He saw the disappointment in his client's face and added, "Don't worry. We'll find game enough here in the Manyara territory."

It was difficult for Nigel to refrain from removing his rifle from the boot sheath strapped to the side of the land rover. He was unaccustomed to following rules meant for the common man. But Big Jim pressed on, not slowing enough for him to take advantage of the situation.

After two hours of driving over rough, rocky terrain Big Jim brought the land rover to a stop. To their front lay dense thorn-filled scrublands dotted with sansevieria plants, giant baobab trees, and a few thinly-veiled streams snaking through the bush.

He knew large herds of elephant traveled here at this time of year. The mating season was in full swing, and there were plenty of bachelor bulls, what they called rogue male elephants, looking to find as many mates as possible.

"We'll march on foot here," Big Jim said. He pointed to a set of tracks near a stream to their right. "Look. Those are fresh."

The three white men walked to the stream and surveyed the ground. Big Jim pointed to what he believed to be marks in the sand made by the bull's tusks.

"This is a big one!" he observed. "You'll have your trophy today."

Nigel wiped his forehead clean of perspiration. "Splendid," he replied. Only his tone belied his physical condition.

"You look a bit under the weather," Caesar observed. "Feeling all right?"

Nigel straightened his composure. "Nothing will keep me from bagging a bull today," he replied, with effort.

Big Jim decided to leave the askaris and wapagazis with the car and lorry. He wanted to travel light, so Caesar, Nigel, and he carried only their rifles and canteens. Their trousers and boots would protect them from the heavy thickets of thorn brush, and they carried spare ammunition in the cartridge loops over the breast pockets of their bush jackets, khaki vests and shirts.

Big Jim checked Nigel's .450 Army & Navy Double rifle. When he was sure they were ready he led the way across the stream, assuring Barake that they would return before nightfall.

"*Kubwa Jim,*" Barake called out. "It is not good you don't bring me with you. Your skill as a hunter is without question, but this Englishman requires more babysitters."

Big Jim was thankful his askari had spoken in native Swahili to keep his client from hearing the insult. He replied in equally fluent Swahili, "I can't argue with you there, but this is for the best. If we have to high-tail it out of here I want you in charge of getting the vehicles prepared. The wapagazis are no good at making decisions."

"That's only because you don't pay them to make decisions, *Kubwa Jim.*"

Big Jim smiled. "Again, I can't argue with you. We'll be back by nightfall," he said, before turning and leading the way into the bush.

Kubwa Jim loved to hunt. He lived for it, in fact.

James *Kubwa Jim* Peck was a man of incredible physical endurance. Standing six feet tall, with jet-black hair combed back, and never falling out of place, women found his piercing brown eyes mesmerizing and seductive. His handsome face and square jaw was capped off with a bronze tan made permanent from his years in Africa. His lean, sinewy frame possessed rugged and raw strength. He personified the real-life image Hollywood depicted of how a *Great White Hunter* should look. Indeed, one definitely had the impression *Kubwa Jim* was not a man to be reckoned with.

After receiving his discharge from the army he traveled to Tanganyika to take part in a hunting expedition. The territory had abundant game, and after bagging his first trophy elephant the physically imposing veteran with chiseled features decided to become a professional hunter.

Tanganyika possessed some of the most beautiful sights in all of Africa. There was Lake Victoria, Manyara National Park, Serengeti and Mikumi National Parks, and the largest game reserve in the world, the Selous located in the south.

North of the town of Runga were lush bush territories, dense with acacia trees, giant baobab trees, and heavy thickets of spiny sansevieria plants, fig trees, impenetrable river grass, and dry sand streams, which the natives called *dongos*.

To many, this part of the world was God-forsaken in appearance. To hunters such as James *Big Jim* Peck and Caesar Wilde it was home.

Much of their time early on was spent wandering the territory to acquaint themselves with the best hunting grounds. The pair hunted through some of the most difficult areas on the continent, forging trails through territory unknown to native and white man alike.

Not since turn-of-the-century hunters Bill Judd, Alan Black, J.A. Hunter, and R.J. Cunninghame had anyone scoured the land in search of game with such intense purpose.

The result paid off handsomely, for his services were much sought by hunting enthusiasts from around the world. In five years' time *Big Jim & Wilde's African Safaris* boasted a client list of England's royal family, American politicians and businessmen, famous actors, writers, artists, European and Asian persons of influence, and just about anyone with the financial means able to afford a month-long safari.

His partner, Caesar Wilde, was a handsome man many referred to as having pretty-boy looks not much different from Errol Flynn. He had a thin mustache above his lip, kept his hair short and slicked back, shining bright with hair tonic, and was renowned as an articulate man who dressed impeccably even in the bush.

Despite his years in Africa he somehow managed to keep his pink-white skin from turning bronze, and his safari outfit always looked crisp and fresh.

"A gentleman should always look his best regardless of surroundings," the Brit would say in defense of his attire. How he managed to keep his shirt, trousers, and boots spotless despite marching through the bush was a mystery to all.

Regardless of his rail-thin frame, Caesar possessed the same physical endurance as *Kubwa Jim*. He could march for days in search of game, a trait that left his clients confident they had chosen the right hunting guide. This was important as clients paid handsomely for the services of professional hunters.

Their reputation as professional hunters was precisely the reason why Nigel Stewart hired them for safari. Thirty days was a long time to be out in the bush hunting, and time was of the essence.

Traveling over territory with little or no roads by land rover and lorry took time. If the hunting guide was unfamiliar with the location of game and had difficulty finding some, his reputation would be ruined and subsequently he would be hard-pressed to find paying clients. Many outfitters were drummed out of the business for failing to locate enough game to satisfy clients, who in turn passed word to fellow hunters never to hire them for services.

Big Jim had no difficulty here. He found enough work to remain booked for hunting safaris year after year.

After marching through the bush for three hours Big Jim suggested they take ten minutes under the shade of a group of acacia trees. Caesar welcomed the rest, but Nigel was not about to admit to anyone how exhausted he was.

"Where are we?" Nigel asked.

"In the Ngorongoro territory," Big Jim answered.

"The Ngorongoro? What's that?"

Nigel spoke heaving deep breaths, and this worried Big Jim. If the Englishman could not make it on his own they would have to make a litter and carry him out. The thought of carrying him for three hours over rough terrain did not appeal to him or Caesar.

I'm starting to think I should have listened to Barake, Big Jim said to himself.

"The Ngorongoro is a sprawling volcanic crater littered with lava rock and dense thickets of thorn brush and scrubs. In its center is a vast veldt of grassy terrain spotted with acacia trees where wildebeest and gazelle graze by the thousands. Mount Kilimanjaro is 50 miles east, and its snow-capped peak is recognizable against a clear blue sky."

"But we're not here for wildebeest and gazelle, and I'm certainly not paying to see Mount Kilimanjaro," Nigel stated between deep breaths.

Big Jim flashed him a look of disapproval. Paying client or not, no one spoke to him in such a tone. His hard stare made Nigel lower his eyes, an indication that he knew he should not cross the line. When he was certain the Brit born with the silver spoon had got the point he explained his intentions.

"Bulls migrate here, too. Few humans venture this far other than the Maasai tribe. Other than a few hunters like Caesar and me, the Maasai know the location of lava pools filled with water during the rainy season. Without this knowledge we wouldn't be able to travel here. Water is a safari's best friend when this far out in the bush."

"I'll drink to that," Caesar said, popping open his canteen.

Nigel took a long drink of water before Big Jim reached for his canteen, pulling it away.

"What the bloody hell do you think you're doing?!"

"Just because I know the location of water that doesn't mean you can drink to your heart's delight," Big Jim said in anger. "You'll make yourself sick drinking heavily in this heat."

Nigel did know better, and did not argue. He removed his broad-brimmed hat and wiped the sweat from his brow. "Are you the first hunter to have discovered this territory?" His breathing relaxed and the color of his face returned to normal from the burning red appearance a few minutes earlier.

"No. This area was discovered in 1892 by a pair of German explorers, who killed wildebeest by the thousands. They grew rich canning the animals' tongue and shipping them off to Italy. But their luck ran out when natives killed them in a dispute. For a time afterwards no white man returned to this territory."

"How did you learn about it?"

Caesar answered. "From hunters Bill Judd and Alan Black. They noted in diaries made available to professional hunters about new territory they had discovered during their time here in the early 1900s."

Nigel knew the history of those names. They were legendary hunters considered the first professional white hunters in their time. He liked the fact they were British descendants, too. Under other circumstances he would have liked to have rubbed this fact in the American's nose if only to spite him.

Nigel looked up at Big Jim. "When do we move on?"

Big Jim grinned. "When you've rested enough."

Nigel rose to his feet fast. "I'm ready now," he blurted, and nearly dropped his rifle.

Big Jim caught it, fearful the weapon might have discharged upon impact with the rocks beneath their feet. "Careful," he warned. "Out here one's rifle is a hunter's best friend."

Nigel didn't like the snub. "I thought water is our best friend."

"Good for you," Caesar said, quickly. "You're paying attention." His intent was to keep these two from having an all-out brawl in the middle of the bush.

Nigel reached for the rifle and Big Jim noticed a red spot on his hand.

"When did you get that?" he asked.

"Get what?" Nigel replied, dumbly.

Big Jim pointed to the red spot on the back of his hand.

"I noticed it this morning," Nigel replied. "Why?"

Big Jim reached for his hand for a closer look. It was bright red and two centimeters in circumference. *This is not good.*

Caesar saw the look on his friend's face and agreed.

"That's a tsetse bite!" Caesar declared.

Those burdensome pests were killers in their own right. Fever and joint aches were only the beginning. Vomiting, loss of bladder control, dementia, and possibly falling into a coma were sure to follow unless Nigel received medical treatment.

Nigel shook his head. "I'll be all right," he lied. "I just need a drink of water to clear my head. Besides, I had my shot for those things in Nairobi."

"That'll keep you from dying," Big Jim quickly pointed out, "but you'll still get sick worse than you can imagine."

"What should we do now?" Caesar asked. He knew the answer, but wanted to hear Big Jim say it.

"We have to go back."

Nigel stood straight as a rod. "Have you gone barmy? I said I feel all right!"

Neither Big Jim nor Caesar believed him and could not afford to chance it.

"We'll have a go for your bull another day," Big Jim said, reassuringly.

But Nigel was having none of it. "I'll be damned if we return without my bull!" he shouted angrily.

The second after blurting out the words Nigel vomited heavily over his feet. Big Jim and Caesar took him by an arm each. "Sit back down," Big Jim ordered.

Suddenly an elephant burst through the dense brush and trumpeted in anger at the disturbance. It displayed the largest pair of tusks Big Jim had seen in recent memory, and it came straight at them, ears flapping madly, and eyes wide with hate. The loud snapping of branches and thickets were drowned by the *tembo's* shrieks as it charged straight for them.

Big Jim rose to a standing position and took aim. He fired both barrels, one right after the other. Puffs of dust plumed off the elephant's head where the 750-grain bullets struck.

The *tembo* was unphased, and continued its charge at full speed, knocking down trees and smashing bushes as it closed the distance between them.

Big Jim reloaded two cigar-sized cartridges, all in one smooth, and very fast motion. The *tembo* raced madly toward him when all of a sudden it swerved to its right, heading straight for Nigel Stewart.

The Englishman raised his rifle and fired, but the recoil knocked him off balance, preventing him from taking aim to fire the second barrel. When he did manage to collect himself the elephant reached him, grabbing him with its trunk. Nigel dropped his rifle and screamed in sheer terror.

Big Jim fired both barrels. *BOOM! BOOM!*

Still, the *tembo* was unphased. It threw the Englishman to the ground and thrust its tusk deep in his chest, skewering him the way a cook would a piece of meat on a stick. The animal raised its giant head and swirled it to one side. The move allowed the limp body of the Englishman to slide off its tusk and to the ground.

The elephant was not finished releasing its wrath on the intruders. It lifted itself on its hind legs with surprising ease and agility before coming down on Nigel with both front legs.

The Englishman cried a quick gasp of pain as his bones snapped and air flushed from his lungs. The last thing he remembered was spitting up a bucket full of blood before dying.

Big Jim was more horrified at this sight than he had ever been in his life. His client who trusted him with his life was now dead. And he was responsible. But this was not the time to grieve.

The *tembo* looked over at Big Jim and cried a long, high-pitched shriek echoing clear across the territory. It was with such force that even the *simbas* stirred and fled.

Big Jim raised his rifle and fired, but the elephant merely swirled its large body and ran. It cried out one last time before crashing through the heavy thickets of acacia and thorn scrubs...and then it disappeared.

"What happened?" Barake asked.

Big Jim flashed a disapproving look. The last thing he wanted was to discuss the events that had cost the life of his client.

What the hell! He needs to know. "The unexpected," he said, with finality. Then he explained in short detail how the *tembo* had surprised them.

Barake stared with disbelief at the limp body of Nigel Stewart lying on a litter in the back of the rover. After listening how the Englishman died he wished now more than ever that he had gone with them. *Perhaps he would still be alive had I been there.*

The askaris and wapagazis surrounded the vehicle with much curiosity, making Big Jim uneasy. Natives were superstitious. For a man of *Kubwa Jim's* reputation to allow this to happen could mean the *Juju* (Big God) was angry with the white hunter. Bad luck was sure to follow all who remained with a man not in favor with *Juju*.

After a moment of silence Caesar asked, "What do we do now?"

Big Jim shrugged. "We go home."

On top of a grassy knoll a single native observed them. Big Jim and the others saw him. He was quite tall for a native, taller than six feet, Big Jim thought. His head was adorned with large plumes of white ostrich feathers, and he wore a dirty, red sarong and sandals. Around his neck were leather strings with bones dangling from them. They were human bones, but too far away for Big Jim to see that they were. He held a long wooden staff upright in his right hand, resting on it.

"*Jabilo,*" Barake said, pointing at the sixtyish-looking native.

"I know," Big Jim replied. And the sight of the witch doctor made his stomach churn.

The wapagazis began chattering amongst themselves too fast for the white hunters to understand what they said, but they had a good idea.

"Keep quiet!" Big Jim bellowed furiously. "Barake, get them back to work."

The askari barked orders at the wapagazis and they left in a hurry, mumbling and staring back at the *Jabilo* as they did.

Caesar turned to Big Jim. "What do you think?" He sounded more than a little concerned.

Big Jim shook his head. "The sight of that witch doctor is the last thing we need," he said, wearily. He looked at the body of Nigel Stewart and then turned to look at the wapagazis. "They're going to spread word that *Juju* is angry with me and has cursed me." Big Jim spoke as if he knew he was right. "We can expect our loyal natives to quit on us when we get back," he added, condescendingly.

Caesar disagreed. "I know these blokes consider their magic strong," he admitted, "but the *Jabilos* only have so much influence. "We've given the natives a place to call home and pay them well. Try and be optimistic."

Big Jim thought he knew better. Staring back at the *Jabilo*, who continued looking down at them, an eerie feeling coursed through his veins. "I'd rather be dubious," he said carefully. "After all, too much confidence can get you killed."

Chapter 4

By the early 1950s Hollywood producers and directors traveled to the Dark Continent to film movies about Great White Hunters, thus adding romance to a dangerous trade that few earned a living as full-time professional hunter.

Arusha was Tanganyika's answer to an American Wild West town. With a population of several thousand, it was smaller than Nairobi located in the Colony of Kenya, and lacked the advantages of a modern town. Located near Mount Meru, the sister of Mount Kilimanjaro, the town boasted picturesque hills with lush green forests and a flowing river from the nearby mountains.

The community comprised mostly of hunters and farmers. It had two hotels, *Bloom's* the original, and *Cassidy's* the latter. Neither boasted much in the way of amenities. Indoor plumbing had been introduced a mere ten years earlier, but running water and reliable electricity still proved a challenge.

The staff made up for this by providing fresh water in bowls to each room three times daily. The hotel manager employed natives to mount bicycles and pedal for hours in 20 minute shifts to keep the tiny but reliable generators operating whenever fuel ran short.

Only *Cassidy's* offered a reading lounge, and the service in each hotel was exceptional, with native cooks known for serving excellent meals. The beds were comfortable, and the mattresses were imported from Italy. Sheets were changed for washing once a day. The bars in each served everything from brandy, gin, schnapps, and beer to expensive champagne and wine.

The best treat each hotel offered were the verandas, roofed

platforms stretching around the entire building where guests lounged in comfortable chairs overlooking Mount Meru, with its snow-capped peak and river running downhill.

Three grocery stores had been built since the town's conception, but *Mulholland's Store* remained the best where they sold everything necessary for a safari. They sold fresh vegetables, meats, liquor, tents, cots, mosquito nets, rifles, ammunition, and even souvenirs made of ivory.

There was a telegraph office, a small landing strip capable of accommodating a C-47 twin-engine plane, now used by many foreigners visiting for safari and a hunt. Most roads had yet to be paved, and the dwellings were modestly built, some of mud, some of wood, some of corrugated tin roof with whitewashed stone walls and wood, and all sturdy.

What struck most first-time visitors was the colorful mixture of Europeans and Asians. German remained the town's primary language from its time when the territory was known as German East Africa. However, its citizens came from all over the world. There were Indian shop owners, Greeks, British, Italians, and native Maasai and Meru tribes people living in harmony in what many believed to be *Paradise* found.

Travel by horse and saddle, and ox-pulled wagons were still common despite the introduction of land rovers and lorries two decades earlier. Farmers grew healthy wheat and grain fields, coffee, corn, fruit trees, cocoa, citrus, and anything else needed for a town to thrive comfortably. Indeed, if one were to visit Tanganyika it was impossible not to pass through Arusha.

Kubwa Jim drove the lead land rover into town and found it bustling with activity. Vehicles of all sorts cluttered the streets, and hundreds of people on foot, some on horseback, visited the shops aligning the streets. Here vendors sold goods ranging from blankets, trinkets, dried fruit, clothes, vegetables, and canned goods, to rifles, ammunition, horses, and in some cases children to perform day labor.

The street vendors were mostly Indian, some Arab, and a few Greek. Whereas the Germans, Italian, English, and Belgian settlers put up shops in whitewashed buildings with corrugated roofs and glass windows. How people from all parts of the world managed to live in harmony in such a desolate place was enough to leave a westerner thunderstruck.

Big Jim pulled up alongside an Arab's Dak, or shop setup, which was little more than a tarpaulin roof held up on four six foot poles. His goods laid spread on a rickety wood table.

"What's all the fuss?" He spoke in badly accented Arabic.

The Arab's name was Mohammed. He was 50 years old with his head wrapped in a heavy turban that looked too big for him. His upper body was covered in a bright white robe two sizes too big as well, and his baggy trousers drooped at the seat, with his leggings wrapped skin tight to his ankles.

"Another Hollywood film shoot," replied Mohammed. He was abrupt and aloof.

Big Jim knew why. They did not like one another.

Along with being full-time professional hunters, Big Jim and Caesar performed duties for the Tanganyika Game Department, tracking and arresting poachers. Big Jim caught Mohammed in the Selous Game Reserve poaching for ivory along the Luwego River several months earlier. The Arab was very sloppy about it, too. He hunted with two boys, armed with .350 Mauser repeaters, not ideal for hunting elephants, but able to kill them nonetheless.

Mohammed avoided serving jail time for agreeing to divulge information about other poachers more successful than he, but he never forgave Big Jim for turning him in. The ivory would have paid handsomely on the black market.

Big Jim shook his head with disgust at the hectic sight of people. "This place is becoming more like Nairobi by the day," he commented.

"I don't know about that," Caesar said. "There hasn't been a film crew this size since 1950 when they filmed *King Solomon's Mines*."

"Yes, and I'd hoped it to be the last."

Caesar did not push the subject. He knew Big Jim was upset at not being hired by the MGM film company to help locate animals and sights for the film. That contract went to competitor hunter *Stan Lawrence-Brown Safaris*.

Big Jim's concern for the moment was reaching the commissioner's office. He had to report the death of Nigel Stewart and make arrangements for the deceased to be returned to England.

"We'll never get through this crowd," Big Jim declared.

"Not in these vehicles," Caesar agreed. "Tell you what, old boy. You remain here with the rover and lorry, and I'll foot it over to the commissioner's office."

That suited Big Jim fine. He was not looking forward to writing how his poor judgment cost the life of his client. Not only was his reputation at stake, he stood to lose his license if the investigation found him negligent.

Caesar disappeared into the crowd while Big Jim sat exhausted in the land rover. To his right was *O'Malley's*, a decent restaurant with an even more decent bar.

"Stay with him," Big Jim said to Barake.

He saw no point sitting still in the car with the deceased lying on a stretcher in the back with a blanket covering him, so he left Barake to watch over him and entered the bar to quench his thirst.

He climbed the wooden steps leading to the deck where patrons sat at tables under the shade of the veranda, and noticed a rather tall, handsome woman with light-colored skin and dark, curly hair staring his way. Any other time Big Jim would have appreciated receiving such a seductive stare, but for the time being his only concern was to down a few shots of bourbon.

"Hi-ya, handsome," the woman called out.

Big Jim stopped for a second and offered a slight nod in her direction before entering the restaurant.

He sat at a table by a window facing the street with a small level of privacy. O'Malley brought him a glass and bottle.

"Thanks, Sean," Big Jim said, pouring himself a full glass of bourbon.

"You bet," replied the proprietor.

Sean O'Malley was a fortyish big, husky man, standing well over six feet and three inches. His face was adorned with a three day shadow meant to hide the scars on both cheeks. No one dared ask how he came by them for his Irish temper was widely known in Arusha. His muscled arms were the size of logs and he wore a long-sleeved button down shirt stretched tight across his muscled chest. Were it not for the slight paunch in the waist he would have had the spitting image of the *Statue of David*. Alas, years spent operating a restaurant had its toll and his appetite grew with the years.

Sean looked out of the window and saw a group of people standing by Big Jim's vehicles. The body covered in a tarpaulin drew their attention, and his.

"Trouble in the bush?" he asked, curious.

Big Jim shook his head. "I only want to tell my story once, if you don't mind," he answered.

Sean O'Malley rubbed his cheeks. He understood the need for privacy. "No troubles, friend. Let me know if you want some grub."

The Irishman returned to his kitchen while Big Jim finished his drink and poured himself another. Before he put the bottle down the woman from outside appeared and took a seat across from him.

"Will you pour me a glass, too?" she asked. The woman stared directly with a slight smile pursing her full lips. She even brought her own glass, holding it out for him.

Not forgetting his manners, Big Jim shrugged and filled it one quarter full. They clinked glasses and took a quick drink.

"Cheers," said the woman, smiling seductively. She spoke with an air of confidence which Big Jim found rare in women. "I'm Ava."

"James," he replied, taking another drink. He preferred this over Big Jim with women. It sounded mature.

Ava put her glass down and placed both elbows on the table, resting her head on top of her folded hands. "I take it you're a *Great White Hunter*?" Her question was laced with a touch of sarcasm and curiosity.

Big Jim nodded. "In Arusha you're a hunter, farmer, or both."

Ava pulled out a cigarette from a silver case and lit one. "Care for one?"

He shook his head. "Never cared for them."

"Good for you," she said, smiling with a slight tilt of her head. "They're dreadfully bad for you."

"Then why smoke?"

"Because they're dreadfully bad for you," she replied, quickly.

Now it was Big Jim slightly smiling. "Do you enjoy doing things dreadfully bad for you?" He laced his question with her same touch of sarcasm.

She paused, locking eyes with his. A moment later her face adorned a broad smile, exposing sparkling white teeth. "It's lots more fun than doing what's right."

Big Jim studied her for a moment. Having such a beautiful woman sit directly across from him was enough to take his mind off his current predicament. "You're just what the doctor ordered," he said.

"Why? Are you sick?" she asked.

He glanced out of the window at the body of Nigel Stewart wrapped in the tarpaulin in back of the land rover. "I could very well be after my report with the commissioner."

Ava saw the body, the natives standing watch over it, and the attention it drew from people walking by. "Care to talk about it?" Her smile faded and a look of concern came over her.

Big Jim thought about telling her, but... "I'd rather explain it once, so I'll save it for my report."

Ava appeared hurt by the rejection.

"Thank you, though," he said quickly. The last thing he wanted was to hurt her feelings.

The smile returned to her face. "I love Africa!" she declared. She reached for her glass, downed the contents, and held it out for more.

Big Jim poured her glass half full. "Been here before?"

She nodded with enthusiasm. "I was here last year working on a film called *Snows of Kilimanjaro*."

Then it came to him. *"You're Ava Gardner!"*

She recognized true surprise when she saw it. His was genuine. "Did you see the movie?"

He nodded. "Yes."

There was a slight pause before she said, "And?"

Big Jim wanted to be kind, so he nodded and said, "It was good."

She watched him curiously. "What *didn't* you like about it?"

His cover was blown and there was no going back, he knew. "I've no disrespect for you," he began. "I think you're a fine actress."

"But?" She wasn't letting him off easy.

He paused, contemplating if he should continue. *Aw, the hell with it!* "The movie was definitely better than what Hemingway wrote. Why he chose to write a short story versus a novel is beyond me." He stopped, collecting his thoughts before continuing. "I suppose I didn't like how the lead actor and I didn't get along well enough to work together."

Ava straightened in her chair. "You didn't get along with Greg?"

Big Jim was about to explain when two distinguished gentlemen approached their table.

"Bunny—Greg—Fancy finding you here!" Ava held up her glass to her apparent companions.

Big Jim recognized them, in particular Bunny Allen, and acknowledged them with a nod, but did not rise or offer to shake hands.

Bunny flashed a malicious grin. "Trouble in the bush," he said, glancing out the window at the body in the land rover.

Big Jim answered with a cold stare. "What's it to you?"

Bunny shrugged. "Nothing. Don't suppose it'll help you much in the way of promoting your company."

Big Jim knew he was right, but was not about to discuss the matter with a competitor hunter.

Bunny's real name was Frank Maurice Allen from Buckinghamshire, England. He arrived in the Colony of Kenya in 1927 to be a hunter. Like James 'Kubwa Jim' Peck, Bunny Allen personified the image of the *Great White Hunter*.

He was tall, clean-shaven, and kept his light brown hair cropped short. He was not muscular and brawny like Big Jim, but looked confident and capable of handling himself. He certainly was not a man to be trifled with. He was christened the nickname Bunny as a boy for his knack of trapping rabbits better than anyone else in all of Buckinghamshire. The name stuck for the rest of his life.

His reputation for adventure, compassion to the natives, his love of Africa, and being extremely gentlemanly British to the core earned him respect and admiration. And his list of clientele was unmatched. It included U.S. congressmen and businessmen, to heads of state such as the Prince of Wales and other famous figures.

The two disliked each other intensely due to their successful hunting companies. The mutual respect was there, but the British in Bunny wore Big Jim out when he acted as though he was born with a better pot to piss in. The other thing was Bunny's reputation for being a Lothario. He believed it to be disrespectful to take another man's woman, though he never broached the subject with Bunny.

The man standing beside Bunny needed no introduction. He recognized Gregory Peck from having met him in late 1947 during the filming of another Hemingway short story, *The Short Happy Life of Francis Macomber*. Five years later the man still looked to be one of the handsomest leading actors in Hollywood, or so the ladies thought.

Big Jim knew the actor had selected David Lunan over him to be his stand-in for the *Twentieth Century Fox* film shot the previous year. Big Jim submitted a bid to manage camp for the film crew, with the intention of drawing attention to his safari company. He lost out to *Lawrence-Brown and Lunan Safaris, Ltd.*, and did not like the snub handed down by Gregory Peck.

Rumor had it the actor did not want him as his stand-in because they had the same last name. "I don't want anyone confusing us as being related," the actor supposedly said.

Ava invited them to sit down, but the actor declined. "Thank you, no. I have to leave. It was a good safari, but it's time to return home."

"How was the shooting?" Ava asked. Her enthusiasm surprised Big Jim. He took her for an animal-lover, not a hunting enthusiast.

"Not bad at all! I bagged a leopard, lion, cheetah, and rhino."

"Can't wait to see them on your wall," she said, and took another drink from her glass.

The actor looked at Big Jim, and then out the window at the body in the back of the rover. Turning his attention back to Ava he said, "See you around, dear," and kissed her on the lips.

She watched him leave, as did many other female patrons in the restaurant. She turned to Bunny, who remained standing in front of them. "Sure you won't join us, Bunny?"

"I've actually come to collect you," he said, in his usual energetic tone.

Ava explained to Big Jim. "Bunny here is assisting with the management of the camp and the director and producer probably want to discuss scenes with us."

Big Jim already knew this. The *MGM* film, *Mogambo*, was directed by John Ford and produced by Sam Zimbalist, both known for being hands-on people.

"I'll be along in a minute," Ava said, dismissively. "I want to talk a bit more with my friend here."

Bunny glanced at Big Jim, nodded, looked at Ava one more time, and left.

"I don't think he appreciated you dismissing him like that," he said.

"Oh, he'll get over it," she said. "What's going on between you two?"

Big Jim shrugged and downed the contents in his glass. "Competitor hunters don't always see eye to eye."

"Is it because he got the contract to manage the camp sites for *MGM*?"

This broad is as smart as she is pretty. "I guess it's no secret," he confessed.

But Big Jim was not the only hunter disappointed. Other companies sought the lucrative contract to oversee film sites and quarters for the crew. Bunny's connections and reputation won over everyone else's, and Big Jim still smarted over it. Losing some employees to Bunny did not help matters either.

"There'll be other contracts," Ava offered, soothingly.

Big Jim refilled his glass. "At least until the craze Hollywood has over African safaris runs its course." He poured her another drink. "Kind of soon, isn't it—to be in another film shot in Africa?"

Ava let out a laugh. "Yes, but in Hollywood if you don't keep working, people forget about you. And like you mentioned, there's a craze for filming here."

Big Jim did not think anyone would forget someone as lovely as her.

Then out of the blue she stood, finished her drink, and set down her glass. Before turning she stared for an intermittently long time at Big Jim. With a tilt of the head she said, "Hope to see you soon, handsome!"

Big Jim watched her leave, as did many of the male patrons who turned their heads to watch the most beautiful foreigner in Arusha leave.

In the corner of the restaurant Big Jim failed to notice the medium-height skinny woman with short brown hair sitting alone, observing him with much curiosity. She was dressed in clean, tight-fitting khaki jodhpurs tucked into polished knee-high boots. Her blouse was a long-sleeved crispy white shirt tucked in at the waist. On the table was a glass of water, a half-eaten sandwich, and notebook, which she opened and began to write.

A smile pursed her lips as she did.

Chapter 5

Natives often turned to professional white hunters for help in dealing with troublesome animals. This did not endear the tribe to the Jabilo, or Medicine Man, for it demonstrated their lack of faith in the Jabilo's ability to handle such issues. Thus, an unsteady co-existence between hunter and Jabilo made the situation no better for the tribe.

The natives walked toward the river single file. The women, four in all, walked between the two men who carried long spears with a wide three-inch double-edged blade, three feet long on the throwing end. The women walked steadily, balancing two foot high clay pots on their head. Their skirts ran from ankle to waist, but their torso was adorned with no clothing other than row after row of thick beads around their neck.

The men wore sandals and loincloth, nothing more. Their bodies were well-defined from having eaten healthily for most of their lives, the result of being superb hunters capable of providing their tribe with an abundance of meat.

The group of six reached the river and took a moment to rest under the shade of mimosa and ficus trees. The native bringing up the rear untied a leather pouch strapped to his waist and opened it. Reaching inside he grabbed a handful of *posho*, maize quite commonly eaten among natives. It was mixed with corn, vegetables and meat, turned into a doughy substance and carried in leather pouches for one's rations when traveling.

The leader of the group was named Mikaili (*mee-kah-EE-lee*), of the Wakamba tribe. His name translated in English was Michael. Mikaili in Biblical Swahili stood for *God-like*. Though Mikaili was no god, he certainly was a fine specimen of a warrior. He stood well over six feet tall, with bulging leg and arm muscles that would have made a professional wrestler envious to be endowed with similar attributes.

The younger warrior was named Mirembe, an impressionable 18 year old who, like many in his tribe, looked to Mikaili as the main hunter.

Under normal times Mikaili would not have been walking women to the river to fetch water. But these were not normal times. The past few days' word spread village to village of an unrelenting creature terrorizing the territory. A description of the creature proved sketchy, but from what Mikaili determined it appeared to be a mad buffalo.

Cape buffalos were dangerous, Mikaili knew, but did not behave in the manner described by natives. They were timid by nature, and fed on grass, shrubs, and other plant life. They did not disturb crops grown by villagers, nor did they approach native settlements. They lived in large herds, keeping mostly to themselves. Their natural enemies were lions and crocodiles, but the buffalo proved a dangerous foe, using its large horns adorned on its head to fight its predators, as well as stomping them with its large hooves. It could run up to 37 miles per hour; grow up to six feet tall at the shoulder and as long as 11 feet from head to rump. Weighing as much as 1,500 pounds, when the buffalo charged it came at you like a thunderous locomotive.

This creature could not possibly be a buffalo, Mikaili said silently. *My people are wide with imagination.*

And this was true, much to his frustration. The Wakamba, Nandi, Kikuyu, Swahili, and Maasai to name a few, were still as superstitious as their ancestors centuries earlier.

It's no wonder we live as we do while the white man take full advantage over what the Juju has blessed us with. Mikaili shook his head at that thought.

Just then a loud piercing shriek echoed across the valley, followed by a deep, throaty moan equally bone-chilling.

"Ni mnyama!" (It's the beast!) one of the females shouted.

The woman scurried about the trees searching for cover when

Mikaili shouted, *"Kuwa bado!"* (Be still!)

The two men stood still, clutching their spears with the blades pointed in direction from whence the cry came. Only their eyes moved to and fro, searching the terrain for a sign of the animal they knew was sure to come.

In the distance a form appeared atop a grassy hill. The four-legged creature stopped and stared in their direction. It was black with a large set of horns on its head, and Mikaili recognized the animal the moment he saw it.

"Nyati," he said silently. *So this is the creature everyone has fretted over?*

"We should return to the village," Mirembe suggested.

Mikaili shook his head. "We haven't filled our pots with water," he replied, never taking his eyes off the *nyati*. Then he added, "I have to admit the animal seems larger than most."

Indeed it was. At over four hundred kilometers the *nyati* should have been little more than a speck in the distance. However, this one appeared to be so huge they could make out its large curved horns and see its tail wagging madly even at such distance.

"I don't like this, *Wakuu*," said the younger warrior. "We should leave *now*."

Mikaili was not the village *Wakuu* (chief), though he was sometimes referred as such. Much as he hated the thought of turning back without filling their pots with water, an ill feeling came over him.

"Yes...I believe you're right," he said, finally.

The group gathered their things and hurriedly followed the trail back. When Mikaili turned for another look at the *nyati* he called out for everyone to stop.

"What is it?" Mirembe asked.

"Look," Mikaili said, nodding in the direction of the hill where the animal was.

Only the *nyati* was gone.

Quickly picking up their pace, they did not get more than a few feet when the same piercing shriek they heard earlier brought them to a halt.

"It's to our front!" one of the females exclaimed. Fear laced her every word.

"That's impossible!" Mirembe declared. "It could not have traveled that distance in so short a time."

Mikaili raised his hand. "Be calm," he ordered.

He held his spear at the ready in both hands. If the *nyati* did appear he could not risk throwing his only weapon. He would have to let it charge him and remain still. Only when the animal was close enough to trample him would he throw himself to the side, stabbing the buffalo in the neck with his spear while in midair. With luck—and a lot of it—he might cut the animal in the throat, causing it to choke to death on its own blood. It was unlikely the buff would die a quick death, but Mikaili knew his options were few when facing one of the most dangerous animals on the continent.

An interminable tense few moments passed before Mikaili moved forward. He only managed three steps when the sound of something crashing through the dense thickets to their front caught their attention. They could not see the animal, but the trees and bushes shook wildly as something huge had tore through them.

The females ran off in different directions and the younger warrior backed away.

"Stay together!" Mikaili shouted.

It was no use. The women were too frightened to think clearly. One of them managed to get 20 feet when the *nyati* burst through the dense brush in full charge. Its large hooves thundered over the grass and rock, and its breathing made an eerie rhythmic staccato of huffing and puffing.

The woman turned and screamed in sheer terror at the sight of the huge creature bearing down on her. The *nyati's* eyes were wide with anger and hate, and the mere sight of the beast forced her to freeze.

Mirembe drew his spear back and prepared to throw.

"*No!*" Mikaili shouted. He knew the younger warrior would not be able to retrieve the spear once thrown.

Too late!

The spear struck the *nyati* in the leg near its left shoulder. The animal cried out, but did not stop its charge. Nothing could have stopped it. The creature lowered its massive head and slammed into the woman with a dull thud.

When the buffalo stopped a cloud of dust engulfed its huge bulk, temporarily making it invisible. An instant later it ran back to the fallen woman, trampling over her and crushing her beneath its hooves. It came back a third time and swung its head low, hooking the lump of flesh with its horns and tossing the limp body high in the air. The life drained from the young woman in an instant, and when she landed on the rocks there was no doubt in Mikaili's mind that she was dead.

Mikaili ran to Mirembe. "Go! Run to the river and climb the trees!"

"I want to stay and fight," the young warrior replied.

"What with?"

Mirembe knew in an instant there was nothing he could do without a spear, so his natural instinct kicked in and he ran for dear life. He reached the ficus trees and started to climb when he heard the *nyati* bellow another cry. The next thing he saw was the huge animal charge Mikaili. It was fast—faster than the *duma* (cheetah), he thought.

Mikaili readied himself. He trembled slightly from adrenaline, and gripped his wooden spear tightly. He only stood one chance.

The *nyati* left a huge dust cloud in its wake as it charged at full speed. Its eyes appeared bloodshot with a black spot in the center where the pupil would be. It huffed and puffed like a steady locomotive, never losing tempo despite running across uneven terrain.

The animal's stench of mud, dung, and death reached Mikaili's nostrils, and he struggled to hold back bile building in his throat. "What in the name of *Juju*?"

A feeling of uncertainty overcame him. He doubted he could move fast enough to keep from being trampled to death by the large beast. With nothing else to do, Mikaili pulled back his spear, drew a bead on the *nyati's* massive shoulders, and threw his weapon.

The blade pierced the thick, coarse hide, and Mikaili prayed it found the lungs in the same way a Spanish matador thrust his sword into the shoulder blades of a bull being fought in the ring.

The *nyati* did not waiver in any way. It lowered its head and smashed into Mikaili. The blow knocked him back a good ten feet.

To his own amazement he was *not* dead. Mikaili fought hard to suck in air, the pain excruciating due to his cracked ribs. Next he crawled for cover behind a tree. When the *nyati* returned it stood menacingly over him, swinging its large head to and fro in an attempt to hook him with its horns.

Mikaili knew if the beast was successful he would be finished for certain. Then out of the corner of his eye something glistened in the sun.

My spear!

It lay a few feet from him. The large beast continued swinging its head wildly, frustrated over its lack of success. When it lifted its head to bellow another cry, Mikaili quickly crawled to where his spear lay. He gripped it tightly and held the blade toward the beast.

The animal turned to face him, grunted loudly, and charged, keeping its head low.

The last thing Mirembe saw before climbing the trees was Mikaili's body sailing through the air. For a moment it appeared as though he had waved goodbye, but Mirembe realized the flailing arms were that of a dead man with no control of movement. Mikaili hit the ground and bounced like an empty straw basket.

The *nyati* slowed its pace before coming to a halt and turned around. Then it ran back to its victim and trampled over Mikaili thrice for good measure before stopping and bellowing a deep-throated cry. Mirembe felt his body shiver when the sound reached his ears.

He could have sworn the creature stared in his direction before trotting off and disappearing in the thick brush.

Chapter 6

In Africa a professional hunter's reputation is everything. It is said a man who will stop at nothing to protect his reputation can be more dangerous than a charging elephant. And yet a man filled with self-pity can be even deadlier.

Big Jim could hardly wait to return to his plantation. If there was ever a time he needed a rest it was most certainly now.

They drove onto his property and stopped in front of the main house where a number of natives observed them from the school he had built to teach the children English. Under normal circumstances they would gather around the lorry to help unload the gear and carcasses collected. Such was not the case this time.

Caesar thought better than to remain outside. "Come on," he said. "Let's get out of the sun and have a drink. The sooner we put this behind us the better for everyone." He tried to sound upbeat, but under the circumstances…

The white hunters left the unloading of the vehicles to Barake and the wapagazis he supervised. The way Big Jim felt, the sooner he got behind closed doors to have that drink, the better off he would be.

Kubwa Jim's home was lavishly furnished by most standards. It was one of the largest homes in Arusha. When he first acquired the property he had the main house with tin roof, corrugated metal walls, and wooden shudders torn down.

"I'll be damned if I'm going to live in that sweatbox," he declared.

Within a year he built a modern home constructed of white

clapboard walls, glass windows imported from Italy, and a sturdy roof. The home was elevated four feet above ground on thick logs cut from the finest trees in the territory. Acacia trees surrounded the home for shade; there was a garden in his backyard maintained by female natives, and a veranda stretched all around the building.

Big Jim wanted to keep his furniture modest, but his business partner from England had expensive tastes. Caesar ordered the finest furniture, carpets, and décor for the home shared with his American friend.

"If we're going to make a name for ourselves in the grand world of safaris, we must make certain our clients are comfortable," he declared.

The dining room was large enough to accommodate up to twelve persons, with crystal glasses and ceramic china. The cushioned chairs had red velvet covers, which Big Jim detested.

"Too fancy for my rump," he politely informed Caesar.

Pictures of famous hunters such as R.J. Cunninghame, Carl Georg Schillings, and Alan Black hung on the wall along with stuffed heads of a *nyati* (Cape buffalo), a *chui* (leopard), and a Bongo. The trophies reminded most hunters of the unusual bond they developed for the animals they tracked and killed, and their presence made for good conversation over dinner with anxious clients.

Big Jim agreed to whatever décor Caesar thought best for the guest rooms, parlor, and dining room. However, his office remained off limits to the Englishman.

It was located in the northeast corner of the home. Two windows allowed him a view of the backyard and garden. He had a desk with three chairs, two in front and his own, and a sofa for two, which had yet to be used. He never invited anyone other than Caesar here.

"Everyone deserves their own Shangri-La," he told a curious client.

A cabinet stood in the corner where he kept his supply of gin, bourbon, wine, and champagne. No carpet covered the polished wood floor.

They would be wasted under Big Jim's boots, Caesar knew.

The walls were adorned with photographs of famous hunters such as Bill Judd, his favorite white hunter, Leslie Tarlton, Kenyon Painter, and Teddy Roosevelt, and a rack with two rifles hanging on it, one a .256 Mannlicher-Schoneaur, the other a .450 Army-Navy Double. Behind his desk a glass-encased drawing of *Mbuga za Peponi*, the name of his plantation, hung on the wall.

The hunter went straight to the cabinet in the corner, pulled out two glasses, poured a half glass of bourbon for Caesar, and a full glass for himself, and handed Caesar his drink.

"Many thanks, old man."

Big Jim drank a large amount from his glass and stared at the drawing of the plantation. It was a good drawing, made by a native with a knack for detail.

Located two miles north of Arusha, the plantation boasted ten acres of fertile land. A tribe of thirty natives lived in mud huts on the northwest tip of Big Jim's property. They worked the fields of wheat, corn, millet stalks, coffee, fruit, and the corral of animals slated for shipment to Europe, Asia, United States, and Latin America to fill requests for zoo orders.

This provided Big Jim and Caesar a handsome profit. With food grown from their fields they were able to sell to grocers in the market. The money earned from zoos for wild animals they captured and shipped overseas allowed them to enjoy financial stability. This permitted Big Jim to occupy himself as a full-time professional hunter while Caesar supervised the plantation.

A school was erected for the natives' children, and even those living outside the plantation sent their children here to learn English and western education. They studied under a sturdy wood roof held up by ten foot high thick, round poles. The structure had no walls, and was also used for group meetings with tribal elders for important discussions concerning the tribe. Well-made tables and benches, and paper and pencils were donated by the City of Arusha to keep the school open.

Things were good here and the natives dubbed the plantation *Mbuga za Peponi*, Swahili for Garden of Paradise.

"Hasn't been much of a paradise lately, has it?" Big Jim said. It was more a statement than a question.

Caesar knew what troubled him.

The weather had been bad this year. Not enough rain came and the minor drought cost them dearly in crops. The price for coffee had dropped. Vendors in market grew their own food stuffs to acquire independence from white farmers who charged outrageous prices to Arab, Indian, and African businessmen attempting to scratch a living in the cities and towns of Tanganyika.

Big Jim's long silent stare at the drawing made Caesar uncomfortable. "Are you all right?"

"When was the last order received for animals to be shipped to America or Europe?" Big Jim asked.

Caesar took a seat, and another drink. "About four months, I think. Why?"

Big Jim shook his head and walked around his desk, sitting heavily in the chair. He took another drink. "Damn shame. We're going to need the money."

His report to the commissioner over Nigel Stewart's death meant an investigation must take place. During this time his license was suspended pending verdict.

Every hunter knew the dangers of safari, and this was more of an attraction for Europeans and Americans out to bag a wild animal from Africa. Even when one took every precaution the possibility of sudden death loomed everywhere in the bush.

"At least we won't have to worry about back-stabbing from the competition," Big Jim noted with some relief.

Caesar agreed. No outfitter took advantage of a competitor's misfortune when it came to a death in the bush. It was the sort of thing that could happen to any one of them, and if negative publicity spread it meant bad business for them all.

"Better for everyone that we stick together," Caesar said. "So long as the commissioner's report declares no negligence on our part, all will be good."

Caesar studied Big Jim long and hard. "What else is troubling you?"

Big Jim did not have to think long. "This life is changing right before our eyes, and there's little we can do about it." He spoke in a monotone Caesar never heard before.

"How do you mean?"

"In a word—*Hollywood*."

Caesar knew what he was driving at. Ever since the life of a *Great White Hunter* made its way in the cinema business had increased tenfold. Any businessman would welcome this news, but not professional hunters.

"Hunting is not a business," Big Jim said. "Though we must operate as such, taking people unaccustomed to the bush to hunt game for fun is no simple task. Lately our clients are motivated by what they see on the silver screen. They don't have the passion we have for hunting; therefore they never appreciate the experience."

He downed the rest of his drink, got up to refill it, and returned to his chair. "The men want to dress like us, don a wide-brimmed hat, hold a double rifle, and bag one of the Big Five for no reason other than to have a photograph taken beside the animal they shot and killed." He paused before adding, "And the wives, bored with their husbands, want to drift into an ill-fated affair with us."

"That part isn't so bad," Caesar said with a touch of humor.

Big Jim scoffed. "The hell you say! It only creates trouble. The woman enjoys a moment of reprieve from their dull husband who's busy tracking game instead of paying attention to her. And the white hunter ruins his reputation by sleeping with her."

A mistake Big Jim made once, with a self-promise never to repeat.

"It's been a tough year," he continued. "And we've no assurance the next will be better."

Caesar shook his head. "This self-pity is insufferable," he said with disgust. "When did you become so negative?"

Big Jim did not intend to be negative. He merely reflected on their series of misfortune.

"I suppose something good will fall on our lap soon enough."

Caesar took a drink from his glass and nodded. "I'm sure of it, Old Man."

Big Jim's face grew distorted. He looked as if he'd swallowed sour grapes. "Why do you insist on calling me that?"

Caesar chuckled. "Come now, I thought all you Yanks had a sense of humor."

"We do when we hear it," Big Jim said, condescendingly.

Caesar got up and refilled both their glasses. "I'll visit the commissioner in the morning and see if he can shed light how long this investigation of theirs will take. With luck we'll be back in the bush in no time."

Big Jim remained skeptical. *Still there's always the unexpected,* he told himself.

Chapter 7

Africans believe a man cursed by a Jabilo can bring bad luck to them.
Thus, the cursed one is cast out of the tribe until the curse runs its
course or the Jabilo removes it. Either way it is a long, lonely fight
for the one cursed.

Mary Watkins got out of the beat up Ford pickup driven by a native from town who knew the way to the *Mbuga za Peponi*. She thanked the Lord silently when her feet touched the ground. The driver offering to take her for a small fee not only knew the way to the plantation, but how to run over every pothole along the way.

Taking a moment to stretch, she wondered if she could deduct from the driver's fee the hospital bill she was likely to receive for having her spine straightened after such a tortuous ride. The driver holding out his hand for his money made her think otherwise.

After paying him five East African Schillings she grabbed her bags in the back of the pickup and bade him farewell. "Thanks for the lift," she said, forgetting he understood little English. I probably would have gotten here in better condition on horseback, is what she really wanted to say.

There was a knock on the door.

"Kuja katika," (Come in) Big Jim said from behind his desk.

Barake entered the spacious office. "A girl here to see you, *Kubwa Jim*."

Big Jim blinked twice. "Msichana? Nini msichana?" (Girl? What girl?) he asked.

Barake shrugged. "She only said she's here to see *you*," he replied in intentionally slow English.

Big Jim had forgotten Barake preferred speaking English with the white men. It set him apart from other natives, showing off his education.

Big Jim looked at Caesar, who sat comfortably on the sofa across from his desk, and whose curiosity was piqued.

"Well, show her right in," Caesar said, seeing how Big Jim sat as though incapable of finding the right words.

Big Jim recognized her the moment he saw her. *The girl from O'Malley's.* He remembered seeing her sitting in the corner of the restaurant reading or writing in a book, or something like that. *What does she want?*

"Good evening," she started. "I'm Mary Watkins." She spoke like they were supposed to have heard her name before. "I'm afraid I don't speak Swahili, but I take it you both speak English."

Caesar chuckled. "You speak well," he said, extending his hand.

Mary responded with a firm handshake of her own. "Pleased to meet you."

"How can we help you?" asked Big Jim, getting right to the business at hand.

Mary opened her bag and pulled out a folder. "I work for the *Los Angeles Outdoor Adventures* magazine," she said with a touch of pride. She handed a copy of the magazine to Big Jim, who remained standing behind his desk. She made certain to open to the page with her picture among a group of other persons, all designated employees of the magazine mentioned.

Big Jim read in silence her short bio beneath her picture.

Mary Watkins was born and raised in San Diego, CA. She attended and graduated from UCLA in 1950, earning a degree in Journalism. After which she embarked on a year-long trip around the world, gathering information about wildlife in places like the Brazilian jungle, Galapagos, New Zealand,

South Africa, and Madagascar to name a few. She is an overseas journalist for the magazine.

Big Jim lifted his eyes to meet hers. "You're a reporter?" he said, with a touch of astonishment.

Mary stiffened, but not enough to show it. I'm a *journalist*, she wanted to correct him. This was not the time to let petty issues dictate the tone of the conversation, she knew, so she let it pass.

"My magazine sent me to Africa for a story about white hunters," she explained. "With all the excitement over movies such as *King Solomon's Mines* and *Mogambo* there has been a sudden spike in the lives you live. People want to know more about you, not just what they see in the movies."

Caesar let out a laugh. "Those movies hardly tell the story of hunters in Africa," he said, defensively, "but I must admit, a lady or two as beautiful as Grace Kelly and Ava Gardner have crossed paths with us from time to time."

Mary glanced at Big Jim, who lowered his eyes, but only for a moment. "I'm sure you have," she said, with an assurance meant to embarrass a third party.

Caesar motioned for her to sit, which she did. Big Jim and Caesar took their own seats while Barake stood by the door closed behind him, arms folded across his chest. He looked as though he were on guard.

"I'll get right to the point, Mr. Peck," she began. "Our magazine has selected your organization for a story about hunting safaris in Africa. Movies are meant to sell tickets and entertain people who won't leave home for a chance to experience life beyond city limits. Most people believe they can't possibly afford a safari vacation, so they dismiss the idea without ever looking further into the possibility of taking one. Our magazine wants to change that by writing facts."

"How exactly?" Caesar asked, relighting his pipe.

"How much does the cruise cost to come here?" she asked without skipping a beat.

Caesar lowered his eyes in thought. "I suppose that depends where you're traveling from," he replied.

"Ah, but you have no idea how much it costs," she pointed out matter-of-factly. "This is precisely what my magazine wants to provide readers. We want them to know the price of a plane ticket, the price of a cruise, what type of clothes to bring, what type of weapons are used, and the price for your services to guide them in the wild."

Big Jim leaned back in his chair puffing on his cigar. "I can already tell you some of that," he said, nonchalantly. "The price for the service of two hunters varies from $65 and $100 per day, depending on the type of safari the client wants."

"What types are there?" Mary interrupted. She desperately wanted to jot down notes while he spoke, but knew it would be better to look him in the eye while he spoke. If they agreed to what she had to offer there would be plenty of time to write notes for her story.

"For instance, a photo shooting safari does not require hunting, so the risk is less dangerous. That type of safari will run around $65 for the services of a hunter to find game for people to take pictures and such."

Caesar, not wanting to be outdone in the presence of a pretty young lady, chimed in. "Whereas, a shooting safari requires tracking, finding, and shooting game. Here the risk is far greater, so our prices are much higher. But don't forget other prices of the package."

"Such as?" she asked, urging them to continue. She thoroughly enjoyed hearing what they had to say.

"Now hold onto your skirt, young lady," Big Jim said, holding up a halting hand. "We haven't agreed to give you a story, or anything else for that matter."

If Mary felt insulted she failed to show it. "Come now, Mr. Peck," she said, flashing a smile of encouragement. "What harm can there be talking about it?"

"Depends on what you intend to write," Caesar interjected. "In case you haven't heard, we've had a run of bad luck."

"That's enough!" Big Jim snapped. "We don't need to advertise how we run our business." He stared disapprovingly at his longtime friend, a clear sign he did not wish to divulge anything more.

However, neither knew Mary Watkins. She did not get where she was by being easily put off. "If you're referring to the recent death of your paying client," she began, carefully choosing her words, "I could be the answer to your potentially harmful business problems."

The two hunters blinked twice. After an interminable moment of silence Caesar made his inquiry.

"How exactly do you propose to help us?"

Mary shrugged as though the answer were obvious. "I read your report to the commissioner at the Game Department," she said, matter-of-factly.

"Damn Gary Hayes to hell!" Big Jim cursed.

Gary Hayes was a game warden working for the commissioner at the district office. Big Jim filed his report with him and specifically asked to keep the incident under wraps for as long as possible.

Why would he betray me like that? he wondered. *He knows what this can do to me if the investigation is not handled correctly.*

"Mr. Hayes believed my story can help you," Mary said quickly. She could see from their dismayed expression that they failed to understand. She was reminded how her mother used to say, 'Never look a gift horse in the mouth.'

"How exactly can you help us?" Big Jim asked. He practically spat the words.

It was all Mary could do to keep from rolling her eyes. People have yet to learn the power of journalism, she told herself. "Taking an African safari is the adventure of a lifetime," she began, rising from her seat. To their astonishment she walked to the cupboard and poured herself a drink. She returned to her seat and took a sip from her glass. "Hmm! You choose good bourbon," she commented with a smile.

"Glad you like it," Big Jim said curtly. "Will you come to the point?"

Mary had every intention to do precisely that. "You need good publicity, pure and simple." She paused for effect. "People don't understand the dangers of a safari, and you can't very well advertise them or risk frightening away potential clients. I can write in plain detail how hunters choose to face off wild beasts and risk certain death lest they keep a clear head, and hire a good professional hunter. But it's the *risk* of death which draws a special breed of man…" Mary paused again, carefully choosing her words. "…And sometimes a special breed of woman…" she could not help failing to exclude her gender, "…to take on that risk."

Big Jim scratched his chin. "Go on," he said, his curiosity piqued.

Hook, line, and sinker, Mary told herself. "My story will consist of intimate details of what you face when on safari," she explained, in a tone laced with the passion of someone believing in what they do and say. "Readers will learn it's not only the romantic scenery and adventure of life in the bush which draws hunters, but the very notion of facing death that is equally attractive. I will describe every aspect of camp life, including traveling over rough terrain and the type of foods they eat. In short, my readers will learn if a man loses their life against a wild beast, it's not because of the failure of the hunter to protect the client, but rather the superior cunning of the very animal which man seeks to kill."

Don't say another word, Mary told herself. *Too much talk kills it. Let the words sink in and hear what they have to say.* She may have been considered young for a journalist, only 25 for that matter, but she learned fast.

Big Jim looked over to Caesar, who shrugged approvingly. He finished the remains of his glass, got up and walked to the cupboard, and poured himself another drink.

"The prices for licenses have to be taken into consideration," Big Jim began. "The Game Department has limits on how many animals may be shot and killed. To hunt one leopard, a lion, one rhino, buffalo, and an elephant can run as much as twelve hundred dollars in licenses."

"This does not include bird licenses and other game, such as the Thomson Gazelle, wildebeest, and the like," offered Caesar. "Licenses will be necessary to hunt those animals for food, especially on month-long shooting safaris."

Mary put down her drink, pulled out her notebook from her bag, and began writing notes.

"There's also the running of the camp to be considered." It was Big Jim again. "It's the hunter's responsibility to manage the camp, make certain there's enough equipment, bearers, cooks, and vehicles on hand in order for the client to live comfortably whilst in the bush." He leaned back in his chair collecting his thoughts. A moment later he continued. "I'd say a full month on safari may run $35,000 to $50,000."

Mary sat dumbstruck. *$50,000!* The magazine owner and her editor were the only people on the planet she knew capable of coughing up that amount. "If I write those figures," she began, carefully, "no one will go on safari."

She spoke with a certainty Big Jim did not appreciate. "I beg to differ," Big Jim said, defiantly. "We manage to stay busy year-round. I understand not everyone may afford a safari, but then safaris aren't for everyone."

Realizing she may have damaged his pride, Mary changed the subject. "And this is what my magazine wants," she went on, "information for our readers to learn what it takes to come here." She observed their reactions. *Good*, she said silently. *I have their attention.* "Take for instance, the *Big Five* in Africa. What are they?" She already knew of course, but wanted to hear it from them and write it in their words.

Big Jim motioned for Caesar to explain.

"They are considered the most dangerous animals to hunt," the Englishman said with pride. "Elephant, Cape buffalo, lion, rhinoceros, and leopard comprise the *Big Five*. Many clients fail to collect them on a single trip. It takes some a lifetime, in fact, to bag them all in order to fill their study with trophies."

"Why do people persist on hunting for trophies?"

Big Jim held up his hands. "That could take a fair amount of explaining—*and time.*" He paused for effect. "You mentioned your magazine wants our organization to give you a story about hunting on safari?"

Mary nodded enthusiastically. "Yes sir! And we'll pay handsomely."

"How handsomely?"

"Ten thousand dollars."

Big Jim glanced in Caesar's direction. "You want to pay us ten thousand for a story." He was incredulous.

"Not only a story," she replied, "but to take me on safari for a first-hand look at life in the African wild."

"It's referred as African *bush*," Caesar said, puffing on his pipe.

"You see, that's precisely the kind of information our magazine wants to write about. The *real deal*." She noticed their behavior to be somewhat reluctant. "Is anything wrong?"

"Ten thousand won't pay for much of a safari, Ms. Watkins," Big Jim said, resting his elbows on his desk.

"But I don't need much," she explained. "All those licenses and fees won't be needed on this safari because I won't be hunting. I'll be there for a story, writing how you do things in the *bush*, as you call it. And we won't have to stay a whole month out there. I'd say a week should be long enough."

Big Jim tapped his fingers on his desk, irritating Caesar in the process.

"Can we let you know our answer in the morning?" Caesar asked.

"Certainly!" She rose to her feet. "I only have a small favor to ask of you."

They stared back patiently.

Finally she said, "Do you suppose I could rent one of your rooms for the night?"

Her question surprised the hunters, but they were used to surprises.

"Certainly," Caesar replied, enthusiastically. He turned to Big Jim and said, "What do you say, Old Man?"

Again with the 'old man' business! He shrugged. "Of course, we've plenty of room."

Mary beamed. "Great!" She started to leave, but stopped and stood before them as if wanting to say something. *How can I put this without being forward?* she wondered.

Caesar saw her discomfort and said, "What is it, my dear? Speak up."

She shrugged. "Will you be having dinner any time soon?"

Big Jim and Caesar looked at each other and laughed.

"We dine in 30 minutes," Big Jim said. *This girl's a clever one.*

Chapter 8

Hunters consider the Cape buffalo (nyati) the most dangerous of the Big Five because it seldom can be stopped on charge.

The *nyati* moved swiftly through the tall grass in the swamp. It stopped for long enough to listen and catch the scent of the hunters tracking it. When the animal was certain they were close it disappeared in the swamp, where it knew they could not follow. Not without risk.

The buffalo was a big, dirty animal, smelling of mud and its own excrement clinging to its rear. Its dull, black hide was spotted with patches of dried mud and ticks. The ticks and fleas provided a simple meal for Oxpeckers, tiny birds the size of a blue jay perched on the buffalo's back. They ate until they could barely fly off with a full belly.

When the buffalo reached the opposite end of the swamp it stopped and turned its large head to look back from where it came. Its trail was barely visible through the thick reeds of grass. It was certain the hunters would not follow through the knee-deep water. Most likely they would skirt the swamp for a confrontation on the open veldt. Out in the open the buffalo made a good target.

Not today. Not if the buffalo could help it. It bellowed a long shriek to give away its position. Then it burst through the tall grass and into the open territory of the Manyara National Park.

And then it waited.

The hunter stepped into the smelly, dark water and sank up to his ankle before pulling his leg out. "Damn!" he shouted. "Too deep to follow." He bent his leg at the knee to unload the muddy water filling his boot.

"What do we do?" asked the short, stout man.

"We're not giving up, are we?" asked the taller, rail-thin man. He stood beside the stout man, wobbling on a pair of legs resembling stilts.

The hunter looked at the pair and frowned. They were German and spoke in heavily-accented English, which Stanley had difficulty understanding. *How could I have sunk so low to attract the likes of these Huns?* he wondered.

Before wishing he had never took on the German clients he was reminded how desperately he needed the business.

"No, we're not giving up," said the hunter. "We'll return to the land rover and drive around the swamp. If we're lucky, we might catch the *nyati* in the open."

"What if it remains hiding in the swamp?" the stout man asked. He stared through round-lensed glasses and wore a pith helmet to keep his bald head from being scorched under the sun. He wore a hunter's jacket with cartridge loops sewn over the breast pockets, khaki shorts, boots, and knee-high socks to look the part of a hunter.

The little man cannot look more out of place if he tried, the hunter said silently.

The same went for his friend. Standing side by side they looked like Abbott and Costello in Africa.

The hunter did not like being questioned despite working in a trade where clients bombarded their guides with plenty of them.

"It won't," answered the hunter, in a guttural voice. "It'll go through the swamp to lose us, but we'll catch it on the other side."

Stanley Kowalski once had a reputation which most professional hunters envied, but to look at him today no one would be the wiser. He stood six feet three inches tall with a solid build and slight paunch resulting from heavy drinking. He kept his head shaved bald, and no one dared ask why. When he spoke in his deep, commanding voice everyone paid close attention. And he always wore gray khaki trousers and long-sleeved shirt rolled up to the elbow, a bit of a trademark for him.

Stanley was not a particularly handsome man, and though he never admitted it, this bothered him because he never got the female attention most hunters did when traveling with clients who brought their wives. His face was adorned with a crooked, large nose resulting from multiple breaks from barroom fights. His eyes lay in deep, sunken sockets with black circles, and the corners of his mouth drooped in such a way he was left with a permanent frown. He seldom smiled for fear of exposing his silver mouthpiece, which he bought to replace his decaying teeth. He thought silver teeth would help him stand out in some morbid attractive way.

Rich clients were often accompanied with their beautiful, spoiled wife with no interest in a shooting safari. After the thrill of seeing wild animals in natural habitat wore off, the idea of an illicit affair with a white hunter in the Dark Continent seemed the only way of escaping boredom.

Kowalski was not much of a religious man, and adulterous behavior would not have ruined his day. But the fact remained; his unattractive looks did not make him a bored wife's first choice even if she was willing to have a fling with a *great white hunter*.

Some people have all the luck, he thought.

His frustration over his physical short-comings was relieved in the bush while on safari. At least it used to be. Years ago Stanley had a long list of clients ranging from U.S. politicians and businessmen, to wealthy Europeans. He was known for tracking and finding the best game in the bush. If a client hired Stan Kowalski they were certain to bag the Big Five, returning home with trophies that would leave any dedicated hunter drooling.

His luck ran out when a client refused to carry the Rigby .470 double rifle as he had suggested.

"I prefer my .350 Mauser," the gentleman from New York exclaimed. "It hasn't failed me yet and I don't like the idea of exchanging rifles on a hunt."

Stanley was glad to hear his client had some experience hunting and was comfortable with his rifle, but when hunting a 1,500 lbs.

buffalo one needed a powerful rifle to bring it down. The Mauser, he knew, was better suited for other game like lion or leopard.

However, the paying client had his way, and paid dearly for it. When they sighted a large *buff*, as they were sometimes called, not far from a large herd on the Great Rift Valley escarpment, the New Yorker took it upon himself to shoot without waiting for Stanley to come up with his back up rifle, the .470 double.

The light caliber rifle did little more than irritate the buff, ricocheting off the heavy boss adorning its head. However, the amateur hunter managed to shoot it in the leg, forcing the animal to run for cover in the brush.

Stanley scolded his client for not waiting for him, and more so for not shooting from a better angle. "I told you to aim behind its shoulders!" he shouted. Doing so would have punctured the animal's lungs and pierced its heart. It would not have killed the buff outright, but definitely weakened the animal.

The risk amateurs failed to understand was that tracking an injured animal proved far more dangerous than tracking an uninjured animal. The Game Department insisted no wounded game be left to die a slow, painful death from a rifle shot, and no decent hunter would leave the bush until he was certain the animal was put down. It was part of the *hunter's code*.

The two marched after the wounded buff, and got no closer than 50 yards when it suddenly burst through the brush at full charge. Stanley fired both barrels, but at a speed of nearly 40 miles per hour the buff was practically a living locomotive. It crashed into the New Yorker, killing him instantly before Stanley had reloaded and brought it down with a side shot to the buff's head.

The death of his client brought enough bad publicity to ruin his already shaky reputation beyond repair. Former clients went to competitors like *African Hunting Safaris* in Mombasa, or *Nairobi Safariland*, one of the largest companies on the continent. More competition followed with the likes of *Ker and Downey Safaris, White Hunters Ltd.*, and Edgar DeBono's *Big Game Hunting Ltd.* Then there was his most hated nemesis, James *Kubwa Jim* Peck and his *Big Jim and Wilde's African Safaris* company.

With his reputation ruined, Stanley did what most did—he

turned to the bottle. His list of clients and friends disappeared. Natives no longer worked for the *Bwana* (big boss) with bad medicine. They turned to successful hunters like Bunny Allen, David Lunan, Syd Downey, and of course *Kubwa Jim.*

Stanley managed to stay afloat with a client from time to time, but only because he kept his prices 40 percent lower than most outfitters. He was never able to hire more than three natives to serve as porters. He didn't have the money to keep his lorry and land rover maintained, and the numerous breakdowns in the bush added to his growing frustration. Even his canvas tents were worn with holes, and the cots to sleep in were falling apart.

His misfortune did not allow Stanley to provide a memorable safari, and anyone with money kept clear of him. Anyone other than the likes of *Abbott and Costello*, that is.

"At least they pay," Stanley mumbled.

"How is that?" asked the stout man.

Stanley shook his head and waved off the question.

Stout Man's name was Georg Weismann, a restaurateur whose successful chain dominated Bavaria and Munich. Thin Man's name was Joachim Strasser, a financial adviser for the Berlin bank that put up the money for Weismann's business. The two developed a fast friendship over the first two years of business and chose to celebrate their success with a shooting safari on the Dark Continent.

The buff was where Stanley said it would be.

"Nyati!" shouted the Askari.

"Pipe down!" Stanley scolded him.

Too late. The animal saw them.

Weismann winced upon closer inspection of the buff. "He's much larger than expected."

Stanley agreed. It looked the size of an elephant. "Impossible," he mumbled.

No one seemed to do anything, and this made the Germans nervous. "Aren't we going to wallop it?" Strasser asked.

Nothing would have pleased Stanley more, for once they had their prize he could take them home and be rid this duo of clowns.

Approaching the animal with stealth was out of the question. It had seen them and stood menacingly facing them.

Stanley checked their surroundings. *No place to run for cover if the nyati charges*, he thought. The trees were too far and without low limbs for them to climb. A hilly knoll off to the left offered boulders they could climb or hide in crevices, but the *nyati* could outrun them and likely trample them to death.

"We have to take down the buff here," he said, speaking in a hushed tone. "There can be no retreat for us." He watched the pair's reaction and did not like what he saw.

"What do you mean by that?" Weismann asked, nervously.

"I mean you have to *kill it*. Or be…" He chose not to finish his sentence.

It was Weismann's turn to bag the game. Stanley opened his Rigby .470 double rifle's breech and verified two cartridges were inserted. *It pays to be sure*, he told himself. The 400 grain cartridge was enough to send the .470 bullet head clear through the buffalo, tearing up its vitals. But Stanley knew even if they managed a clean shot the buffalo remained a threat.

In his time he had witnessed buffalo having their heart and lungs torn to shreds by well-placed shots, and still continuing to charge. Once he saw a buffalo have its snout blown clean off. It disappeared in a cloud of red dust kicked up upon crashing to the ground. A few interminable moments passed before it emerged like a dark spirit conjured by a *laibon* (witch doctor). The buffalo charged, killing a gun bearer and injuring the client before Stanley managed a shot through the animal's throat, the kill-shot that brought it down finally.

No repeats, he prayed upon reflection of that horrible time on safari when anything that could go wrong did.

He motioned for Weismann to come closer. "Stand beside me," he ordered, and pointed in the direction of the buff.

Weismann hesitated. His rifle slipped in his sweaty palms, clattering on the rocks by his feet.

"Idiot!" Strasser commented.

"Shut up!" Stanley said quickly. "Remember, if you don't bring it down on the first volley, it'll bolt into the tall grass or worse—*charge.*"

"What if it bolts off?" Strasser asked.

Stanley gritted his teeth. "I'll have to go after it," he said slowly, and with a tone indicating he preferred not to go that path. *The bastards are practically pissing their pants,* he thought.

He motioned with his finger to Weismann and said, "Pick up your rifle and come here. The game has been brought to bay, now's your chance to wallop it."

Weismann walked nervously to where Stanley stood. Their eyes locked on the buff staring back at them. It eerily stood still, tauntingly, menacingly, and oddly, curiously.

"Let's move," Stanley said, nodding in the direction of the buff.

Neither had any idea that they were being observed by Mokonzi, the old Kikuyu jabilo. He stood in the bush, out of sight and silent, wearing the traditional headdress and robes of a chief. He leaned on his six foot long wooden staff with which to assist him on long journeys from village to village, and watched.

About this time the buffalo should have retreated, thought Stanley. They were intelligent animals and completely aware of when in the presence of an enemy.

The closer they got to the buffalo the more Stanley wished they had not continued the hunt. He thought about the land rover. When tracking animals in open terrain it was preferable to have your vehicle nearby. It allowed you to escape unharmed.

Stanley halted their march.

"Why have we stopped?" Weismann asked.

Kowalski did not answer right away. Instead he stared at the buffalo with much curiosity before slowly shaking his head. "I don't like this," he said, warily. A moment later he followed up with, "We're going back."

The German appeared thoroughly shocked. "Why?"

"This is no ordinary buffalo," Stanley replied.

This should have been obvious from the start. The closer they got the larger it appeared. It was damn near the size of an elephant,

Stanley thought. *That's impossible! They don't get this big.*

Its thick hide covered with black coarse hair glistened in the sun, still wet from wading in water. And its stench was overwhelming.

"Mein Gott!" Weismann exclaimed. "What on earth is that smell?"

Mud, excrement, the smell of the swamp—*and death.*

Stanley turned to his client. "This is as close as we get."

Weismann took two steps forward, looked back at Stanley, who prodded him with a nod of the head, and raised his Mauser to take aim. He squeezed the trigger and the barrel exploded with a sharp crack.

Stanley never took his eyes off the buffalo. He saw a puff of dust come off the animal's head. "You hit it!" he declared.

The buffalo dropped with a crash and moaned a long, mournful bellow. The ground shook beneath their feet from the vibration of the animal's impact, and this caused Stanley to wonder what in hell was happening. The red dust disturbed by the animal's bulk engulfed the animal completely.

After an uneasy pause Thin Man looked to Stanley and said, "What now?"

"We make certain its dead."

Marching toward the animal, Stanley knew something was wrong. There's no way that .350 Mauser could bring down an animal of that size, he told himself. And yet it did!

They marched toward the animal and the askari followed a few paces behind. He called out to Stanley, "Bwana," but the white man did not turn to answer. A feeling came over the askari and he knew they should leave immediately.

When they reached 50 yards from the cloud of dust still hovering over the animal they heard a low, heavy groan come from where the buffalo lay. Weismann looked at Stanley as if to ask, what's going on?

A sudden wind blew the dust cloud away and the giant buffalo stood before them, menacing in all its form. Its small eyes appeared bloodshot with two black pupils in the center, and the boss adorning the animal's head was the largest set of horns Stanley had ever seen. Its hide seemed to be dripping dark crimson ooze to the ground.

Blood?

"What in God's name are you?" Stanley mumbled.

The beast lifted its front right leg and tapped it on the ground twice, an indication that it prepared to charge. Stanley snapped out of his momentary trance and raised his double rifle. His right forefinger touched the trigger and he slowly squeezed.

Suddenly a score of buffalo burst from the tall grass in the swamp, heading in their direction. They looked to number well over 50.

"Where the hell did they come from?" Stanley asked aloud. "Shoot over their heads!" he commanded.

They raised their rifles and fired, but the charging herd drowned the noise from their weapons, failing to disperse the herd as Stanley hoped.

"What do we do?" Weismann screamed.

With nowhere to run there was little they could do. Stanley looked over to the askari, whose expression was solemn. When he turned to face the larger buffalo he saw it still staring, never moving an inch. It was as though it had commanded the herd to attack while it watched an inevitable outcome.

Weismann panicked, dropped his rifle, and ran to where Strasser observed the scene. He had not run more than 20 paces before the herd reached him. The buffalo lowered its massive head and upon hooking the man's legs with its sharp horns, lifted him off the ground, tossing him ten feet in the air.

Weismann screamed a high-pitched shriek and fell on top of other buffalo that gored him before trampling him to death.

The askari made no attempt to run. When the herd reached him he took the brunt force of the lead buffalo with the knowledge there was nothing he could do except die.

In an act of defiance from certain death, Stanley opened the breech of his Rigby double rifle and reloaded two cigar-sized cartridges. He snapped the breech closed and took aim at the beast in command of the herd.

And fired both barrels simultaneously.

BOOM! BOOM!

Chapter 9

The summoning of evil spirits to exact revenge is seen as nothing more than superstition among those living in modern tribes…And yet there are those who believe.

Mokonzi sat on the ground silently staring at the fire. It kept him warm on this cold night, but his thoughts were not on how to keep from freezing.

No.

His thoughts dwelled on how to seek out and destroy the white hunters.

Thus far the natives believed—truly *believed*—in the *Mnyama* (Beast). It proved difficult for the *jabilo* not to laugh aloud over the ease with which they could be manipulated.

After all these generations past, he said silently, they still believe. *Nzuri* (Good). *It will be to my advantage.*

Word spread like wildfire of the *nyati* that destroyed the villagers' crops, and with their primary food source destroyed the village faced starvation. The hunting accident *Kubwa Jim's* client suffered would add fuel to the curse of the *Mnyama*, and the latest hunting tragedy with the bald hunter, Kowalski, would leave no doubt as to the power of his black magic.

How next should I strike? This was the question plaguing him.

The tribes were falling in line with fear. They scurried for help from the government against the beast wreaking havoc against them. It would only be a matter of days before chiefs sought his magic to rid the territory of the curse. But he needed something more to solidify his power as *jabilo*.

I need a victory against the white hunters.

The death of the Englishman was a blow to the hunter's trade, he knew, as was the attack on the bald hunter and his safari. The white hunters will be scurrying like rats to protect their reputations and trade, Mokonzi reasoned. He achieved an important victory early in his vendetta to destroy the white hunters.

But that is not enough! I need one of them to die! Only then will my power be unquestioned. Mokonzi only needed to choose his next victim. *The Mnyama would take care of the rest.*

But which hunter? This was the question plaguing him for there were many.

There was the tall, imposing Jorge de Lima, a Brazilian who made his living as a professional hunter selling ivory. He was by far the best known, having hunted every corner of the continent. Well-educated and aristocratic in nature, Jorge de Lima had the natural ability of drawing people to him. People of the highest court in American and European society sought his services, only to be disappointed upon learning de Lima preferred hunting alone and rarely took on clients.

I would not know where to begin looking for him in any case, Mokonzi realized. *The lunatic never remains in one place long enough.*

What about the Italian owner of Big Game Hunting Ltd.? He is a possibility.

Edgar DeBono proved to be one of the best hunters in his own right. He never hunted with other white hunters, instead relying on African askaris and wapagazis to make his clients comfortable. He was fluent in several languages as well as numerous African dialects, and had the good fortune of a reputation for thwarting poachers. Killing him would certainly bring the *jabilo* the attention he sought.

There was also the white hunter David Lunan, who gained fame as Gregory Peck's stand-in for the film *The Snows of Kilimanjaro*. Donald Ker and Sydney Downey of *Ker and Downey Safaris* were also potential targets.

Mokonzi shook his head at the thought of seeking them out. They were surrounded by too many. I need to be careful how I expose the *Mnyama,* he told himself. *If too many outsiders see the beast first-hand the mystique will vanish. No, I must kill a white hunter in the bush far from the crowds. People fear what they cannot see.*

But which hunter? Who could give him the attention he sought? Who had challenged his power the most?

It did not take long for the answer to come to him.

James *Kubwa Jim* Peck and Eric *Mchangi* Rundgren were the Game Department's most experienced animal control hunters in the territory. Both earned their living as full-time professional hunters, and on occasion their services were called upon for *cropping* large herds as part of the Kenya Game Department's efforts for controlling hordes of buffalo, wildebeest, and gazelle from over-grazing or destroying village crops.

Rundgren was a Norwegian inspired by famed hunters Leslie Tarlton and Bror von Blixen. Natives christened Rundgren with the nickname *Mchangi* meaning *to be always here and everywhere* with good reason. He never stopped hunting. The man lived for it, acquiring a reputation as towering as his six feet and 220 pound bully-boy frame commanded. The natives loved him, as did some clients. But there were those who disliked him for his lack of manners and intimidating behavior.

Kubwa Jim was similar in reputation as a professional hunter, Mokonzi knew. He performed control work for the Game Department and the villagers sometimes sought his help to shoot troublesome elephant, hyena, lion, and leopard that destroyed crops or killed their women and children. Some lion were bold enough to enter villages in the middle of the night and make off with a child or lone man walking among the mud huts. Some natives told stories of how they heard a knock on the door of their hut and upon opening it were startled to find a leopard glaring back.

Mokonzi relished such stories. *They will only help in my quest of unquestioning power.*

The *jabilo* scratched his head. *Why do people call the hunter James Peck, Kubwa Jim?*

Rumor had it the white hunter faced off with a bull elephant that nearly pummeled him to death, but the hunter's cunning got the better of the *tembo*. Natives also were impressed with how the white hunter was able to seek out and find the biggest game in the territory. None of his clients were disappointed with his services, and he paid his askaris and wapagazis better than most. Thus, the natives called him *Kubwa Jim*, meaning Big Jim.

It does not matter why, Mokonzi said to himself. *The death of a hunter of Kubwa Jim's reputation will be enough to create the fear I need so that my people turn to no one other than their jabilo.* He paused and his lips pursed into a malicious grin. *To me!*

The quiet of the night was disturbed by the crackling of the fire and the sudden bellow of a Cape buffalo. And Mokonzi's smile grew wider.

Aha! The beast comes.

Chapter 10

A journal helps keep experiences and events in perspective when reflecting on where we were and what we were doing. Also, there are certain subjects better left unsaid. Hence, putting pen to paper allows you the opportunity to broach the subject in a later appropriate time and place.

Big Jim awakened at the crack of dawn like usual. He rarely slept longer than six hours a night, preferring to make the most of the day with his eyes wide open rather than lying in the comfort of a bed.

He entered his study right as Kendi [KEHN-dee]; a 15 year old native girl brought him a tray of coffee, toast, marmalade, and fruit.

"Shukrani Nyingi, Kendi," (Many thanks, Kendi) Big Jim said. He walked around his desk and poured himself a cup of steaming coffee. The coffee was grown on his plantation and he was quite proud of it, too.

She walked to the door, turned to face him and said, "Kitu kingine?" (Anything else?)

Big Jim shook his head. "Hapana, mimi si unataka kuwa inasikitishwa." (No, I do not wish to be disturbed.)

Kendi softly closed the door behind her, shaking her head at the thought of him preferring to speak in native Swahili to her and the natives rather than English. All the children living in the nearby villages attended the school built on *Mbuga za Peponi*, and all were proud to have learned to speak English.

Why go to the trouble of learning how to speak the white man's language if they choose not to speak it with us? Kendi was left to wonder.

Big Jim looked out the window, admiring the sunrise. He lit his pipe, puffed it thrice, and opened the top right drawer in his desk. He reached inside and pulled out a worn, leather-bound journal, and opened it.

Things could not be worse, he wrote. *I lost my client in the bush—a first for me. A blasted elephant we tracked got the better of me. I fired two shots at the tembo, but failed to drop it. For reasons I cannot fathom, the tembo turned and went after my client, Nigel Stewart. An Englishman and not a bad sort considering he was born with a silver spoon.* Big Jim stopped, questioning whether he should leave that last part in. He did. *The man was anxious to bag an elephant,* he continued, *but all clients are.*

Big Jim put down his pen, puffed on his pipe twice, and reached for his mug of coffee for another drink. The aroma filling his nostrils reminded him of happier times, and he smiled, but only for a moment. He took another drink, this time making a squeamish face when the still hot coffee burned his lips. He put the mug down and picked up the pen.

Already the natives are claiming Juju is angry with me. After losing contracts to Bunny Allen this is the last thing I need. It will be difficult for me to save face, especially if I cannot be hired for a safari. I submitted my report to the Game Commissioner, but it could be some time before his investigation is complete. I will have to rely on my work here on Mbuga za Peponi to hold me over. Too bad about that. I still enjoy hunting more than anything in life.

There was a knock at the door and Caesar entered. "Morning, Old Man!" He held his own mug of coffee in one hand and a piece of paper in the other. "How was your night?"

Big Jim stopped writing and reached for his coffee mug. "As good as expected," he replied, shrugging. He motioned with a nod to the paper Caesar held. "Finished?"

"Hot off the press," Caesar said, handing it to him.

Why the hell are you so happy? Big Jim wanted to ask. He read the report in silence, occasionally drinking from his mug. Midway down the page his stomach churned. The details of Caesar's

Accidental Death Report were all too vivid for Big Jim, and the more he read the worse he felt. He set down his coffee mug. Suddenly it no longer satisfied his taste.

"Anything wrong, Old Man? You look as though you're about to bowl over."

Big Jim lifted his eyes to meet Caesar. He felt slighted the way Caesar sat comfortably in the chair across his desk. "Are you daft? Our client was killed. Our license is suspended and the natives are spreading rumors how *Juju* is angry with me." He paused, waiting for a reaction from Caesar, who gave none. "Do you have any idea how this affects our outfitting company?"

Caesar knew where Big Jim was going with this. Despite living in modern times Africa clung to superstition and witchcraft. With the coincidence of failing to acquire lucrative contracts with the movie industry and losing a client in the bush, natives would abandon the *Mbuga za Peponi* out of fear they would suffer same fate as the white hunter.

"This sort of trouble never lasts," Caesar reasoned. "Our boys and girls have nowhere to go. They know they live a comfortable life with us. At least here their mud huts and crops face no danger against being raided by elephant and buffalo." Caesar leaned back and lit his pipe. "You worry too much, Old Man." He said the last part with a touch of sarcasm.

Big Jim shook his head. *One of these days I'm going to strangle that S.O.B.*

Mary Watkins awakened at 7:00 AM, yawning and stretching slowly in bed. *I can't remember the last time I slept this comfortable,* she thought.

Her sense of adventure mind boggled family and friends, never remaining in one place long enough to develop lasting friendships. Her mother had given up the idea of playing with grandchildren years ago.

"How can anyone raise a family when they're gallivanting across the globe?" she would tell friends when asked how her daughter was doing and when she planned to marry.

Mary opened the wooden shudders to her room and let the sunrays spread their magic. The garden looked like a wonderful place to explore. So did the open-roomed school, the corral of horses and cattle, and the cages of wild animals ranging from anteaters, chimpanzees, and African Wild Dogs, to orangutans, baboons, and a baby rhinoceros.

Mary wanted to explore them all, but first had to tend to business. She washed her face in the bowl of water on the dresser in her room, changed into a pair of tight-fitting khaki trousers tucked into ankle-high boots, and a white blouse see-through enough for a second look at her perky breasts.

After running a brush twice over her hair and brushing her teeth she opened the door and ran into Kendi, nearly knocking the tray of coffee and breakfast she was bringing to her.

"Good morning!" Kendi said, pleasantly.

Mary appeared more startled than Kendi. "Oh, I—I'm sorry." She struggled for words. *There's never a translator around when you need one*, Mary said silently. A few awkward moments passed before she managed to say, "I—I—am looking for James and Caesar." *I hope she understands English.*

Kendi laughed a high-pitched squeal. "They're in the study," she said in slow, but clear English.

Mary blushed. She reached into her trouser pocket and pulled out a piece of paper. *Why I can't remember the simple things*, she wondered. She read her scribbling, searching for the right words. "Ahsante," (Thank you) she said, finally.

Kendi laughed again. "You're welcome."

Caesar opened the door to the study, inviting her to join them. Big Jim, ever the gentleman, rose from his chair and motioned for her to have a seat. They spent the next few minutes asking Mary about her experiences and what she thought of Africa. Big Jim poured her a cup of coffee from a set of china in the cupboard.

In the short time Mary explained her passion for journalism and travel both Big Jim and Caesar concluded she was capable of enduring a safari.

"Don't get me wrong," Big Jim started, "I've taken women on safari before. I want to be sure you understand the hardships accompanying bush travel."

"Yes," Caesar added. "It's not all what you read about in books and magazines, or watch in the cinema."

Mary did not appreciate being taken for a *daisy*, but kept her opinion to herself. "I'm offering to pay my way and then some," she said, confidently. "Why the hesitation?"

Big Jim puffed on his pipe, unconcerned if the smoke bothered his guest. "As Caesar and I stated, traveling in the bush is difficult. You won't have amenities like the *Norfolk Hotel* in Nairobi."

"And yet you've accepted my offer," she quickly interjected.

Big Jim nodded, still puffing on his pipe.

"Why?" she asked.

He glanced at Caesar, who shrugged as if to say, go ahead and tell her.

"The money and publicity will prove helpful until I overcome the challenges we now face," he said, with a touch of resignation.

"What do you mean?" Mary asked, curious. Jim started to explain and she cursed herself for not having her pencil and notebook on hand.

He told her about native superstitions and how losing his client cost him face, something a man in his position cannot afford to lose.

"Now there's a blasted rumor about a *Mnyama* in the form of a *nyati*, tearing up the villages," Big Jim explained. "They believe I'm being punished for my work with the Game Department."

"What work is that?"

Caesar took charge of the conversation here, telling her about Big Jim and Eric Rundgren, the man known as *Mchangi* to natives. "The Game Department hired them for control work." He saw her expression and knew she did not understand. "From time to time they hire hunters to shoot game to scale back population explosion. Huge herds of buffalo and elephant destroy wheat fields and other crops. Lion and leopard are after cattle, goats and sheep, even people. Anyhow, the Game Department hired them to shoot a couple thousand—"

"—*A couple thousand!*" Mary looked to be as astonished as she sounded.

Big Jim reached for his coffee mug and refilled it. "Believe me, it's not something hunters brag about, let alone even broach the subject."

Caesar recognized Mary's expression. "You must understand our crops and livestock are our livelihood. Even natives, after all these centuries and long before we arrived face similar difficulties. Without this action entire grain, millet stalks, coffee fields, and other vegetables are destroyed overnight."

Mary put down her coffee cup and felt her stomach churn. She wanted to change the subject, but that was contrary to her journalistic nature. "So how does this play in with native superstition?"

"They believe a *jabilo* has summoned the *Mnyama* to seek revenge against Rundgren and me for killing game indiscriminately."

"According to you it's not indiscriminate, but under direction of the Game Department."

Big Jim nodded and said, "That's not how they view it."

"And what's this *nyati*?"

Caesar informed her it was Swahili for Cape buffalo, and further explained that the *Mnyama* had chosen this form to represent the largest number of animals killed in their control work."

Mary scratched her chin. "I thought a *Jabilo* is a medicine man villagers rely on to cure the sick with spells, or cast away evil spirits and bring rain and good luck?"

Big Jim told her this was true. "However, every so often they tend to forget their place. They don't appreciate how natives turn to hunters for protection against lions and leopards, or a rogue elephant tearing up their fields."

"Or the buffalo," Caesar added.

Big Jim reached for his journal and replaced it in his drawer. He relit his pipe, puffed three times and leaned forward, resting his elbows on the desk. "I'm bringing you along because you're paying me money I'll need in the near future. Your story will generate interest in our company and keep me in the business of hunting."

"Which is our passion," Caesar said with pride.

Big Jim nodded. "At the same time, killing the *Mnyama* will regain confidence from the natives and keep them from leaving the plantation. I need them to work the fields and tend to the cattle."

Mary straightened in her seat. "Are they slaves?"

Big Jim reddened with anger. "Certainly not!" He practically spat the words. "I pay wages, sometimes in currency, other times with food, and often whichever they prefer."

Caesar chimed in quickly to help get off the subject of slavery. "Natives happily put up their villages on farmers' and hunters' plantations for protection against wild animals and other tribes that sometimes raid a nearby village for women, children, and food."

"Which means," Big Jim interjected, "they *choose* to be here." He paused, watching the young woman carefully. *I'm not so sure having you on safari is a good idea after all.*

"But we don't make slavery," Caesar finished, and with conviction.

Mary accepted the explanation. "Good to hear."

"Be sure to write that in your story," Big Jim said. It sounded more like an order than a request.

Chapter 11

Vengeance is seldom planned with enough consideration to escape unscathed.

The group of natives reached the river and jumped in, oblivious to the danger crocodiles and hippopotamus posed, their thirst overcoming judgment. They were a ragtag group, ranging from early teen age to early twenties, dressed in loincloth, sandals, and some with a robe worn across one shoulder, some without.

Only one African remained on the shore, watching the others submerge in the cool, murky water, drinking to their content without consideration of bacteria or disease. He crossed the territory suffering the same challenges of hunger, thirst and danger, yet he appeared unphased. His meager clothing was neither disheveled nor filthy like the rest, and he appeared well-fed and healthy despite eating no more than a handful of his *posho* each day.

Maybe we can catch some catfish and have a decent meal, he thought.

As if the men in the water read his mind, they were tossing small fish nets in the water and pulling out sizable numbers of fish. A few used spears to thrust in the schools of catfish, but the nets proved most successful. A short time later the fish were cleaned and cooked over a fire from the end of sticks.

One of the men walked over to the one standing alone and handed him a cooked catfish still on the smoldering stick. "Will you sit with us?" he asked.

The man took the fish and shook his head. "No," he said, in a commanding tone.

His name was Mashaka (mah-SHAH-kah), and meant 'trouble' in Swahili. Mashaka was born and raised in Nairobi and one of the few in his group with an education. He did much to earn his name as a boy, always fighting others in school, and stealing food and other goods and gave them to his mother. Mashaka's mother did the right thing by making him return the stolen items and refrain from bullying others, but that did not keep Mashaka from doing whatever came to mind.

What Mashaka had in mind now was to be chief of his tribe. Not any tribe, but the one he created beginning with this ragtag group of skinny, dirty, hungry, and illiterate natives who had no tribe to call their own. Outcasts to a man, they followed Mashaka because they looked up to him. He was good with words, with people, and knew what to say to make them believe in *him*.

Karanja (kah-RAHN-jah) was the unofficial second-in-command, and only considered so by the others due to Mashaka spending the most time with him. He wanted to believe in Mashaka for he promised them a village they would one day call their own. They would establish it by the sea, or a lake, or a river, any place where water and food were abundant. They would build mud huts, marry, and raise children.

…And live like human beings.

After years of living as outcasts, struggling for work, no family to turn to for support, Mashaka presented them the opportunity for a home they could call their own.

Only first they had to earn it.

"Are you certain about this?" Karanja asked, his voice tense with worry.

Mashaka did not blame him for doubting. Karanja was the smartest among the group, and he was not ready to *believe*. "Still doubt the power of *Juju*?" he asked. His lips pursed into a smile.

"I believe in *Juju*," Karanja said evenly. He paused a moment before adding, "I remain uncertain about *you*."

Mashaka stiffened. This challenge was unexpected. He looked over to the others who remained busy eating their fish and rice by the fire.

Good, they're out of earshot. "When we have proven to the

jabilo we are worthy," he said slowly, "*Juju* will bless us with the strength we need to build our village and gain the confidence of our people."

Karanja had no doubt Mashaka believed so, but he was not so certain. Attacking the white hunters was beyond their skills and he saw death following their actions. But not just any death—*their deaths!*

The others in their group went along with Mashaka's plan because they had nothing else. They did not even have an idea where they would get their next meal. Mashaka played on this to get them to follow him in his quest to become a village chief.

The plan was simple enough. The *jabilo* summoned the *Mnyama* for revenge against the white hunters who destroy the wildlife for sport. By attacking the plantations they are demonstrating support for the *jabilo* and respecting the wishes of *Juju*. A victory here will bring more followers and soon Mashaka will have enough men to build a village. Women were sure to follow, and they would bear children, thus making the village ever larger.

And I will be the chief, Mashaka told himself.

"We must earn our reward," he said curtly. "Only with the *Jabilo's* blessing will we receive what we seek." He then added in slow words, "And he will not bless us until we demonstrate to *Juju* our full support."

After an awkward moment Karanja nodded slowly. "I understand," he said in a subdued voice. Only he did not agree what they were about to do was in their best interest.

Sunset came shortly after, no more than two hours, and the men were edgy. Mashaka knew this was dangerous. None of them were trained to fight, and they had no rifles, only spears and long knives, mostly dull bladed.

It is still necessary, he told himself in an attempt to convince himself those who may die tonight would do so for a good cause. *His* cause.

They gathered on top of the hill overlooking *Mbuga za Peponi,* hidden by thick brush and acacia trees. The plantation was not alive with activity. The main building where the white hunters lived looked dark. Only the kitchen windows were lit, not the rooms where the owners ate their meals, sat and drink, or slept.

The natives who work for him must be in the kitchen, Mashaka thought.

He looked to the north of the plantation where mud huts were located, fifteen in all, and large, too. The natives who worked the fields and tended the animals occupied them. Some cooked dinner over small fires while others went to sleep. Only a few gathered in front of a large mud hut, mumbling stories to one another.

Mashaka was not angry with these people who worked for the white hunters. At least *they* have a home, he said silently.

And quite a home it was! This was Mashaka's first time seeing the *Mbuga za Peponi* from a bird's-eye view. He had no idea how large it was. The main clapboard building with the corrugated roof obviously was where the white hunters lived along with clients. The structure was lifted off the ground and supported by three foot wide stilts and a shaded veranda stretched the entire building.

On the western side of the plantation were the fields of millet stalks, corn, coffee, wheat, and vegetables. It was here the natives worked to earn their keep. Acacia trees and bushes were studded here and there, providing a natural look to the property. On the lower east side was a pond close to the corral and kennel where horses, cattle, and cages of animals were held before being released back to the wild or shipped to zoos outside of the country.

On the southern side close to the main gates to the property was the school. How the others in Mashaka's group longed to have learned to read and write. The structure was maintained in good condition, its corrugated roof supported by long wooden poles. The wooden floor was not suspended off the ground like the main building, but it appeared to be in good form. Rows of benches and tables were provided along with books, pencils, and paper. It was an open structure with no walls, like the kind people would gather for lunch while out on a picnic.

How did they get to be so lucky? he wondered.

A glimpse at his men indicated they had doubts about what they were about to do. Even in the dark of night he could see their expressions in the moonlight. Mashaka started to open his mouth to speak when a deep, guttural bellow came from behind them. The sound was followed by heavy snorting and hooves pounding the earth as whatever creature this was made its way toward them. They all faced the heavy Leleshwa brush and Msasa trees, wondering what animal approached them.

Karanja looked at Mashaka, who stared back an empty look, one that said he had no idea what was happening—or about to happen. Mashaka raised his spear over his shoulder, preparing to throw it in a moment's notice, and his men started to do the same.

Then without warning the brush and trees exploded!

The beast charged full speed at 40 miles per hour. Its hooves pounded the earth like thunder, snapping trees, dead wood, and kicking up a heavy cloud of dust in its wake. It shrieked a loud, angry cry, the kind distinguished only with hate.

Mashaka threw his spear, and saw it bounce off the beast's thick boss adorning its head with a long pair of razor-tipped horns.

Karanja and two others threw their spears and saw they failed to pierce the animal's thick, coarse hide.

"*Throw your spears!*" Mashaka cried to the others.

It was too late. Fear had sunken in and the remainder of his men ran screaming in the night.

As if the beast knew who it sought, it turned toward Mashaka. In a matter of seconds the beast would be on top of him, ready to crush him beneath its thick, heavy hooves.

"*Run!*" Karanja shouted.

Instead, Mashaka dropped to the ground and the beast ran directly over him, missing him entirely. He had no time to thank *Juju* for sparing his life for the animal spun around and came back for him. This time, however, it did not have the rush of speed on its side. When it struck Mashaka the blow was not enough to kill him. It was not even enough to knock him off his feet. Mashaka did the only thing he could, and that was to hold on for dear life to the animal's boss.

Karanja looked on in horror as the beast, an animal he made out to be an oversized buffalo, swung its head this way and that, trying to dislodge its intended victim. With no apparent luck, the beast dropped its head and rammed Mashaka to the ground.

Mashaka's body went limp and he felt the air in his lungs drain as the beast rammed him again. He tried to cry for help, but no words came. When the beast pummeled him a third time he felt like his insides were about to explode.

"*Nooo!*" Karanja cried out.

The beast swung its head in Karanja's direction, its crimson red eyes boring into him. Karanja could practically feel the evil from its stare, and he froze from fright.

Mashaka lay hopelessly on the ground and watched the beast charge Karanja. Right before it struck it cried a deep, throaty shriek echoing clear across the valley. The last thing he saw before closing his eyes was Karanja's body being thrown back and to the ground. Then the beast hooked him with its horns and tossed him high in the air.

Karanja's sense of feeling left him now. He did not feel the shock of hitting the ground when his body landed on the rocks and dirt. Nor did he feel the razor-tipped horns dig into his fleshy stomach, spilling his intestines. Right before closing his eyes he witnessed the huge beast rise on its hind legs, moving its front legs in the air like a stallion demonstrating its dominance. It shrieked another piercing cry before landing on Karanja, crushing his body to a pulp.

Chapter 12

*Many white hunters steadfastly denounced hunting as a form
of sport. For them hunting was a way of life defined by the special
bond formulated between hunter and prey. Only those who have
hunted will understand this.*

Mary Watkins reveled riding in the front passenger seat of the land
rover with Big Jim at the wheel. Caesar was kind enough to allow
her his usual seat to witness how his partner would handle the many
questions she was bound to ask. They always asked a mountain of
questions on safari.

"What type of tree is that?"

"It's a *Msasa* tree. You can always tell by the rosy-red, chocolate
leaves hanging on the branches."

"And those?"

"They are *M'swaki* bushes. The natives make good use of the
olive green thickets."

"How so?"

"They make toothbrushes from the stems of those bushes."

Mary pointed in the direction of a large number of trees. "What
are those trees called?"

Big Jim drew a breath before answering. "*Fever* trees," he said.
"They grow as high as 60 feet, and can be identified by their bright
yellow trunks. They're the only tree I know that shreds its bark like
the brittle parchment of a snake shredding its skin."

Mary raised an eyebrow and nodded twice. She would never
admit how she detested snakes, and fought the urge of squirming
at the mere mention of one.

Mary caught sight of the snow-capped peak to their north east. "Is that *Mount Kilimanjaro?*"

Big Jim nodded. "The natives call it *Mount Kili.* It's the highest point in Africa."

"How high?" she asked.

Big Jim sensed she was testing his knowledge. *You're not going to get under my skin,* he said silently. His mouth pursed into a slight smile and he took his eyes away from the trail momentarily to meet hers.

Mary blushed.

Too bad you're 15 years too young, he thought.

Too bad you're 20 years older, she thought.

"It's 19,340 feet," he said, finally. "The mountain above Arusha is *Mount Kili's* sister, called *Mount Meru.* She's 14,979 feet. Both are extinct volcanoes and draw a lot of attention."

"Yes, especially from Hollywood film-makers," Caesar interjected.

Big Jim glanced over his shoulder. "So you finally decided to speak," he challenged.

Caesar responded with a sly grin before taking a swig from his ever-ready flask.

They spent the next two hours traveling north to the Serengeti. During this time Mary asked the question Big Jim dreaded most.

"Why are you called *Big Jim?*"

He kept his eyes on the trail and shook his head as if to say, not again. "You have the honor, Caesar," he said, speaking over his shoulder.

Caesar chuckled. I'm going to enjoy this, he told himself. "*Kubwa Jim* is Swahili for Big Jim. He got the nickname for surviving the toughest and biggest elephant any hunter faced." Caesar's brow furrowed. "I take that back. Eric Rundgren may give Big Jim here a run for his money. The natives call him *Mchangi Rundgren.*"

"And that means?" Mary asked.

"Means there, here, and everywhere you look. Rundgren is a Dane about the same size as Big Jim here, except he's a bit stouter whereas our lad driving is fit as a bull."

Big Jim did not bite the bait, but managed to shake his head.

When they arrived at the southern edge of the Serengeti Big Jim ordered the askaris and wapagazis following in the lorry to set up camp. A nearby river provided plenty of fresh water and guineafowl were everywhere. They would provide a good meal for the night and help to save on provisions.

While the natives went to work setting up camp, Mary took her satchel and meandered over to the river. Finding a nice log to sit on, she plopped herself down and removed her broad-brim hat. The cool breeze felt good against her face and she wiped the perspiration off her forehead with a handkerchief. Then she pulled out her notebook and began to write in her journal.

Africa is truly the land of adventure. If I were on the far side of the moon I could not feel more detached from civilization as I do here. In Nairobi and Arusha I was amazed how people from all over the world live in harmony. I suppose this feeling is due to my selfish notion that only in America can people of all races live in such proximity without killing one another.

I made contact with the white hunters in Arusha and have hitched a safari with a man named James Peck. The natives call him Kubwa Jim, but I think James suits him. He and his partner, Caesar Wilde, have had a run of bad luck. A client of theirs was killed by an elephant while on safari and the natives believe them to be cursed.

I only caught wind of this yesterday, but the natives here are still superstitious. They believe a witch doctor, called a Jabilo, has cursed the white hunters for killing off the wildlife. This could be nothing further from the truth, but I suppose it has to play itself out before things return to normal. They agreed to have me on safari because my magazine company is paying a sizable fee which will help them until the Game Department clears them of wrongful death of their former client. Until then they are not permitted to have clients on a shooting safari. This journey is for me only, and I will be taking pictures and writing for my magazine.

I think James resents this, him being proud and all. At least he is wise enough to see the benefits of my—.

"Please remember not to stroll off far from camp and without one of the askaris," Caesar said. He saw how he had startled her and apologized. "Didn't mean to cause you to jump. It's just that you never know what wild animals are lurking about."

Mary surveyed their surroundings. "I don't see any wildlife," she noted, carefully.

"One never does when being hunted." He lifted his eyes upwards. "This tree could very well have a hidden leopard high in its branches, lying silently in wait for someone of your size to offer an evening meal."

Mary jumped to her feet, eyes alert, and moved closer to Caesar.

"It's quite all right, dear. I only want you to think about safety before marching off."

A rifles report caught their attention.

"Who's doing the shooting?" Mary asked.

"The *askaris,* our gunbearers, guides, and protectors have the honor of collecting our dinner." Caesar provided Mary with a brief history about the relationship between *askaris*, white hunters, and clients.

"For all intents and purposes, natives in the role of *askari* are an elevation in stature. They don't perform menial labor like the *wapagazi*. Carrying supplies on top of their head is beneath a person of their talent. An *askari* is a crack shot with a rifle, but seldom has the opportunity of proving it. That privilege is reserved for the client and white hunter. Images are a terrible thing to waste. They do hunt guineafowl and *Thomson Gazelle* to provide meat for everyone. At night they patrol camp like soldiers on guard. This is for good reason, for it's quite common for hyena, cheetah, leopard, and lion to stroll into a camp in search of an easy meal. Another important part of their work is locating a potable source of water. Without a working knowledge of rivers and rain pools a long safari is doomed for failure."

"Native cooks are called *M'pishis*, and provide clients with a first-hand taste of local dishes. Breakfast consists of eggs, oatmeal, toast, and coffee. This meal remains simple and light in order for everyone to keep from getting sick on a heavy stomach while marching through the bush or traveling by land rover or lorry over rough terrain."

Caesar took a moment to light his pipe before continuing.

"Lunch is an elaborate meal of *Kumbari a la regal*, which consists of catfish caught from a nearby stream or river, and served with corn and salad on the side. The main meal for dinner is *Nyama Choma*, roasted meat cooked *Maasai*-style with a spear over a fire. Clients love this form of cooking and watch the *M'pishis* in action like children in an amusement park. The meat types range from ostrich, zebra, gazelle, and goat, served with plates of *Kachumbari*, seasoned vegetables, on the side."

Mary struggled to write down every word Caesar spoke.

"Not going too fast am I?" he asked, with a touch of wily sarcasm in his tone.

Mary continued writing. "My shorthand isn't too good," she confessed. "All this is interesting. The little details like those make the best of any story." She looked over to where the natives were busy setting up camp. "What do the natives eat?"

Caesar grinned curiously. "You're the first person in quite a while to have any consideration for what the natives eat. Usually they're too busy fussing over the wildlife."

"That's understandable considering where we are," Mary said quickly.

Caesar agreed. He told her about *Posho*, the rations for askaris and wapagazis, and made up in the form of maize mixed with water to create a doughy look. "Mixed with vegetables and meat, it holds them over from meal to meal."

Mary next observed how well the camp was setup. Three medium-sized green double-fly tents were their quarters, each with one to themselves. There was a large tent for the kitchen mess, another for the dining, and a third for bathing. Smaller ones were used as sleeping quarters for the askaris and wapagazis.

Mary observed three Africans reach into the back of the lorry and carry heavy canvas bags. "What are those?" she asked, curiously.

"Cooling bags," Caesar replied. "They keep the food cool, not cold mind you, but enough to keep perishables fresh."

"Not to forget the beer," Big Jim interjected with a touch of humor Mary had not yet seen. He surprised her by approaching in silence.

She noted in memory details for later entry in her journal how they lacked nothing in the way of equipment. Wooden tables and chairs for dining, food preparation, and sitting by the fire were hauled in the lorry and set up by the wapagazis. She took particular notice of a canvas wash basin held up on a wooden tripod next to a tree with a mirror hanging from a knife stuck in the tree trunk.

When the wapagazis had finished setting the tables and chairs they went about cutting large thorn bushes.

"Why are they doing that?" she asked, still in her inquisitive tone.

Big Jim lit his pipe. "It's called a *Boma*. We take the thorn bushes and form a fence around camp for protection from predators."

All Mary could say was, "Wow! Things really are dangerous around here, aren't they?"

Big Jim nodded. "You'll be safe enough. Let's have some lunch. Afterwards we'll take a short march for game."

"I thought you aren't allowed to hunt until the investigation clears you?"

Big Jim stiffened. He did not like being reminded of having lost a client.

Caesar took notice of his friend's discomfort and answered in his place. "As we pointed out before, this isn't a 'shooting safari.' No licenses are required for taking you on a photographic trip."

Mary stopped in her tracks. It occurred to her that her magazine editor would like photographs of hunters in action. Her story was about white hunters in Africa, not wild animals in their natural habitat.

Big Jim blinked and looked at Caesar. "I think we can manage something without drawing attention from the Game Department," he said self-assuredly, and then continued walking to the dining tent.

Mary looked at Caesar. "What does he mean by that?"

Caesar shrugged. "Guess you'll have to wait and see." He was smiling when he said it.

Chapter 13

Poaching of African wildlife has decimated many species. Some argue the most threatened of all species is the elephant. Its ivory is priceless, and in a land where much of the population lives in abject poverty, the lure of riches is too great to ignore. To the surprise of many, professional hunters have done much to curb poaching by working for the Game Department, which manages Africa's national parks. They issue hunting licenses, enforce the protection of threatened species, destroy poachers' traps, and arrest those caught in the act of illegal poaching. This part of their life can be more dangerous than facing a charging Cape buffalo, lion, or bull elephant.

"Poachers!" Big Jim cried.

There was no doubt in his mind that this was the work of poachers; the scum of the earth so far as he and all professional hunters were concerned.

While traveling along the escarpment of the Manyara National Park the sound of gunshots caught their attention.

"Another shooting safari?" Mary asked from the back of the rover.

"Possibly," Caesar replied.

Big Jim did not think so. The gunshots sounded erratic, and whoever was doing the shooting appeared to be wasting cartridges with impunity.

"Let's have a look," he said, sternly.

They drove on for another fifteen minutes over rocky terrain surrounded by scrub thorn brush and many varieties of trees. Mary recognized the species from books she had studied during the boat ride across the Atlantic. There were Msasa trees, made recognizable by their rosy dark-red leaves. The ever-present acacia trees dotted the landscape, easily identified by their umbrella canopy and spindly limbs. The ficus trees where the species commonly found along rivers offering shade to animals and humans alike.

I wish I could take a photograph with my Brownie, she said silently. But they traveled too fast and their path was quite bumpy over the rocks.

Big Jim ordered the caravan of vehicles to a halt when they reached a *dongo*, what the natives referred to as a dry riverbed or sand stream. On the other side before them was *river grass*, also called *tall* or *long grass*. During monsoon season the grass looked dark green, but this time of year was dry and it had turned light brown. The field of grass remained thick and dense, and as high as ten feet, making it impossible to see what awaited them on the other side.

Big Jim was glad the lorries made it over the rough terrain. *Last thing we need is a vehicle breakdown.*

"Taabu, you remain with the woman," Big Jim ordered. He turned to Caesar and said, "Come on."

Big Jim took his Mauser .350 repeater and Caesar carried a .256 Mannlicher rifle, both easy to reload in case they found themselves in a bind.

Mary climbed out the back seat of the rover and pulled her *Brownie 127* from her leather bag. Taabu said something in Swahili, which she did not understand, but knew well enough that he did not want her venturing after the two *bwanas*.

"Don't worry," she said, in a tone emphasizing she was not going to make trouble. "I only want to photograph the *Great White Hunters* in action."

Taabu understood the white peoples' language along with the sarcasm in her voice, and a thin smile cracked his lips.

After five minutes of walking through the tall grass Caesar wished it was he who had remained with the woman instead of trailing his longtime friend. "This is worse than a swamp infested with crocs," he complained.

Big Jim turned and shook his head, flashing an expression for him to keep quiet. "You know better," he whispered.

Still, he agreed with the Englishman how the trail proved formidable. The grass was so thick you could not see more than an arm's length in front of your face, and its blades were sharp and cut into their exposed faces and hands. Their long-sleeved shirts, trousers and heavy boots came in handy for this type of trail; that much was certain.

Slivers of light shone through the blades indicating they were near the edge of the field of grass, and they stopped and listened. Only the sound of wind rustling through the grass reached their ears at first. A few moments later they heard it.

Voices!

Big Jim and Caesar had lived long enough in Africa to recognize the dialect. Swahili was the most commonly spoken language on the continent, and easily recognizable in spite of the many variations spoken tribe to tribe.

Big Jim turned to Caesar, released his right hand from its grip around the barrel of his Mauser, and spread his fingers wide.

Five. That was the number of men he guessed they faced. Caesar nodded his understanding.

When they pushed forward enough to see through the field of grass the sight was horrific. A huge bull elephant lay on its side, blood trickling from its giant head from the many bullet wounds it had received, and a few spears jutted from its side. Big Jim guessed the spears were laced with poison to help bring down the behemoth.

Not far away lay another elephant, not quite as big a tusker as the bull, but with enough ivory to make the poachers water at the mouth. It was a female elephant and still alive. It laid on the red, dusty ground, struggling to rise while the poachers danced around the fallen giant, arguing over which of them was in turn to claim the animal theirs to kill.

Spears jutted from its side, the same as its mate, along with numerous, flowery red holes on its head where the poachers shot it. One of the natives stepped close to the *tembo* and stabbed it over and over with a spear. The others laughed at the scene, decrying the man for a fool to believe this was the way to kill such a creature. The elephant managed a final shriek of defiance from its trunk before another stepped forward with a rifle and fired a kill-shot at point-blank range. The bullet smashed through its skull and into its fist-sized brain, reducing it to a pulp. The elephant's body stiffened, and then went limp.

Big Jim and Caesar had seen this type of poacher before. They were natives belonging to no particular tribe, instead choosing to loot and pillage for profit. The price of ivory had skyrocketed in recent years, and to date there were land giants aplenty to provide them with enough riches to keep them out of the fields or working for the white man for the remainder of their lives.

"Shameful how they haven't learned to dress despite having earned their ill-gotten gains," Caesar said in a hushed voice.

Big Jim agreed. This sort of native did not earn money to enrich their lives, but to live for the moment. They spent their money on drink, women, and more of the same until the money was gone. After a couple of weeks of living their filthy lives in this manner they were back in the bush earning their keep in precisely the same way.

Big Jim reasoned this sort of person had a life expectancy of five years. After which they died of disease, be it from malaria, black water, dengue fever, sleeping sickness, tick fever, or from being mauled by a lion or leopard, or trampled to death by a charging bull elephant.

This group was the most rag-tag either hunter had crossed yet. Two wore khaki shorts and torn blue jerseys, an indication they were former gun bearers for a white hunter's safari company. They likely were not askari, but wapagazis. Any native capable of being an askari would never stoop so low to poach. But wapagazis were another matter. Few moved up from carrying luggage on their heads and receiving barked orders from a *bwana*, be it from a white or black man. This was reason enough for them to turn to poaching for a living.

Big Jim was reminded of the saying, *better for a bull to die in the ring against a matador, than a cow in a slaughter house.*

The other three wore filthy robes and sandals, armed with spears and *pangas*, large throwing knives more useful against man than beast. Big Jim reasoned they were Kikuyu or Kamba tribesmen, certainly not Nandi. The Nandi were the best askaris and possibly bravest hunters in all of Africa. None would lower their dignity by turning to poach.

Both white hunters flipped off the safety switch to their rifles, raised them to shoulder level, careful to only allow the tip of the barrels to pierce through their shield of tall grass, took aim—and fired!

Both natives with rifles were knocked to the ground flat on their backs. Their cry of agony was more piercing than the death cry of the female *tembo*. The other three ran to retrieve the fallen rifles. They had no intention of fighting with spears against rifles in the way their Zulu ancestors had against the British. The victory at Isandalwana in 1879 had taught the Africans never to tempt fate.

Another two simultaneous gunshots fired from the tall grass kicked dirt into their faces right when the natives reached for the rifles. It was apparent their foes intended the shots to be a warning not to press their luck.

The ruse worked. Instead of putting up a fight, the three scantily-clad native poachers went to their fallen men, helped them to their feet, and ran like the devil chased them. The shoulder wounds were not life-threatening, and did not slow down their pace. It was not long before they disappeared in the thick African bush.

Big Jim remained at the edge of the field while Caesar returned to the vehicles and brought them all to the sight of the carnage of fallen elephants. True to her blood of wanting to be a reporter, Mary jumped from the back of the open-top rover and started taking photographs with her *Brownie 127*.

"I say," Caesar started, "You don't waste time."

Mary ignored the comment, moving from one position to another and taking snap shot after snap shot of the giant elephants. After several more shots she stopped, moved up to the bull, and reached out and touched the deceased animal on the side of its head near the bullet holes that killed it. After what appeared to be an interminably long time, Mary turned and faced Big Jim and Caesar.

"Why?"

They noticed a tear slide down her cheek after asking.

Big Jim pointed to the ivory tusks. "Those," he said, definitively. "They're worth as much as gold in Asian markets."

Mary nodded twice, understanding his meaning.

"Why don't you take another photograph," Big Jim suggested.

Mary shot him a look of astonishment. Caesar did, too.

As if he knew what she were thinking, Big Jim quickly followed up with, "The more people know how poachers destroy wildlife for illegal profit, the better chance we have of the law putting pressure on the black market, which funds poaching."

Mary thought for a moment, and then said, "But you kill these same animals for trophies. I saw them in your office in your home. You sell your services for people from all over the world to come here and kill for pleasure, and to take their prize back home for display in a den, or museum." She paused for effect. "How are you different?"

Big Jim had been caught off guard. Never in his dreams did he believe he would be compared with that of a poacher. His face paled, but only for a moment. When he gathered his thoughts he opened his mouth to speak, but was cut off by his English friend.

"I beg to differ, my dear," he started, clearing his throat. "You're way off the mark." Caesar shouldered his rifle and stepped closer to her. "We hunt for sport, yes. But the bond developed between hunter and beast differs in ways only a hunter can realize. It has been in man's nature to hunt since the dawn of man. Our placing the head of a trophy, as you called it, on a wall does not demean our respect for these creatures. To the contrary, it reminds us of the respect we have for such animals we faced off with." Now it was Caesar who paused for effect. "You see, it's man's nature to hunt. Yes, we may buy our food in a local market, but to hunt for our meal leaves us with a sense of satisfaction only a true hunter may realize." He followed up with, "Just because we're civilized doesn't mean we've lost all our natural instincts."

Big Jim was grateful for the intervention. He added, "Not to mention that the kills we make feed villagers in need of meat." He waited for Mary to turn and face him before saying, "Not all tribes can visit a local market for food, you know, and elephant and buffalo make a tasty treat for the natives."

Mary was not one to be easily won over, but something told her these two were men of honor and true to their word. "Thank you for the clarification," she said, smiling gratefully. "However, you can't expect me to believe there are no hunters who shoot for the mere fun of it. Surely there are those who want to brag about their shooting experience by hanging the head of an animal on their wall."

Both hunters had this sort of discussion before. Usually it was with the wife of a client tagging along for the ride, but who disapproved of their husband killing for sport.

"Yes, that's true," Big Jim started. "I can't make the distinction with a client who books our services through a telegram, but once I've been introduced I pretty much know their true intentions."

Mary was intrigued. "And you still take them on safari?"

"My dear," Caesar began, calmly, "it would never do to cancel a contract with a client once we've agreed to it. Not without cause anyway. If a person wants to bag a wild animal for the sole purpose of bragging rights, no one will stop him. But let me remind you, if we have that sort of person on safari they're not likely to go on a shooting rampage under our management."

"That's right," Big Jim said quickly. "Professional hunters can manage clients in a way that people can appreciate the thrill of a hunt and learn to respect animals versus killing them for the mere thrill of it, as you put it."

Mary believed them, but the sight of the dead elephants made her ill. For the first time since arriving in Africa she was left to wonder if this safari was a good idea.

Chapter 14

Despite generations of living side by side each other, native suspicion runs deep in many tribes. It is not uncommon for them to believe much of their problems have been forced upon them by the white man. This suspicion has prevented relations between them from moving forward, and caused death and despair.

Gary Hayes read the report twice and still did not believe it. "Has the entire village gone mad?" he asked, in disbelief.

The chief commissioner sat behind his desk going over papers. The report Gary, a full-time game warden and part-time hunter, held was one of many the commissioner read since arriving for work in the district office in Arusha.

"And what exactly is your definition of sanity?" the commissioner challenged. "Spending your entire adult life in Africa chasing poachers and protecting wildlife?" He snickered. "You stand a better chance of being mauled to death by a leopard or trampled by a bull elephant than you have of collecting your pension."

Gary did not like being reminded how his chosen profession was seen as a poor choice among the civilized world. *What the hell does anyone know?* "Better to live life to the fullest than being coddled with a silver spoon," he shot back.

Now it was the commissioner stiffening. His name was Roger Forsythe, an Englishman and son of a nobleman close to the British royal family. It was rumored that Roger's father had been knighted by the King and was elevated to the title Lord Forsythe in large part due to his actions in the First World War. The senior Forsythe fought Kaiser Wilhelm's army in what was then German

East Africa, and took part in the surrender of German forces led by General Paul Emil von Lettow-Vorbeck.

In truth, the German general fought through the entire war undefeated. His victories embarrassed the British military, and many officers who fought with little distinction were presented with high accolades in an attempt to downplay the superior leadership of General von Lettow-Borbeck.

Roger Forsythe's father had been one of the lucky officers to be awarded with medals, promotions, and a knighthood. He was even granted a large spot of land in the former German East African territory, where he spent the remaining years of his life raising his family and making a name for himself in the newly-christened Tanganyika Territory.

Roger was educated in England, but felt his roots came from Africa. Much to his father's disappointment, the junior Forsythe returned to the Dark Continent where he pursued a career as a professional hunter, later game warden, and now chief commissioner of the Nairobi and Arusha districts.

The district office was located in Nairobi two blocks from the esteemed *Norfolk Hotel*. It had recently gone through an upgrade from white-washed stone walls and corrugated roof to clapboard wood and shingled roof. Even the windows and doors were imported from England. As professional hunting grew the need to improve appearances for all government offices did, too, and Roger was relieved to be working behind a sturdy desk.

At least I can put the benefits of my education to good use here, he told himself.

Standing at five feet and five inches, Roger was not a physically imposing man. What he lacked in size he made up for in good looks and elegant manners. He kept his blond hair plastered down with hair tonic, brilliant in the sunlight, and his sky-blue eyes captivated women. Despite spending most of his life in Africa his skin remained a pinkish-white, unlike others who turned bronze. Roger did not spend much time hunting for his services were sought by the government when it became apparent his organizational skills were precisely what the Game Department needed.

When he received promotion to chief commissioner he changed

his work attire from khaki shirt and trousers to a suit and tie. This made him and the manager of *The Safari Hotel*, another Englishman named Ben Benbow, the only two men in all of Arusha to dress in such out-of-place style. It was not uncommon for locals to place bets on which of the two would give up the coat and tie for something more practical considering this was Africa. To date, no one had collected their winnings.

Roger put down the papers he held on his desk and leaned back, adjusting himself to a comfortable position. "I'll need you to visit this village about fifty miles north of here. Do you know it?"

Unfortunately I do. Gary nodded. "You don't believe this report?" he asked, still astonished by its content.

Roger shrugged. "Doesn't matter what either of us believe until after you've conducted a thorough inspection," he said quickly. "Word of an *incident* has reached the governor's desk and he wants us to investigate immediately." Roger was a bit more curt than usual.

Gary sighed. *Why argue?* "If I leave now I can return by nightfall and have my report on your desk by morning," he said, wearily.

"There's a good chap for you!" Roger said, beaming.

Gary had traveled to Kupendeza back when the road was less developed. *How long ago was that?* he wondered.

He remembered back in the day when roads were little more than pot-holed, rocky trails carved by roaming herds. Since then the dirt road had been leveled by a government work crew and he could not remember the last time he had traveled such a distance without feeling as though his spine was jolted to and fro.

It was mid-afternoon when he arrived on the outskirts of the village. He brought the Chevrolet land rover to a stop and switched off the engine. Staring at the village of Kupendeza, he slowly spoke the words, "What in God's name...?"

Total devastation lay before him. What was once a village of numerous huts and one modern home built and owned by the village chief named, Omel, had now become a waste land.

This looks like someone took a giant plow-share and uprooted the entire village, he thought.

"It was the *Mnyama*," said a voice from behind.

Gary turned swiftly and found himself staring into the face of a boy. "The what?" he asked, carefully.

The boy stared blankly ahead, never looking Gary in the eyes. "The *Mnyama* destroyed my village," the boy repeated. "It killed my father. It killed my mother and brothers and sisters. It destroyed everything."

Gary could not argue. All of the huts had been knocked down, including the modern home. Even the field had been uprooted and the crops destroyed. A few people walked in a daze here and there, pacing back and forth as though searching for something or someone, even bumping into one another. But most of the natives were gone.

"Where is everyone?" Gary asked, softly.

The boy did not answer right away.

Gary touched him on the shoulder. *You look hungry and thirsty.* He retrieved a canteen from the land rover and offered it to the boy. At first the boy did not respond. A moment later he took the canteen in both hands and drank heavily, spilling water down the sides of his mouth.

Gary pulled the canteen away. "Take it easy, son. You'll get sick. Now tell me your name."

The boy wiped his mouth dry. His eyes seemed to come to life, and his breathing steadied. When he managed to look Gary in the eye he said, "My name is Tayari."

Gary knew the name. In Swahili it meant 'ready.' "And your father? Where's he?"

The boy stared blankly.

Gary knew better than to push him for more information. "This village called Kupendeza means 'delightful,'" he said in a subdued voice. *Only there is nothing delightful about it now.*

Tayari agreed and nodded slowly, leaving Gary to wonder if he had read his mind.

Tayari finally looked up at the white man and started to speak.

"You must leave," he said with finality. "Your presence has brought the wrath of the *Mnyama* upon us."

Gary knew what *mnyama* meant. He spoke and understood fluent Swahili. "Did you see this *Mnyama*?"

The boy stared blankly. After an awkward pause he nodded. "Go. Your presence will damn us all."

Gary touched him on the shoulder. "We can help," he said, soothingly.

Tayari stepped back away from him. "If you stay you'll die along with the rest of us."

He sounds like he means it. "You can't possibly believe that," Gary replied. "We've been in Africa for generations now, living side by side with you."

The boy shook his head. "Go! You don't belong here." He paused again before saying, "Look at what has happened to my village, my home."

"You can't possibly believe we're responsible," Gary said, shocked at the notion the natives would think such a thing. A moment after saying so he was reminded how the commissioner told him, *"It only matters what they think."*

Tayari glared at Gary. "If you remain here we will all die," he repeated with tears welling in his eyes.

Gary started to say something. He desperately wanted the boy to believe the Game Department could help, but thought better of it. *What's the use? This boy's mind is made up.*

He walked back and climbed back in the land rover. As he started up the engine he said, "We're not going to look the other way, son. We're going to find the creature that did this and put it down. You have my word."

Tayari watched the white man drive off and believed he meant what he said. But something told him the *mnyama* would not be easy to kill.

Chapter 15

There is a saying among hunters. The return of a favor may be worth less its value for the trouble you have while giving its return. And some people never learn for the better.

The next morning Roger read Gary's report in silence in his office in Nairobi. Gary took note of Roger's suit and tie. *Looks like I still won't collect on that bet.*

Roger finished reading and put down the papers on his desk. He got up, walked to the table across the room, and poured himself a cup of tea. For Gary he poured coffee.

"Too bad you Americans don't appreciate the finer tastes in life," he said, handing Gary his cup on a saucer.

"Too bad you English don't appreciate the simple things," Gary countered.

Roger managed a smile. He returned to his desk and sat down heavily in the chair. "So what do you propose?"

What do you mean, what do I propose? Gary flinched. "The only thing we can do is hire someone to track and kill this *Mnyama*."

Roger took note of his non-committal tone. "You think we're chasing a ghost?"

Gary sighed. "As you said, it doesn't matter what either of us believe. We've conducted a thorough report. The village of Kupendeza is no more. The survivors have spread a rumor that a terrible beast they call *Mnyama* is on a rampage."

Roger's Swahili was not so good. "What does *Mnyama* mean?" he asked, bemused.

"It means 'beast.'" He paused for effect. "They believe an angry *jabilo* has summoned this beast for revenge."

"What revenge?"

Gary collected his thoughts. *I don't want to confuse him more than he already is.* "Apparently this witch doctor is angry with local villages for turning to white hunters for help against troublesome elephant and buffalo destroying crops. Word has it that this *jabilo* is punishing the natives for their lack of faith in him."

Roger thought a moment, and then shook his head. *How in the world have these people survived for so long?* He did not need to ask the question aloud, nor did he require an answer. He knew well and good that superstitions ran deep in Africa. The matter needed to be handled with care.

"Who's on our list for favors owed to us?" the commissioner asked.

The list he referred to was of safari outfitters in debt to the Game Department for generous permits allowing them to hunt in territories with plenty of game for their clients to have full advantage. In exchange, the outfitters agreed to cropping herds or taking down a troublesome elephant or buffalo at no charge to the Game Department. It was their way of scratching each other's back.

Gary sipped his coffee. *Needs milk and sugar.* He got up and walked to the table for some. Taking a drink, he thought for a moment and said, "Ker and Downey are too busy to investigate. They've got clients up to their armpits."

Roger hated that saying. *You Americans are so uncouth.* "What about Bunny Allen?"

Again Gary shook his head. "He's managing a large camp for the film company shooting a movie called *Mogambo*."

Roger repeated the name. "*Mogambo*. I'll have to be sure and see it. I understand the lovely Ava Gardner is starring in this cinema."

The two took their seats again opposite each other sipping their coffee and tea. Finally it came to the commissioner.

"James Peck!" Roger said sharply.

"What about him?" Gary asked, befuddled.

"I hear he had a spot of trouble recently. He lost a client, an Englishman no less. And his license has been revoked pending conclusion of the investigation, yes?"

Gary did not like where this was going.

Roger took note of Gary's behavior and continued. "Tell him if he chases this imaginary *Mnyama* and brings it down, at least to the satisfaction of the natives believing such nonsense, we'll reinstate his hunting license."

Gary nodded. *What the hell. We've done this before.* "I'm sure that'll sit well with him."

"Where is he now?"

"I hear he's out in the bush taking a journalist on a photo shoot."

"He's not in violation of his parole?"

Gary raised a halting hand. "He knows better," he said, reassuringly. "He's to do no hunting until we conclude our investigation on the death of Nigel Stewart. This safari he's on is a photo shoot only."

Roger nodded. "This is even better! He's already in the bush. He can take on this *Mnyama*, bring it down, show the carcass to the natives, and we'll have this thing put behind us once and for all."

He sounded as though it were as easy as pie.

Chapter 16

*In Africa they have a saying. 'Vengeance only leads to more death. All
too often it is the one seeking revenge that loses their life.'*

Mutia [*moo-Tee-uh*] was determined to seek and find *Kubwa
Jim*.

"But Mashaka wanted to kill the white man," declared Rabo. He
was a thin, well-muscled nineteen year old African from Uganda.
His parents christened him the name Rabo because it meant
'luck' in Hausa of West Africa. Rabo's mother could have chosen
a common Swahili name, but she wanted something more for her
first-born son and the name struck a chord with her.

"Do you not think I know this?" Mutia retorted, angrily.

"Then why do we—?"

"I had a vision," Mutia cut in. He stopped marching for long
enough to look Rabo face to face. "My vision said we were wrong
to follow Mashaka," he explained. "The white hunter is not the
enemy. The *Mnyama* is the enemy."

With Mashaka lying injured from the attack of the beast and
Karanja dead, Mutia took charge of what was left of what they
believed would be a future tribe, now reduced to three Africans.
Rabo turned to Mutia for leadership because he was the elder, and
his name meant 'honored one' in the Kamba tribe of Kenya.

Rabo stared in total confusion. "Mashaka said his vision was to
serve the *Jabilo*. If we did this for the *Jabilo* we'd be blessed with
good luck by *Juju*."

Mutia was beginning to realize how backwards they all had been
by clinging to native superstitions. The *Jabilo* worked both ways, he

knew. On the one hand, natives turned to them for spells to cure the sick, or a blessing for a good season of crops, more rain, and good land to build their villages.

On the other hand, there was the *Jabilo* who was completely self-serving. He was the medicine man, or witch doctor that carried a grudge against those who did not look to him for everything. Indeed, when a *Jabilo* had the confidence, or fear, of a tribe he was certain to have a full belly of food served to him by the natives each night. It was not much of a life, but better than going hungry, especially at an old age.

"What do we do?" Rabo asked, with a touch of desperation.

Without hesitation Mutia replied, "We seek the white hunter called *Kubwa Jim*."

Rabo looked over to where Mashaka laid under the shade of a tree. All three had been injured by the *Mnyama*, but Mashaka's wounds were more severe. He was lucky to be alive. They all were. And Karanja's death had been the worst.

"And when we have found him, what then?" Rabo asked.

Again, Mutia did not hesitate to answer. "We join forces with him and seek and destroy the creature." He watched for Rabo's reaction. Then, staring him directly in the eyes, he added, "Only together will we defeat this demon."

The impressionable young native was beginning to believe Mutia was right, and that Mashaka's vision had been interpreted wrongly. But he knew their condition compromised a speedy journey across the veldt.

Mashaka's ribs were broken, and his left leg sprained. Mutia had a deep gash in his right thigh. An inch to the right of the cut would have severed his artery, killing him for certain. Rabo had been knocked down by the buffalo and very near trampled, but the animal went after Mashaka with a vengeance, like it knew he was their leader.

"What does Mashaka say?" Rabo asked curiously.

Mutia looked over at their chief, who still lay asleep. For the first time he doubted the man's leadership and capabilities. He shook his head out of disgust. "There's nothing left to say," he said, flatly. "It's what we all must do."

Mashaka opened his eyes slowly. A strange feeling made him feel he was being stared at. Sure enough, Mutia and Rabo stood over him. The chief lifted himself on his elbows. He looked at them as if to say, what?

Without saying a word they helped Mashaka to his feet. Mashaka grunted in pain. He felt his ribs scratch against his stomach, and he nearly doubled over. They handed him his staff and wrapped his upper body with his dirty blanket. Then they picked up their leather satchels, water bags, leather pouches of *posho*, and *assegais*, short heavy spears with a double-edged blade up to six inches across its widest part and two feet long. They also carried *pangas*, long and heavy throwing knives also good for cutting through heavy brush.

Mutia nodded to Rabo, who assisted Mashaka in their march into the bush, and thus continued their journey as they sought to finish a fight they hoped would render them a place they could call home...So long as they proved victorious.

Chapter 17

Most hunters will agree a charging lion is one of the most frightful events to experience. Time and again the big cats have mauled, maimed, or killed a hunter tracking them. Even when hit multiple times with powerful rifles the lion continues to charge.

Big Jim watched with concern as Barake and Davu approached the *simba* lying in wait for them in the bushes. The big cat's tail swung wildly and it growled savagely, curling its lower lip. Big Jim knew these were sure signs the lion was close to attacking the two natives, and he raised his Westley-Richards Double Rifle to shoulder level, drawing a bead on the animal in his sights.

Mary remained with Caesar, Nyeusii, and Idirisi by the land rover. Taabu, the other askari, was left to look after their camp with the majority of wapagazis. Mary watched the scene unfold with her camera, a new *Brownie 127* by Eastman Kodak. It was quite popular with outdoor enthusiasts looking to capture a special moment on film. Simple in design, the *Brownie* was a small box-like camera with a meniscus lens and curved film plane. It was easy to operate and the 127 film was more than enough quality to capture good shots in black-and-white.

Before embarking on her journey Mary insisted her editor provide her with a more expensive camera, but her editor encouraged her not to let the low-cost price of the *Brownie* undermine its tough durability. To date she was pleased to have listened to her boss.

Putting her eye to the viewing lens, she snapped a shot of Barake and Davu inching closer to the lion. The clicking sound of the *Brownie* echoed loud enough to stir the big cat, and it released another growl.

Caesar touched her shoulder from behind, motioning with a shake of the head for her to refrain from taking another shot.

"Sorry," she silently mouthed.

Big Jim shook his head without taking his eyes off the lion. *Gonna have to paddle that girl's bottom.*

Big Jim received a message from a native runner working for the Tanganyika Game Department the day before about a troublesome lion terrorizing the nearby villages.

Sorry to put you out, old friend. Stop. *We have word of a Simba making things rough for natives in the lower Serengeti.* Stop. *Understand you are traveling in the vicinity and would appreciate if you took care of the situation.* Stop.

It was signed by Chief Commissioner Roger Forsythe, a man who was neither friend of Big Jim nor an enemy. The hunter new the commissioner was not a man to trifle with, and also knew him to be fair. In a way, Forsythe was doing Big Jim a favor.

The loss of his client was a serious occurrence in the hunting trade. No one wanted to see him lose his license. The dangers of hunting were discussed with professionals and novices before embarking on each and every safari. Everyone knew death lurked around each tree, over every hill, and in every dense thicket. And still people came to hunt in Africa.

There was something about the *Dark Continent* which drew people from all corners of the earth. It had romance. There was danger and adventure beyond anyone's wildest dreams. Hollywood provided people a taste of this in the cinema, but there was nothing close to the real thing as an African safari.

Although Big Jim and Caesar's competitors would prefer less competition, to see him go under in such circumstances was disagreeable for all, especially seeing how the same thing had occurred with every hunting company on the continent at one time or another.

Barake and Davu continued to inch forward with small steps clutching spears with the blades facing the *simba*. It was an old cat, but healthy from enjoying easy kills in the nearby village.

Thus far two adult males, one female, and three children had been killed by this lion. As Big Jim explained to Mary on their journey to the Serengeti, lions and leopard were known to enter villages and towns in the middle of the night and attack unwary people. They were drawn by the smell of fresh cooking, or dogs, and of course small children. Stories of people living in town answering a knock on their door in the middle of the night, only to be dragged out into the street and mauled to death by a 400 lbs. lion were commonplace among the natives.

Caesar explained to Mary how only the old or sick lion made a habit of creeping into towns and villages to attack people. "People make for an easy kill," he said, speaking in a flat, toneless voice. "A healthy, active lion remains in the bush, protecting its harem of lionesses. When they grow old or sick a younger lion takes over and the former cannot risk injury going after a zebra or gazelle. The zebra can kick more powerfully than a mule and a broken jaw would spell the end for a cat."

Mary thought he sounded like a teacher explaining a lesson to a child. "So the lion goes after people because we aren't much of a threat?" she asked.

Caesar nodded. "It doesn't occur with much frequency these days, but it does happen."

And Mary knew this to be the reason they were here going after the lion approached by Barake and Davu. She watched as the pair walked closer to the animal. The scene unfolding before her was incredible.

Suddenly the lion lurched forward three feet, growling menacingly.

The natives froze.

Big Jim's index finger touched the trigger of his double rifle ever so lightly. He knew he could not fire effectively at this distance. At best he could wound the lion, but to kill it outright would be sheer luck.

Barake better get it right, he whispered to himself.

Then the lion bolted forward, growling and baring its teeth, closing the distance between it and the two natives with lightning speed. Barake and Davu remained frozen, clutching their spears. The lion leapt high in the air, its forward legs reaching out and baring its claws.

Barake moved to his left and out of the lion's path. At the same time he thrust the blade of his spear into the lion's throat. Davu dodged the animal by moving to his right and quickly thrust his spear into its heart. The lion loosed a high-pitched cry that sent chills running down Mary's spine.

The big cat's body went limp and fell to the ground with a hard thump, skidding a few feet before coming to a stop. The two Africans stood still, their adrenaline running high from the experience, which nearly cost them their lives.

Mary regained her composure and snapped a photograph. The clicking sound of the *Brownie* awakened everyone from their silent trance.

Big Jim lowered his double rifle. His eyes met Barake and Davu, who grinned back at the white hunter. "Old tactics never die," he said aloud, but not enough for the Africans to hear.

Davu reached for the staff of his spear stuck in the lion's chest when suddenly the big cat jumped to its feet. It growled in a low, heavy murmur, gurgling blood in its throat. Barake had enough time to pull his spear out of the lion and prepared to plunge it into the cat when the lion swiped the spear from his hands. Another swipe knocked him back, and he clutched his chest where the claws dug deep into his chest.

Then the lion swung around facing Davu. The African took a defensive stance, drawing his long, heavy two pound knife, the *panga*, from the sheath at his side. The cat spat out blood when it growled again and Davu stared into its eyes. He was close enough to see his reflection in the animal's eyes and could not help but wonder if this was his last few moments on earth.

The lion lunged for Davu! At the same time a shot rang out from Big Jim's double rifle. Two flower-like holes appeared on the big cat's side following the dull thud of the 750-grain bullets striking its hide. The animal cried out a high-pitched cry before skidding to halt inches from its intended victim.

Davu drew a breath. His entire body trembled. When he looked over to Big Jim he saw the white hunter grinning.

"That was a one-in-a-thousand shot," Big Jim said, proudly. He looked over his shoulder where Caesar and Mary stood. "Did you get your photograph?"

Mary blinked. "No," she said, trembling from excitement and fear. When she calmed herself she grew embarrassed from missing the opportunity for a rare photograph of a hunter in action. *What will my editor think?* She quickly said, "But I'll be sure to write about this in my journal." Although Mary did not know Big Jim well enough to judge, she could have sworn he expressed a look of disappointment.

Chapter 18

The Westley-Richards .577 Double Rifles were manufactured with one purpose, to bring down the largest beasts on the continent. Its reliability made it a favorite among professional and amateur hunters.

Mary still felt the rush of witnessing the lion's death and had trouble putting pen to paper. Ever the true journalist, she made due.

'It's amazing how these people live,' she wrote. *'The natives have primitive methods that remain effective in killing troublesome lions, and yet they rely on the weapons of white hunters, which proved helpful today.'*

She put her pen down and took in the scene of their camp. The dead lion was loaded in the back of the lorry and brought back to the village where local natives came to see it. They wanted to be sure the devil-cat was dead. The villagers seemed to give all the credit to Davu and Barake, ignoring Big Jim altogether. Fortunately for Barake, his wounds were not life-threatening, but the scars on his chest would remain with him for life along with the memory of nearly being sliced in half by the claws of a *simba*.

Mary was awakened from her reverie by the sound of approaching footsteps from behind.

"Didn't mean to intrude," Caesar said. "How goes your journal?"

Mary closed her book and rose to her feet. "You're not bothering me. I can't concentrate now anyhow."

Caesar looked at her curiously. "I hope you're not too disturbed by the killing of the lion?"

Mary paused and shook her head slowly. "I don't think so," she replied with a hint of confusion. She faced Caesar and explained. "In America we see lions as 'king of the beasts,' and when we hear how they're frequently hunted it raises concern." She paused for reflection while turning to observe the scene of natives gloating over the dead cat.

Caesar patted her shoulder. "They're magnificent," he declared. "They also happen to be a damn nuisance." He motioned for her to take her seat on the fallen tree and took a seat of his own on a boulder.

Mary opened her journal again and prepared to write as he explained his knowledge of the lion.

"They're beautiful, cunning creatures," he began in a tone much like a schoolmaster speaking with students. "The moment you disrespect them you die." He let that statement hang for a moment to be sure she understood his meaning. Then he went on about a particular hunt he and Big Jim went on while in the Selous Game Reserve.

"We had our share of close calls, but then every professional hunter does. Each animal poses a particular danger over the other. In the case of a *simba* one must guard himself against a creature blessed with speed, cunning, and agility. While on safari in the Selous Territory we learned a pride of lions had acquired a taste for human flesh. They don't usually eat humans, but certain tribes make it too good for them to pass up."

Mary was all ears, and kept up by writing in short-hand.

"Some tribes leave their elders alone in the bush to die in peace, only they don't die as peacefully as they were intended. On occasion a *simba* will come across such a person and turn them into a meal. The big cats will eat anything, flesh, blood, bones, clothes, boots— every part of a human and their belongings that you can imagine. Well this pride of lions, about six if memory serves me, notched three to five kills a day for weeks before the Game Department caught wind of the tragedy taking place in local villages."

"Why didn't the natives contact the government sooner?" she asked, curious.

"They were too frightened to travel through the bush. In any case, James and I were asked by the Game Department to see if we could handle the matter."

"And you said, yes," she abruptly cut in.

Caesar nodded and lit his pipe. "One does not ruffle feathers with the Game Department," he said matter-of-factly. "Seeing how they issue licenses and permits it pays to remain on their good side."

Mary jotted down a few words in her journal. "So what happened in the Selous Territory?"

Caesar drew on his pipe and exhaled slowly. His pupils seemed to dilate as he reflected on that incredible journey that seemed so long ago, yet lingered like it had taken place only yesterday.

Big Jim followed the spoor through the heavy brush of thickets with Caesar in tow not more than ten paces behind. No askaris or wapagazis accompanied them. Caesar thought it best to have Barake and the other veterans remain with the clients in camp and ensure they kept out of trouble. The clients wanted to join the hunters, but Big Jim did not want to risk losing a client to a pride of lions. Their disappointment was soothed by the prospect of having Barake track an African Bull elephant with heavy tusks; every hunter's dream.

"They should be close," Caesar warned.

Big Jim agreed, nodding twice. His eyes remained to their front where the pride of lions was sure to be. The question was where?

Where are you? Big Jim wondered.

He could feel their presence and it made his skin crawl. The feeling always amazed him. Despite years of hunting he remained awed at how the effect of tracking dangerous animals had on him. The thrill of danger was as addictive as a drug, he knew.

… Which is a primary reason we hunt.

At first they thought they were tracking one lion. Then it became apparent there were two, perhaps three. Soon the spoor and tracks revealed a pride of six, possibly seven or eight lions. Big Jim thought about retiring and reporting his find to the district commissioner, but decided against this.

Surely the Game Department would close off the territory until the danger was settled.

This was something Big Jim and Caesar could not allow. If two of the most renowned professional hunters could not resolve the issue, then what point would there be for clients to hire them for a shooting safari?

Big Jim was committed and both he and Caesar knew it.

A hunter's sixth sense is developed very quickly in the African bush. It's quite inescapable. The hunter peered through the brush and tall, spiny acacia trees and found nothing. Yet he knew they were there.

Caesar caught Big Jim's attention with a soft whistle, sounding more like a guineafowl bird lost in the heavy brush of thickets. He motioned to their front and when Big Jim peered in the same direction he saw it.

One hundred yards away lay a knoll of boulders surrounded by acacias and brush. It was the perfect place for a pride of lions to make their den. Big Jim acknowledged with a nod and the two hunters inched forward. Some fifty yards later they halted. What caught their vision confirmed their worst fear.

Three lions marched out of a cave one by one and plopped themselves on the warm boulders, sunning themselves. They licked their chops the way the big cats did after consuming a meal. Then another two lion appeared from the den, lying next to the others.

A pride of five!

The hunters knew this was no good. They could shoot two, and hit a third if luck proved to be on their side. The uninjured *simbas* were sure to take off, leaving the safety of their den. The last thing either hunter wanted was a drawn-out hunt for man-eating lions.

Caesar crept closer to Big Jim and whispered, "What do you think?"

Big Jim never took his eyes away from the pride of lions. "We've no choice but to go for two of them. If possible, we'll get a third. The others will bolt. We'll report to the district commissioner this and he can send a party to track and bag them."

"That won't satisfy him," Caesar declared. "The commissioner has given us a job and will expect us to finish it by killing this pride."

"That's out of the question," Big Jim declared. "We've got clients to take care of. It could take two, perhaps three days to track and destroy the ones that get away."

Caesar knew this was not the time to argue, and the *simbas* did make a good target. After feeding they would be lazy, unable to move swiftly over uneven terrain. He started to take a position a few feet away when movement to their front caught their attention.

A big cat appeared twenty yards to their front. It was a male lion, making its way to the den. It moved slowly because it dragged something heavy in its jaws and the object caught on the thorn brush here and there. Suddenly the object in the lion's jaws moved freely. It squirmed as if trying to escape. The black shape let out a yelp, and then the arms and legs of the object became unmistakable.

"Dear God in Heaven!" Big Jim muttered.

"That's a man," Caesar whispered.

"Quiet," Big Jim muttered soft, but firm.

The native was near death and delusional from blood loss and cuts to his back and neck. Big Jim figured there must have been a village nearby and the poor man had been dragged from his hut, or perhaps attacked while fetching water or searching for food. *Simbas* were bold enough to enter villages if they had a taste for human flesh.

And this cat does, he said silently.

Caesar knew better than to talk at a time like this. A lion's sense of hearing was acute, and to speak risked giving away their position.

To hell with it! "Are we going to *do* something?"

Big Jim remained silent, watching the African being eaten alive as though mesmerized.

The native cried a low-pitch scream, and the lion put its large paw over his mouth to silence its prey. It opened its jaws wide and bit deeply into the man's throat, crushing his larynx and biting through his vertebrae. The dark crimson ooze spilled out of the native and the lion started licking the blood before it dried.

Caesar had seen enough. "If you aren't going to do something then I—"

Big Jim stopped him by holding out his arm. "Don't be a fool!" he said sharply. "He was already dead."

Caesar stared perplexed.

Big Jim explained. "The man's movements were reactionary. He was dead and didn't know it. Even if we managed to free him from the *Simba* he's lost too much blood to survive a journey across the veldt to a hospital." He waited for Caesar to let his reasoning sink in and then added, "We can't afford to lose the element of surprise."

Caesar grunted, licked his lips and nodded. "I suppose you're right," he said with reluctance.

The two hunters had worked together long enough to know what needed to be done. They moved away from each other no more than ten paces. The heavy shrub and thickets allowed them no more, and remaining in one another's sight was important for their survival.

Big Jim checked the cartridge loops on his hunter's vest for assurance he had enough ammunition for the job at hand. Perspiration beaded heavily on his forehead before dripping into and stinging his eyes. His 16 lbs. Westley-Richards double rifle became heavier as the sweat in his palms made it difficult to hold the weapon in a firm grip.

A large tearing sound caught his attention. It was the *simba* biting into human flesh. The feline beast chewed the native like it was a huge feast. It snapped through bones, too, creating a popping sound when its powerful jaws closed on the remaining pieces of what once was a man, and now small lumps of sinewy flesh, blood, and bone.

Big Jim sized up the cat and determined it was the largest of the pride. Its black mane was uncommon for this territory. He reasoned it must have traveled from Uganda, taking up residence in Tanganyika. This breed of lion was more common in that territory.

He pulled back the hammers to his double rifle and adjusted the rear express standing sight for the twenty yard distance between him and the animal. He would have to make the first shot count for he knew a healthy lion such as this could cover the distance between them in about three seconds.

An amateur hunter would be a fool to try and bag a lion under similar circumstances. The Westley-Richards double had a powerful kick and few hunters could fire the second barrel with any accuracy after the first shot. Its 750-grain bullet with a muzzle velocity of 2,050 feet-per-second was designed to bring down the biggest, toughest, and most difficult to kill animals on the *Dark Continent*.

Big Jim learned long ago that if you chose the wrong weapon when hunting *simba* you would learn it to be a mistake quickly, and you only made one mistake against the large cats for they did not allow you to escape in order to live and make another.

Caesar lifted his own rifle to shoulder level. His was a .470 Rigby Double that fired a 500-grain bullet at 2,150 feet-per-second. In the bush this rifle proved as reliable as the Westley-Richards.

Both hunters took aim, squinted their non-firing eye, without closing it completely, and touched the trigger to their rifles with their forefinger.

The simultaneous *BOOM* from both rifles sounded like thunder directly overhead. Their eyes blinked, as everyone's did when firing a weapon, but they held their rifles aimed in the direction of the *simba* to their front.

The bullets slammed into the side of the lion's chest, tearing through muscles and bone. The big feline cried a high-pitched snarl and jumped five feet straight in the air. The pride resting on the boulders bolted for cover in the den and bush. When the lion landed it shifted its body in the direction of the hunters—*and charged!*

Big Jim squeezed the second trigger.

BOOM!

Caesar did the same.

BOOM!

A second later the lion lunged for Big Jim the remaining ten feet between them, jaws wide open and its front legged large, fat paws with long claws fully extended. Big Jim dove to his right to miss the full weight of the beast. Had he not done so the 400-plus lbs.

cat would have landed on top of him, crushing him with its bulk before sinking its teeth in the back of his neck as they instinctively did when killing the two-legged animals with fire-sticks.

Big Jim cracked open the rifle stock and ejected the spent shells from the barrels. He had less than two seconds to reload before the angry cat swirled around to charge again. Times like this made him wish the Game Department permitted hunters to carry pistols, but that would take away the challenge of man versus beast.

He removed two cartridges from his vest, but the *simba* lunged toward him and swatted the double rifle out of his hands. The cat pounced on Big Jim, knocking him on his back and opening its jaws wide. Right as the cat was about to bite Big Jim quickly shoved his hand deep in the animal's throat in a move designed to keep the big cat from closing its mouth and biting him.

Caesar snapped shut the breech to his .470 double rifle and took aim at the *simba*. His close friend lay not more than ten yards from him and looked to have his arm inside the cat's mouth up to his elbow. He caught Big Jim's glance.

"What are you waiting for?" he shouted. "SHOOT!"

The rifle roared two simultaneous booms followed by a ball of orange flame. The heavy weapon kicked furiously in Caesar's arms, but he managed to hold it steady.

The first slug struck the cat in the side of the head, blowing out its left eye. The second slug entered the animal's ear and blew open its fleshy, heavily-maned top of the head where its skull would be if the lion had a skull to mention. The *simba* roared and collapsed its full weight on Big Jim—and clamped shut its jaws.

Big Jim cried in pain as the sharp teeth dug into his forearm.

Caesar ran to him, keeping watch on the pride disappearing in the brush. Lion were a peculiar sort. Sometimes they retreated in the face of danger, other times they met it head on. The last thing they needed was one or more of the pride to attack. When he was certain none were within sight he rested his double rifle on the carcass of the big cat and grasped its snout. With little effort he pulled back the lion's snout, allowing Big Jim to remove his arm from its throat.

Big Jim grunted in extreme agony as he pulled out his arm.

"Remind me not to do that again," he scowled.

"Hang tight," Caesar said, reassuringly.

Next he moved behind Big Jim and wrapped his arms beneath his armpits. "This is going to be a bit tricky," he warned.

"Do what you've gotta do," Big Jim replied.

The weight of the *simba* was too great for an easy removal from beneath it. Caesar pulled left, then right, then left, then right again. He kept this up several times before feeling Big Jim begin to slide out from beneath the cat. After several moments he managed to drag Big Jim free.

"I can't believe I allowed that to happen to me," Big Jim bellowed, furiously.

Caesar grinned. "Don't be hard on yourself. That move damn near saved your life. With your hand deep in the *simba's* throat it couldn't bite." Caesar pulled out a handkerchief. He never hunted without one, and Big Jim wondered how the Brit managed to keep it crisp and clean. "Where the deuces did you learn that trick?" he asked, curious.

"I've stayed alive by thinking fast on my feet," Big Jim replied, curtly.

The sharp edge in his voice did not go unnoticed, leaving Caesar to wonder if his injury was worse than it appeared. He checked to see if his arm were broken.

"Only a flesh wound," the Englishman said, coolly. "We'll get you back to camp and properly clean and bandage your wound. After a shot of penicillin you'll be up and ready in no time."

Big Jim watched as his friend tightened the tourniquet and wrapped the cuts on his forearms with his handkerchief. "Looks like I'll have something to remember this cat from now on," he said, with scorn.

Caesar laughed. "Don't look at it that way, Old Man. Now you'll have one more story to keep the clients interested while sitting around the campfire."

Chapter 19

*Many professional hunters have said there is nothing romantic
about the African bush. Lions are considered a nuisance, hyenas
are determined and deadly, and elephants are dangerous and swift,
capable of trampling you in the blink of an eye. Death awaits the
careless and it is the hunter's responsibility to keep his clients alive.*

Mary sat in the privacy of her small, double-fly tent. There was
room enough for two, but Big Jim allowed her a tent for herself
seeing how she was the only female in their group. Caesar made
certain the wapagazis provided her with all the comforts one
expected on a full safari. She had a cot with mosquito net, a small
wooden table and chair with a lamp hanging overhead, and her
suitcase of belongings beneath the cot.

She took this moment of privacy to do what she loved most. She
wrote in her journal. *If everyone traveled to Africa they would soon
form the opinion Hollywood has misled the public,* she wrote.

*The simba is Swahili for lion, and they are not referred to as
King of the Beasts. Rather they are a menace to society in the way
the gangsters were seen during the American bootlegging days
of the Prohibition Era. Caesar enlightened me how a famous
early hunter by the name of Leslie Tarlton killed nearly 300
lion. Some were killed on a shooting safari with paying clients;
others were by request of local villages and the government
Game Department. In his time, Mr. Tarlton was considered a
hero by the natives for protecting them from dangerous simbas
threatening their lives, but he never liked discussing the fact he*

shot and killed so many lion.

I believe his reasons were due to the hunter's code, which is to say tracking a wild beast for sport is no simple task. In the early days of safaris the odds were stacked against the hunter. You could shoot a lion square in the chest and it still charged with its tail wagging madly, claws outstretched, and jaws snarling. So long as the odds were even for man and beast, hunters do not believe shooting for sport is wrong. In fact it is more natural for man to hunt much in the way their ancestors did for food. But to shoot lions for cropping purposes provided no thrill. No challenge. Mr. Tarlton was not proud of the number of lion he killed, so he never discussed the matter. I find it curious how his fate was to be mauled to death by a lion while on safari doing what he loved most.

Mary stopped for a moment, reflecting on what to write next. She reached for a glass of water on the table, took a sip, set down the glass, and drew in a breath. *So relaxing,* she thought. Then she picked up her pencil and started writing.

Then there is the hyena, called Fisi by the natives. They are not as cowardly as described in books and movies. They hunt in packs and attack with unparalleled ferocity. The hunters have told me they have the most powerful jaws on the continent, and were it not for their short hind legs they would be more formidable than the lion.

The leopard is called Chui, and can climb a tree faster than a lizard. Few hunters have been able to bring down this swift cat with a single gunshot. Natives are fiercely superstitious and believe the chui are reincarnated Jabilo, or Laibon, both meaning witchdoctor who seeks justice against those who insult Juju, their deity.

I find this Jabilo and Laibon to be most fascinating. Villagers turn to them for healing, marrying, acquiring lost cattle and other property, for rain, protection, casting spells for good luck, and much more. Yet these same witchdoctors are feared as devils that punish natives for turning to white hunters for help against

*simbas and fisi and other animals threatening their existence.
It's a form of jealousy that would make one laugh were it not
for the animosity existing between hunter and witchdoctor that
threatens any chance of building a positive relationship between
the two.*

Mary paused, again to reflect on other information she learned
about professional hunters. Under the shade of a tree stood Big
Jim washing himself in an outdoor sink made of canvas, supported
in the center of a folding wooden tripod. It was the latest piece
of equipment used on safari to help clients and hunters enjoy the
comfort of a half-bath during a hot day.

Mary watched the hunter with growing fascination. There was
no mistaking the handsome masculinity of James *Big Jim* Peck.
She found him confident, polite, experienced, and proud of his
profession. Her female curiosity was piqued by this fine specimen
and she wondered why he was not married.

Must be a lonely life, she thought. Then she knew what to
write next.

*They are hunter, guide, doctor, mechanic, poker player, and
gentleman all in one,* she wrote. *When a lorry or land rover
breaks down the hunter makes repairs. When a client or native
is mauled by a lion or leopard the hunter tends to their wounds
same as a doctor. When a client has a question about the wildlife
the hunter always has an answer. In the evening when a client
wishes to play poker the hunter proves to be a formidable player
and always has a good supply of champagne and gin on hand to
celebrate a good day of hunting.*

*What would surprise most people is the way the professional
hunter prides himself as a conservationist. They certainly have
their share of hunting for sport in their blood, but they fiercely
fight poachers and help natives control wild animals threatening
their crops and children by cropping them. This action is seen as
a threat to the Jabilos and Laibon who prefer villagers turn to
them for help instead of the white foreigners.*

Yes, I wrote foreigner. Despite a hunter's love for Africa they are not native here. It is the foreigner who seeks ivory, gold, diamonds, trophies, and anything else that creates a profit. The hunter is by no means a poacher; however their presence threatens the Jabilo's sorcery. Therefore the Jabilo condemns the professional white hunters with their black magic in order to keep hold of their people.

Mary stopped and took another moment to think before adding, *or so they try.*

"Care for a spot of lunch?" It was Caesar. He stood at the entrance to her tent, catching her off guard and startled her.

Mary composed herself. "Y-Yes," she stuttered. She glanced again in Big Jim's direction. "I'm feeling a bit hungry."

Caesar noted her discomfort over being caught admiring Big Jim. "They don't call him *Big Jim* for nothing," he said, jokingly.

Mary's eyes practically popped from the sockets. "I beg your pardon," she curtly replied.

He nodded in his friend's direction. "Not every day he removes his shirt in the presence of a lady," he said, grinning mischievously. "Some time ago he was severely mauled by a *simba* that nearly took off his arm were it not for his quick-thinking. The scars have been a reminder how even an experienced hunter can lose his life in the blink of an eye."

"I haven't noticed them," she said.

"And you never will." Caesar paused to light his pipe. He motioned her to follow him. "It's a conversation he avoids." He could not help noticing how her journalistic curiosity was piqued, so he told her the story of how Big Jim and he searched for a pride of man-eaters and nearly lost their lives in the bush.

When he finished Mary stood awestruck. "I had no idea those beautiful animals could be so cunning and vicious," she confessed.

"Of course not," Caesar said, understandably. "Up to now you've only seen the beasts behind a cage in a zoo. In the bush these cats are home in their environment, and they know how to make the most of it."

"I thought lion turned to hunting people only when they grew old or injured," she admitted.

Caesar shook his head and mentioned the incident in Tsavo during the turn of the century. It was a time when ivory poaching was at its height and the British were constructing a railroad bridge over the Tsavo River needed for transporting trade goods from Nairobi to the coast. An engineer and hunter by the name of J.H. Patterson was assigned the job of building the bridge, and it was not long before he found himself out in the bush tracking the big cats who proved quite disruptive.

"You see, the lions got a taste for human flesh thanks to the Indian coolies," Caesar explained. "The laborers didn't bury their dead and it's believed lions fed on the corpses, hence developing a taste for human flesh." He watched the journalist closely before continuing. "Apparently our meat has a nice salty flavor the felines tend to appreciate."

Mary made a face of discomfort upon hearing this, but Caesar was not one to stop in the middle of a story even for etiquette.

"It took Colonel Patterson several months of tracking this pride before bagging them," he continued. "Then there were another pride of lions hunting and killing humans for food in the Ubena Territory, a beautiful place northeast of Lake Nyassa in Tanganyika. They operated for over a decade before a fellow by the name of Rushby, a game officer, bagged them as well."

Mary appeared flabbergasted. "How many did they kill?" she asked, curious. She clung to every word he spoke.

Caesar looked surprised. He thought she looked like she would not hold her stomach, but apparently misjudged her resolve. *Guess writers are a tough breed after all.*

"Hundreds," he replied, shrugging. "Perhaps thousands. No way of knowing for certain. In the Njombe District in the southern territory of Tanganyika there were over a dozen pride lions responsible for killing up to 1,500 people over 15 years. And this is only the number of recorded deaths. There is no way of knowing how many were killed in remote villages."

Mary shuddered at the thought. "In my short time here I find the romantic image of an African safari to be nothing more than a fraud," she said hoarsely.

Caesar grunted. "You only know what Hollywood shows you

in the cinema. That opening scene in *King Solomon's Mines* when Stewart Granger walloped the bull elephant was no prop. The herd was worked up by the film crew looking for film locations. One of the cameramen got too close to the herd and the bull charged. The professional hunter hired by the film company for escort was a fellow by the name of Stan Lawrence-Brown, a good chap and equally good shot. He saved the lives of those cameramen that day, but the incident continues to rile."

"Why?" Mary asked. She could see the story bothered the English hunter and genuinely wanted to know.

Caesar stopped walking and looked up at the clear, cobalt sky. On any other day he would have appreciated the view of the mountains looming in the distance across the acacia tree and thorn shrub-scarred bush-veldt. A herd of wildebeest and zebra made its way across the tall, dry grass, grazing under the likely presence of stalking lions waiting to catch an unsuspecting calf for a meal.

Nodding twice, he explained his feelings. "We don't hunt for the sake of killing," he explained. "A bond only a hunter understands is developed between him and beast. That elephant was killed for the sole purpose of people looking to make a film."

"Then why stuff and mount the animal on a wall in your study," Mary quickly interjected.

Caesar turned to stare her directly eye to eye. "It's not for show, I assure you," he snapped. "Rather it's more of respect. By making use of the animal's meat an entire village is fed. The hide is made into clothing, and the ivory sold for money to pay for workers." He paused to collect his thoughts. "As for the trophy mounted on the wall, it's to remind the hunter out of respect for what it once was and stood for."

Poppycock! Mary shook her head. She wasn't buying it. "There are professional hunters in America, too," she said, suppressing a smirk. "I find it difficult to believe all hunters are as noble as you describe."

Caesar shrugged. "*You* would," he replied, calmly.

Mary stiffened. "Why do you say that? Because I'm not a hunter?"

The Englishman shook his head. "It's because you have your

mind made up."

Mary appeared to be hurt. "I'm only judging based on what you and James have discussed with me," she said, defensively.

"Perhaps, but do you truly believe us? Or are you simply writing a story to increase circulation of the paper employing you?"

Clever boy! You know me better than I thought. "I'm not sure I know what to believe," she said, flatly. "But I'll let my readers decide. And if you like, I'll allow you to review my journal and provide me with a critique which I'll present to my editor." It was all she could do to keep from flashing a malicious grin. *If you believe that, I'll have one hell of a story for certain.*

Caesar was thoroughly impressed. He did not expect her to rise to his challenge so admirably. He pointed to the shaded tree where a table and chairs were arranged for them to eat. The wapagazis stood nearby ready to serve them freshly caught catfish, potatoes, and a tossed salad. A bottle of champagne was opened by one of the natives, the popping sound of the cork resonating loudly.

"Let's discuss this more over that spot of lunch I've invited you to," he said, grinning.

Mary nodded once. *All too easy.*

Chapter 20

It only takes a moment for a predator to strike. Even an experienced hunter who drops his guard can find himself victim of a leopard, or lion, or hyena in search of food. The African bush faults no one for mistakes. It only asks you pay for them.

Gary Hayes arrived at Big Jim's camp right when they were about to sit down to a meal of *Kumbari a la regal*, which was catfish caught in the nearby stream. Side dishes included corn ears and *Kachumbari*, steamed vegetables prepared by the *M'pishis*, the native cooks.

His land rover looked to be little more than a worn-down jeep, but it still proved capable of getting him through some of the more difficult terrain in Tanganyika.

Big Jim got up from the table and walked over to him. "Gary," he said, offering his hand, "good to see you!"

"And you as well," replied Gary, shaking hands firmly.

Gary Hayes and Big Jim were very much alike. They were both American-born who loved Africa and made their living here. Both served in the army during the War and took up hunting at its close.

Hayes was a tad shorter than Big Jim, but as physically imposing. His blue eyes and blond hair, tapped off with sun-bronzed skin left the impression he could have been a surfer from California. His lean frame and rugged good looks were enough to leave the wives of safari clients drooling for a visit to his tent after dark. On more than one occasion Gary had to avert the flirtations from females by pitching his tent elsewhere from camp and leaving the Askaris to keep the clients safe from predators.

"They should add wives among the list of predators," he once declared to Big Jim after having rejected advances from a British official's wife.

Lately he remained free of such compromising situations by working for the Game Department. Their work consisted of capturing poachers and preserving wildlife. It was not the same as taking clients on safari, but equally dangerous.

"Have a spot of lunch with us," Big Jim offered, and motioned for him to sit at their table.

"Thank you. Don't mind if I do."

Caesar introduced Mary Watkins and the two shook hands. "So you're a journalist looking for a story about professional hunting and life on a genuine African safari," he said with enthusiasm. He motioned with a nod toward Big Jim. "Well, you certainly have the right man to show you the tools of the trade," he added with a touch of confidence.

"Yes, I'm sure," Mary said, agreeably. She noted his khaki shirt with insignia. "I see you're with the Game Department. Must be interesting work I would think."

"And quite dangerous," Caesar cut in.

He explained how the Game Department did more than issue hunting licenses. They tracked and arrested poachers, protected remote villages from rogue elephants that destroyed crops, and hunted troublesome lions, leopards, hyena, and any other predator stirring up trouble.

"Chaps like Gary spend days, even weeks in the bush up to their neck in tsetse flies, coupled with sweat and exhaustion, bouts of malaria, hunger, thirst, heatstroke, biting cold, and facing death from their own gunbearers who turn on their employers if they suddenly have a notion to quit."

Mary displayed a look of shock. "Then why do it?" she asked, carefully.

"It was safer than facing the wives of safari clients," Caesar said, with a good level of sarcasm laced in his tone.

"That's enough of that," Big Jim said abruptly. He spoke in a curt, toneless voice, staring directly at Caesar as if to say, *not another word.*

The *M'pishis* added another plate and everyone ate the delicious meal topped off with beer, champagne, and water.

"What brings you this way?" Big Jim asked between a mouthful of catfish and vegetables.

"Actually, *you*," Gary quickly replied. He did not bother lifting his eyes to meet Big Jim, but knew he was watching him closely. Gary set down his knife and fork, took a long drink of cool beer, and started to explain. "You remember what a *Jabilo* is, right?"

Big Jim nodded. "A medicine man," he answered. Then he turned and faced Mary and said, "It's what Hollywood calls a *witch doctor.*"

Gary nodded. "Right. The natives turn to these *Jabilo*s for help curing the sick with spells, praying to *Juju* for rain, and a number of other things." He stopped to face Mary and said, "*Juju* is their name for Big God, their deity."

"Yes, I know," she said, thanking him with a nod.

Gary continued. "Anyway, the locals believe a *Jabilo* is angry and conjured up a *Mnyama.*"

"What's that?" Mary asked, suddenly curious. She opened her notebook and started to write. *This better be good. I don't have paper to waste.*

"It's Swahili for beast," Big Jim explained. "Natives are superstitious to the last. They believe these witch doctors are in cahoots with spirits, some good, others evil. These spirits are supposedly summoned by the *Jabilo* to wreak havoc on villages out of revenge."

"Revenge for what?" she asked with a keen sense of interest.

Big Jim turned back to Gary and motioned with a wave of the hand for him to continue.

"Could be a number of reasons," he started, choosing his words with care. He lifted his eyebrows at the next thought coming to mind. "However, I believe one of these *Jabilo*s is angry with the professional white hunters in the territory."

"What do you mean one of the *Jabilo*s? How many are there?"

Caesar struck a match to light his pipe. "Every village comes with a *Jabilo*," he explained with a sneer. He puffed twice, blowing the smoke away from the table. "They're a damn nuisance we ought to have added to our list of predators up for fair game."

"That's enough of that," Big Jim said abruptly. "Gary, what's this all about?"

Gary shrugged, looking somewhat embarrassed. "I'd like to ask if you'd have a look into this matter," he said, flatly, staring in Big Jim's direction. "The natives believe this *Mnyama* is responsible for wreaking havoc in one of the villages outside of Arusha. I also received a report from a licensed hunter by the name of Kowalski. Do you know him?"

I know him too damn well! It was a silly question. Gary knew Big Jim was more than acquainted with Stanley Kowalski. The two were rivals, with Kowalski holding a hard grudge against Big Jim for him getting the better paying clients over him.

"How does Kowalski fit into this?" Big Jim asked. He clearly wanted to know.

Gary leaned back, took a drink of beer from his glass, and set it down. "Kowalski lost two German clients on safari." He let his words hang there and the silence among them was most uncomfortable.

"Why do you continue to issue that man a license?" Caesar asked, accusingly. "This isn't the first time for him, you know."

For Caesar to speak aggressively to the man who could revoke his hunting license with the stroke of a pen was a bold move. Fortunately, all present were close friends.

"What exactly am I looking for?" Big Jim asked, looking bemused.

Gary was not surprised Big Jim agreed so quickly to accept the assignment. Every hunter knew when a member of the Game Department asked a hunter for a favor the hunter had little choice than to accept. That is unless the hunter wanted his licenses and fees to rise to an unaffordable rate.

A look of reluctance swept over Gary's face. He obviously had a difficult time explaining.

"Come out with it," Caesar demanded.

Gary threw up his hands in surrender. "Apparently you're looking for the biggest, dirtiest, and meanest *Nyati* in all of East Africa."

"*Nyati?*" Mary said, writing feverishly.

"You have a short memory," Caesar said, grinning condescendingly. "I explained before how *Nyati* is Swahili for Cape buffalo."

"Yes, it is," Gary added. He turned to face Big Jim. "Well, our friend Kowalski said that's what killed his clients and nearly took his own life in the process."

The only thing surprising Big Jim was the fact that Kowalski had escaped. The Cape buffalo was an animal of incredible size, strength, cunning, and extremely dangerous. On more than one occasion Big Jim and Caesar had close calls with the 'Buff,' as they were sometimes called. Big Jim recalled in his early years learning in the professional hunting trade how one of the famous turn-of-the-century hunters, Bill Judd, called the Buff the most fearsome animal to hunt. Big Jim and others agreed seeing how difficult the beast was to stop on its charge even after receiving multiple hits from the powerful Westley-Richards and Rigby double rifles, weapons made with heavy 500 and 700-grain bullets specifically for knocking down the biggest animals on the *Dark Continent*.

Mary jotted down more notes in her journal, wishing she had brought more books to fill with the stories these men had to offer. *At this rate*, she thought, *I'll be a Pulitzer-Prize winner for journalism before I'm 30.*

"Where did this supposed incident Kowalski claims took place?" Big Jim asked. It sounded more of a challenge than an inquiry.

Gary understood. Few hunters appreciated Kowalski's skill for running a safari company, and the fact the Game Department continued issuing him licenses continued to be an embarrassment for those in the trade.

'There's always a market for *poor man's safari* clients looking to save on comforts and a trusty guide capable of bringing them back in one piece,' was the common joke among professional hunters.

Every outfitter knew the loss of a client on safari was bad for their image. For Big Jim, the loss of Nigel Stewart was his first, and he could be forgiven. Kowalski was another matter. No one liked or respected him.

"He's nothing more than a despicable brute," Caesar declared. "He has no manners, he lacks proper supplies, and he can't even play a good hand of cards."

Everyone agreed. Making sure certain clients had comforts of proper sleeping quarters, food, champagne, beer, and the magical ability of entertaining paying customers over a decent game of poker was essential to maintaining the effect of safari. Still, there were persons willing to forgo perks and hire the likes of Kowalski and similar types for no other reason than to save money.

"South of here, in the Manyara Territory," Gary said. "It'd be a big help to us if you went for a look and handled whatever needed to be handled."

I'll bet, Big Jim wanted to say.

Gary was a good friend, but still a warden in the Game Department. Saying no was not an option. One did not disappoint those capable of revoking your hunting license.

"I suppose we can have a look into the matter," Big Jim said, acquiescingly. He looked in Mary's direction. "You'll still get plenty of photographs and have a lot to write about in that part of the territory, same as here," he added, reassuringly.

Mary brightened. "Fine by me!"

A sudden roar caught their attention.

"What was that?" Mary asked, jumping from her seat.

Big Jim rose and reached for the binoculars on the table. In the distance he focused on a group of Ficus trees and thorn brush near the river. The heat fogged the glasses and he wiped them clean. He went back to scanning the terrain.

Then he saw it!

High up in the large Ficus tree was the indistinguishable shape of a large animal. It lay comfortably on a thick branch, its long spindly tail wagging slowly.

"*Chui,*" Barake exclaimed. He pointed in the direction of the tree.

"What's that?" Mary asked, anxiously.

"Leopard," Big Jim answered. He lowered the glasses.

Then she recalled what she had written in her journal earlier. *That's right. Chui is Swahili for leopard. I've got to remember these things.*

"He's probably been watching you the entire time you've been here," Gary noted. "You'd best be sure to post more Askari to keep watch at night."

Why didn't I think of that? Had any other person made the suggestion Big Jim would have felt insulted, but he held his tongue.

Big Jim handed Mary the glasses. She peered in the direction of the leopard and said, "He's beautiful!"

Gary sneered. "Damned nuisance to the natives," he snapped.

She turned and faced him. "How do you mean?"

Gary explained how professional hunters considered the leopard the world's second most successful and effective deadliest killer.

"What's the first?" Mary asked quickly.

Gary glanced in Big Jim's direction. His, how-can-she-ask-such-a-question stare was more than obvious.

"That honor goes to man," Big Jim said with a touch of humor in his tone.

Mary's interest in leopard became apparent. "Tell me why the leopard is considered so dangerous," she said, while opening her notebook. She recalled Big Jim and Caesar's points of view, and wanted Gary's version.

Big Jim stared stoically at Gary. "You brought it up."

Gary shrugged. *What the hell.* "He's called *Chui* in Swahili," he began in a manner much like a park ranger speaking to a group of tourists. "They feed on just about anything whereas other wildlife maintains a specific diet. Couple this with their lithe size and strength they have an advantage over the lion. Leopards can climb a tree faster than a lizard."

I already know that.

"They take their prey high in the trees for safekeeping from other animals looking for a meal," he continued. "They're intelligent, calculating, and move with lightning speed. Their coat gives it good camouflage, making it hard to detect." He stopped and pointed to her *127 Brownie* camera. "You may want a picture," he suggested. "I know people who never get as much as a glance at a leopard in the wild their entire life."

"Are they scarce?" she asked while writing in short hand.

He shook his head. "No, they're very quiet. They'll sit perched in trees for as long as they need to, or at least until they grow hungry. Something must have stirred this leopard to roar. They don't intentionally give away their position for attention."

Barake raised his arm and pointed to their left. *"Jabilo,"* he said.

Everyone turned and saw a lone man stiffly standing atop a hill scarred with thorn brush and a few dried acacia trees. He wore a sarong and a red shawl over his shoulder. In his right hand he held a long walking stick held upright.

"What do you suppose he's up to?" Caesar asked, between puffs on his pipe.

Mary returned the conversation back to the leopard. She was completely enthralled by this magnificent animal. "Can you give me an example of how dangerous they are?" She sounded like a kid having the time of their life on a carousel.

Gary pondered for a moment. "Well, the story coming to mind took place roughly ten years earlier," he began. He folded his arms over his chest while speaking. "In Uganda the natives complained about a *chui* killing people without eating its victims. We don't know why, but there are quite a few instances where a leopard kills for no reason. It's a carnivore, and carnivores kill for food. The *chui*, however, sometimes kills for amusement." He paused for effect. "Or at least it appeared that way."

Mary looked up from her notebook. "What happened to this leopard?"

"No one knows," he replied with a shrug. "Over two dozen people were killed by the same leopard in a three month period. We knew this by the way the victims were killed."

Mary waited with anticipation pleading in her eyes. "How were they killed?" she asked, finally.

After a short pause, Gary said, "They had their throats ripped out."

Mary stared with a blank expression.

"Not a single piece of flesh was missing," he continued, in a flat tone. "It killed simply because it wanted to."

"Like humans do," Caesar chimed in quickly.

The *chui* roared again, grabbing their attention. The six foot long cat did not move except for its tail wagging to and fro. It simply stared in their direction, and Mary felt a sudden chill run up and down her spine.

Gary clapped his hands together. "Well, I've got to be off," he said. "Please keep in touch about the *nyati*."

Big Jim walked him to his car. "Will do," he said, out of earshot from the others. "I take it this will help the Game Department with its decision about my license remaining valid?" He hated to ask, but had to.

This is, after all, my livelihood, he wanted to add. *No sense pushing it though.*

Gary slapped him on the back. "I guarantee it."

Chapter 21

The New Stanley Bar in Nairobi is often frequented by professional hunters. Here one can learn classic tales of true-life hunting stories. One that stands among many is the opinion that a hunter will face no greater danger than tracking an injured leopard in dense bush. In fact, professional and novice hunters are injured by the leopard more than any other animal on the continent.

Gary Hayes drove his land rover across the open veldt at a comfortable 30 miles per hour. He could not risk driving faster over uneven terrain, and the road was more like a trail carved from the giant hooves of elephants on the march.

He was glad Big Jim had agreed to handle the matter in the Manyara Reserve. Actually he knew he would. Hell, all he had to do was ask. Gary could not recall a time when a hunter had refused a request from a Game Officer.

After a month-long of elephant-*cropping* in the Selous Reserve Gary was worn out and thankful he could pass on the job to Big Jim.

Better him than me, he said silently.

Cropping elephant herds was no simple chore, and the Game Department had the responsibility of handling this. From time to time herds grew to incredible numbers and ravaged fields including village crops.

Gary had been assigned to the Selous Reserve, the largest in the world, and faced the daunting task of tracking two separate herds numbering well over thirty each. Driving over volcanic rock, through dense brush, marching through swamps, and all the while fighting other dangers from hyena, lion, buffalo, hippopotamus, poisonous and aggressive mamba snakes, not to forget fever, malaria, hunger, and thirst was enough to drive even the most dedicated Game Officer over the edge.

But Gary managed to get the job done. He brought down fifteen elephants between the two herds, including the bulls. The meat would feed the neighboring tribes that harvested the carcasses, and the ivory was confiscated by the Game Department to prevent poachers from taking advantage of the easy kills.

Fortunately Gary only faced certain death once, and he could not help recalling the incident while driving the long way back to Arusha, where his office was located.

Five Days Earlier…

Boom! Boom!

His Rigby .470 Double rifle exploded. But the bull with a hefty 200 lbs. of ivory tusks did not drop. In fact he did not even flinch. The great behemoth only grew angry and determined to crush the two-legged creature with a stick that spat fire.

The bull elephant charged, screeching a cry from its raised trunk that made the hair on the back of Gary's neck stand stiff. Gary instinctively released the lever to the barrels, discharging the spent cartridges and sliding in two fresh 500-grain bullets the size of cigars. He could not help backing away as the bull stampeded toward him.

The earth seemed to shake and his vision blurred. Were it not for his years of experience he would surely have dropped his rifle and ran for dear life.

And that would have been the end of me; he managed to tell himself, in the heat of the moment. Raising his rifle, he took a mere second to aim and squeeze the triggers one after another.

The first shot stunned the elephant, and Gary saw the puff of dust blow off the massive skull where it struck the gargantuan between the eyes. The second shot fared better. It breached the skull and smashed its brain to jelly. The massive giant stiffened for a brief moment, then dropped like a train crashing on its side from broken track.

Three of the herd ran to the aid of their fallen leader, pushing with their tusks to help lift it back to its feet. It was a futile effort, but a display of love and loyalty from a species with feelings similar to how humans displayed toward each other.

Gary reloaded and fired simultaneously over the heads of the herd, and this was enough to force them to disperse in chaos, screeching high-piercing shrieks from raised trunks as they trampled through the brush.

Leaving nothing to chance, Gary walked up to the fallen giant, placed the barrels of his double rifle against the side of the bull's head and squeezed the triggers for good measure.

BOOM! BOOM!

A smile pursed the corners of his mouth, not from joy over killing a bull elephant with trophy-class tusks, but rather from having the task of *cropping* herds completed and heading home in one piece.

If I had my way I'd pawn cropping to every professional outfitter than risk doing it myself, he told himself.

After driving past a row of termite heaps, rock-hard mounds, some as high as six feet, something ahead caught his attention. Gary's vision was blurred from the heat and he could not make out the figure.

What the hell is that? he wondered. *For the love of—not another tembo to knock down,* he prayed.

He brought the land rover to a stop and grabbed his binoculars from the glove compartment. Peering through them he made out the distinguishable curved horns on the boss of a Cape buffalo.

"You're one damned big *nyati*," he said aloud. The *boss* adorning its head was what they called the thick skull adorned with upturned curved horns. It was thick enough to stop a bullet from penetrating to the brain, and the horns were used to fight off lions and crocodiles, the buffalo's natural enemies—next to the professional hunters and clients looking to make a trophy out of its head.

Gary put down the glasses, switched gears to drive, and moved ahead with caution. When he was one hundred yards from the buff he honked the horn. The nearby wildlife of vultures, *Thomson* gazelle, zebra, and giraffe did not appreciate the sound of a car horn. It was unnatural and discomforting to them and in most cases was enough to distract animals and force them to disperse.

But not this time.

This buffalo remained stone-still, challenging all daring enough to cross its path.

This one's lookin' to have its head placed on my trophy wall, Gary told himself. "Have it your way."

He drove the rover closer, stopping a mere fifty yards in front of the beast. Switching off the engine, Gary climbed out of the seat cautiously and reached for his Rigby .470 Double rifle. He opened the breech. It was loaded. He snapped it shut. He walked forward slowly, taking cautious steps.

The thing hasn't moved an inch, he said silently.

The closer he got the bigger the buff grew. It really was a damned big *nyati*! The biggest he'd ever seen.

It looks to be the size of a—! He paused, staring as though thunderstruck. *That's impossible! You're like an elephant. How in the hell can a* nyati *grow so big?*

A sudden breeze blew downwind from the beast and the stench made Gary wince.

"Geez!" It smelled worse than a rotted carcass.

For a moment Gary thought he would vomit. *Can't get sick now, I'd lose the advantage.*

Then he wondered if he had any advantage to begin with. Something told him he should walk back to his rover and drive around the beast. *No sense tempting fate.*

Gary took a step back to do exactly that, but then the beast took a step forward, grunting as if to say, don't move.

There was something odd about the buffalo's eyes. They seemed to glow, and looked completely red. It was as though they were bloodshot.

And what on earth is that oozing from its hide? he wondered. *My God! That's blood.*

A roar to his left caused Gary to swirl and face whatever creature was there. He clutched his double rifle tightly. "Now what?" he whispered.

The heavy thickets and trees were perfect for concealing a lion or a leopard. Gary's guess was lion. They were the number one natural enemy of the buffalo. After man, he corrected himself.

The sound of movement to his front caught his attention and he turned to face the beast again.

"*What the—?*"

The creature was now twenty-five yards closer than it had been.

"*How did you—?*"

The angry cat roared again and Gary instinctively turned to face it.

Nothing.

Silence.

The cat was there, he knew.

He turned to face the buffalo again only this time it was a mere ten feet from him! It stood looming menacingly, towering over him like a great pyramid. Gary's eyes grew the size of hens eggs and felt like they were about to pop from the sockets.

He slowly raised his rifle, but stopped when the buff stepped forward. It seemed to know what he was about to do.

This is no ordinary buffalo, he said silently.

A disturbing pause fell over Gary. He knew what he had to do, but waited for the right moment. *It's now or never!*

He lifted his heavy 12 lbs. rifle to shoulder level and touched the trigger with the index finger of his right hand. To his amazement the *nyati* did not flinch, nor did it move forward to attack.

He exhaled slowly and started to squeeze the trigger.

Suddenly a force with the power of a fast-moving lorry slammed into Gary, knocking him off his feet and onto his side. His double rifle flew free from his grasp. Gary felt sharp knives dig into his chest and legs. He screamed in agony as fear swept through him.

When he looked up he saw the even stare of a giant leopard glaring down at him through its glowing amber eyes. The cat roared in triumph and dug its heavy claws deep into Gary's skin. He cried out in pain, and this seemed to give the *chui* pleasure as it clawed its prey deeper and deeper.

The cat opened its jaws, displaying a full set of dagger-sharp teeth, and roared again.

Gary's eyes widened with fear. He knew what was about to happen and knew there was little he could do. Instinctively, he reached for his knife in its sheath dangling from his belt. His fingers gripped the handle of the weapon right as the leopard clamped its jaws tight around his throat, and then bit clean through his larynx and neck, practically decapitating him. The last thing Gary saw was his reflection in the amber eyes of the leopard.

Chapter 22

Contrary to popular belief, the Cape buffalo are by no means a timid animal that will shy away with the wave of your hands. In fact, they are intelligent, cunning, and extremely dangerous beasts!

Lake Manyara was a sight to behold. The alkaline lake bristled with wildlife. The pink-hued flamingos reigned supreme in numbers over other water birds like the pelican, stork, and cormorants. The lake shadowed with grassy flood lands, sported larger game like zebra and wildebeest herds numbering in the tens of thousands. Giraffe and impressively tusked elephant migrated to this fertile territory along with the buffalo for centuries.

The Manyara Reserve was 127 square miles large with the lake taking over 70 square miles when water levels reached their peak. It was located 80 miles west of Arusha, and Big Jim and Caesar were most familiar with this part of the territory.

"This should make searching for the rogue buff a simple job," he had told Caesar after Gary left their camp two days earlier. "We already know where the herds migrate and won't have to go marching off into nasty bush where the tsetse, mamba, and crocs lay in wait for a victim."

And this suited Caesar fine! Both hunters knew the buffalo had keen eyesight, hearing, and a sense of smell that worked best for them in dense foliage. If the *nyati* found you before you found it, you could pretty much bet your hunting days were over sooner than later.

Mary sat in the passenger side of the land rover with Caesar in the back and Big Jim at the wheel. A Winchester 30.06 was attached on the outside of the car in a boot, resting the way a rifle did with a cowboy on horseback. Mary wore trousers tucked in ankle-high boots at the leg, a crisp white blouse, and a scarf over her hair.

Although he would never admit it, Big Jim thought she looked quite pretty and could not refrain from glancing at her whenever she looked the other way to admire the sights. Caesar caught him staring and grinned ever so slightly. When Big Jim saw Caesar watching him he flashed a don't-even-say-it look and kept his eyes on the road.

"I see why Hemingway calls this place the loveliest in Africa," Mary said, in awe of the view.

Big Jim shook his head. *Him again*, he said silently with scorn.

In truth Hemingway could not have been more right. The Manyara Reserve not only sported a beautiful lake bristling with life, but also a lush green forest, grassy floodplains, jagged volcanic peaks, and steppes stretching as far as one could see.

Inside the forest jungle she saw hundreds of baboon casually lounging in the trees and forest ground. They observed the cars and lorries with mild interest. High in the trees a cacophony of honking came from the hundreds of birds nesting safely from forest predators on the ground.

Big Jim pointed in the direction of acacia woodland. "Look over there."

Mary saw the narrow belt of trees skirting the plain. "What about them?" she asked.

"We're going to drive close enough for you to see the only area where lion climb trees as naturally as they lay in the grassy bush veldt."

Mary perked up. "Lions that climb trees! Really?"

"All lion can climb trees," Caesar chimed, "though they seldom do. They'll climb to go after prey, or to escape a stampede. This lot in the Manyara is known for spending more time than usual in the trees catching up on sleep. They do so frequently enough to catch the attention of outdoor enthusiasts."

Big Jim slowed the vehicle and brought it to a stop so Mary could snap a photo with her *Brownie 127*. After two shots she thanked him and Big Jim got the safari on the move once more.

"Where are we setting up camp?" Mary asked.

"Not far," Caesar replied. He tapped her shoulder to get her attention. "Care for a bit of entertainment?" he asked, flashing a mischievous grin.

Mary perked with curiosity. *Should I be afraid to ask?* "What do you mean?"

Caesar reached into his left breast pocket of his khaki shirt and pulled out a four inch leather pouch. With care, he slid out a classic *Hohner Harmonica* and started to play *London Bridge is Falling Down.*

Big Jim winced. *Not again!* "Must you try your hand at that once more?" he said, fuming. "You'll frighten the animals."

Caesar remained undaunted. "I'll have you know the harmonica is one of the most classic musical instruments in the world." He spoke with sincerity and conviction. "You Americans loved it so much you adopted many songs in your former Confederate States, which required musicians to play this."

Big Jim shook his head. "That may be, but you give it no justice."

Mary laughed. "I think it's great you play the harmonica," she said with encouragement.

"There's a difference between playing and making a mockery of the instrument," Big Jim said, bitterly.

Caesar remained unphased. "It's a privilege to play this instrument."

"Whoever said you played?" Big Jim shot back.

Mary laughed some more. "Why do you like playing the harmonica?" she asked, touching his shoulder with a gentle, encouraging hand.

Caesar did not have to think about the answer for long. "I suppose the history of this caught my attention," he said, reflecting. "A young man by the name of Matthias Hohner created this in 1857. The firm proved so successful you can find the instrument in all corners of the world." He held the harmonica with tender admiration. "I suppose I also find it amazing how such a small instrument can capture the attention of so many."

He started playing *London Bridge is Falling down* once more and Big Jim caught sight of a herd of zebra running away as they approached.

"Look! You're frightening off the game," he bellowed, irritably.

Caesar continued playing, thoroughly enjoying himself. Mary laughed, clapping her hands, encouraging him to continue.

Big Jim shook his head, exasperated by the terrible playing his English friend forced them to endure. "I'm sorry I ever got you that thing for your birthday," he said, with regret.

They approached a bumpy section of road and Big Jim intentionally drove straight through it. The jolt was so terrific Caesar and Mary had to hold onto the car to keep from being thrown clear. The harmonica flew from Caesar's hands and out of the rover.

"Hey, my harmonica!"

"Looks like fate saved us after all," Big Jim said with relief.

Caesar sank in his seat. "I was destined for greatness," he said, regretfully.

Big Jim disagreed. "You're being overgenerous to yourself."

Chapter 23

In Africa the natives wisely approach rivers and lakes with caution for beneath the water's surface lies a danger more frightening than a charging bull elephant. You only have one chance for escape, and only the quick survive.

After traveling through dense jungle, grasslands, and volcanic rock-strewn plain, Big Jim came upon a stretch of the river where a beautiful waterfall drowned out all other sound. The force of the falls was magnificent, and giant plumes of cool mist struck their faces. Plenty of trees dotted the area and even a novice like Mary saw how lovely this made for a campsite.

"This is beautiful!" she said, in a loud voice so that she could be heard over the rushing sound of the waterfall.

I won't argue, Big Jim thought. "One of my favorite places," he said, nodding agreeably.

Mary walked to the edge of the fast-moving water. "Any place here we can go for a swim?" She looked and sounded like a kid who saw the ocean for the very first time.

Caesar laughed. "There might be a place or two in the rocks above offering pools of still water," he said.

"Great!" Mary was beaming.

Caesar looked at Big Jim. "I'll go to the camp," he offered. "You two go for a bath." He grinned slyly and added, "In separate pools of course."

Big Jim could not hide his frustration with the Englishman. He faced Mary, who awaited his answer. "Get your things," he said, trying hard not to appear embarrassed.

Mary did not need to be told twice. She ran back to the land rover and retrieved her bag and ever-handy *Brownie 127* camera. "Let's go," she said, and ran up the rocky hillside in search of a water pool.

Big Jim grabbed a bag of personal gear and the Winchester 30.06 rifle. He started after her, but stopped long enough to flash Caesar a disapproving look.

Caesar remained unphased. He stared back grinning and lit his pipe. "Have fun," he said in a low voice. He most definitely did not want Big Jim to hear him.

They did not have to walk far. Up on the hills along the gorge where the river ran were pools of water in the volcanic rock, perfect for bathing.

"There's a spot for you to bathe," Big Jim said, pointing at a small lava pool where water from the river overflowed, creating numerous small pools. "I'll go on ahead and make sure it's safe," he continued, trying to be reassuring in case she was frightened.

"Are we in danger?" she asked. There was a tinge of excitement laced in her voice, almost as if she hoped for it.

"Probably not," he said quickly. "I only want to make sure there are no wild game nearby that could get riled by our presence."

"What kind of game?"

Big Jim halted. *She doesn't give up.* He pointed to a group of trees on both sides of the river. "Leopard, for one. They're good at concealing themselves in trees." He pointed further up the rock cliff to their right where large boulders formed what appeared to be caves. "Over there's perfect for a pride of lion to make their den." He watched her reaction and thought she looked anxious. He pointed back down the river from whence they came. "Crocodiles are surely down there, so keep here while I have a look to be sure."

Big Jim started his way up the rock cliff running along the river, his trusty Winchester 30.06 in hand.

Mary watched until he was out of sight. Oblivious to modesty, she removed her clothes and slowly walked in the pool, dipping her pink-white body in the cold refreshing water.

"Oohh that feels good!" she said aloud. She could not recall a time when she appreciated such a bath.

The water and sunshine, combined with the feeling other than being rocked back and forth in the backseat of the land rover was overwhelming. She lay in the water up to her neck and after a few minutes of sunning her face she reached over for her bag and pulled out her pen and journal. Putting pen to paper, she began to do what she always believed she was meant to. She wrote.

What a journey this has been, she began.

> *There is nothing* Dark *about this continent. It's teeming with life. The man called Big Jim has agreed to take me on a picture safari for lack of work. His hunting license is under review while the investigation of the death of a client continues. To make up for lack of work he accepted my company's offer for a journey into the bush.*

Mary paused and took in the surroundings once more. "If only everyone could experience this," she said, aloud.

She returned to her journal.

It is striking how close one is to danger here, especially surrounded by such beauty. One can admire the bush veldt, the volcanic plains, the grassy steppes, towering mountains, and lush jungle. And yet, amidst this grandeur death awaits the unsuspecting!

She paused a moment, reflecting on the incident between Big Jim and a rhino two days earlier.

> *The rhinoceros is one of the Big 5 tracked and killed by professional and amateur hunters. In Swahili it is called* Kifaru. *When we began our journey to the Manyara Reserve we stopped for a spot of lunch right outside the Serengeti Plains. Msasa trees provided shade in the clearing next to the long grass in the area we chose. These trees were eerily attractive, with rosy, dark-red leaves. The dried leaves that fall to the ground emit a strong odor reminding one of chocolate.*

What I would do for a Hershey Bar, she thought. Her tongue rolled across her lips deliciously.

Before we set up tables and chairs the sound of animals on the move caught our attention. The grass was too high for us to see and determine from which direction they came, but they were close—too close! The white hunter, Big Jim, ordered me back into the car, and the wapagazis scrambled back into the lorry. Caesar, the other white hunter, and askaris reached for their rifles.

The sound of heavy grunting combined with large hooves pounding the earth reached a crescendo. Before we knew it the grass exploded before us as three Kifaru tore through. I heard the rhinoceros are considered stupid and commonly called Dimwit, by professional hunters, but they are never to be disrespected for the danger they posed.

These creatures are not all different looking from ancestors that died off long ago, and the white rhino can weigh close to 8,000 lbs., or so I am told. The rhino we came across were black rhino, smaller than the white, weighing from 1,850 lbs. to 3,500 lbs. But they are all extremely fast, and can swirl around with the grace of a gazelle, which is precisely what the lead Kifaru did.

The two bulls following it were cows, and the male likely considered us a threat. He came at us with amazing speed, and Big Jim stopped him cold with a shot from his heavy rifle, only he did not shoot the rhino. The shot hit the ground in front of the animal, kicking up dirt into the Kifaru's face. It stood there heaving, straining its eyes for a view of what it was up against. The rhino has poor eyesight and probably stopped its charge for lack of clear vision rather than the danger of receiving a large caliber round in its face. Caesar told me the 750-grain bullet can knock down any of the Big 5 with a single shot so long as you hit the animal in the right spot.

After a few tense moments the Kifaru marched around our camp circling us in a figure eight pattern. It snorted and grunted, charged, then stopped, charged, then stopped again. Even a novice like me could see it sized us up and thought best not to gore us with its horn and crush us with its large hooves. But it had a reputation as pack leader to uphold and made sure we knew it to be a tough hombre to cross. The Kifaru circled us three more times before disappearing in the long grass after the cows.

I asked Big Jim why he had not killed the rhino outright. His answer perplexed me. He said he did not have a permit for rhino. Killing the beast would have cost him his hunter's license. I asked how anyone would have learned of him killing the rhino. He looked over to his askari and wapagazis and said they would have reported him for the reward the Game Department offered those who turned in poachers and violators.

I found this disturbing considering how devoted the natives appeared to the hunters. Then Caesar told me it had nothing to do with a lack of devotion to them. The natives in their employment have families that could use the money and take advantage of getting their hands on some whenever the opportunity presents itself.

She paused before adding, *I suppose people are more alike than realized.*

When I asked Caesar if Big Jim and he would have shot the rhino had it appeared to continue its charge, thus making it a life or death situation, Caesar shrugged and said, 'I'm happy we did not have to find out.'

"Care for a spot of lunch?" It was Big Jim.

His presence startled Mary, and she sat up in the pool exposing her palm-sized breasts. Embarrassed, she slid beneath the water up to the neck, but it did little good hiding her figure considering the water was crystal-clear.

"Didn't mean to embarrass you," Big Jim said, suppressing a smirk.

Mary took the towel he handed her and wrapped it around her. After the shock dissipated she blushed at the feeling of excitement coursing through her. Her heart skipped a beat when she looked at Big Jim standing before her with his shirt off. Apparently he had found a pool to wash off, too. He had on his trousers and boots, but looked striking bare-chested.

He certainly is quite a sight to behold, she thought, but would not dare say so aloud.

Then she saw the scars on his arms and recalled what Caesar had said about how Big Jim never displayed them—to anyone. "How did you get those?" she asked.

Big Jim froze, clearly taken aback. He reflected and shrugged. *Stay mellow*, he decided. "I'd rather not discuss it," he said, flatly.

"What happened?"

He stared back stoically. "Do you really want to know?"

She grinned, anxiously. "Not if you'd rather not discuss it," she lied.

Big Jim turned his back to her and Mary dropped the towel and changed into her clothes. Something about the way he patiently stood waiting for her made her take her time about it, almost like she teased him. A sly smile pursed her full lips, and she ran her tongue over her upper lip deliciously taunting the professional hunter, but not so he could see her.

"Okay, I'm ready," she said, sounding like the captain of a cheerleading squad.

He turned and faced her. Pride and remembering his place as guide kept him from admitting how pretty she looked.

How long has it been? he wondered. *Don't do it!* he said, scolding himself. *This will only bring trouble.*

"Let's go," he ordered, and led her down the rocky hillside back to camp.

When they reached the bottom she saw the river flowing slowly nearby not far from the waterfall. "I'll be right back," she said. "I want to go and wash the dirt from my feet." And she ran like the wind toward the river's edge.

Big Jim quickly called out to her. "Mary, stop!"

Too late!

A giant-sized croc leaped from beneath the water, scrambling toward Mary at an incredible speed she did not imagine possible. Stunned by the sight of the prehistoric-looking creature, Mary stumbled backwards and fell on her haunches. The croc reached her, jaws opened wide and clamped down on her arm. She screamed a high-pitched wail that turned the white hunters and Africans stomachs' over.

Big Jim raised his rifle to shoulder level. He pulled back the bolt and slammed it forward, chambering a round in the breech. *No good*, he told himself. He had a clear shot for the croc's head, but a frontal shot was like tossing tennis balls at it. The skull of a crocodile was thickest in its front.

An askari, observing the scene from the campsite, picked up his spear and ran for Mary and her attacker. He jabbed at the crocodile's head, aiming for its eye, but missed. The deed still did some good, for the croc released its powerful grip on Mary's arm and lunged for the native.

Mary scrambled away in a hurry while the African askari held the crocodile at bay with his spear. He may have well used a toothpick in its place, for this was about all the good it did, save for the distraction allowing Mary to escape.

The native jabbed thrice at the crocodile, but this only angered it. The reptile steadily moved toward the African, jaws open with intent on having a meal. Right when the native turned to run the croc lurched forward, clamping its jaws shut on the man's leg. He screamed in agony so loud and deafening no one would forget his cry if they tried.

Big Jim reached the crocodile on its right side, aiming above its eye.

KA-POW!

The bullet struck the reptile right above its eye, piercing the thinnest part of the skull, Big Jim knew. The brain exploded into jelly and the croc opened its jaws in a death cry, only making no sound. It was enough time for the African to wrench his leg free and scramble away. The jaws to the crocodile slammed shut and it lay in sudden stillness.

Big Jim looked over at the askaris and wapagazis, worried over what they had witnessed.

Caesar saw how they took note over the white hunter's actions, and shouted for them to disperse. "Kupata nyuma kazi yako!" (Get back to your work!) he commanded.

"This is the last thing I need," Big Jim cried. A sheen of perspiration beaded on his forehead, stinging his eyes.

"There's no way they can report this to the Game Department so long as they remain with us," Caesar said, breathing hard from the dash he made to Mary.

Big Jim pondered that. The natives were loyal, but only to a point, he knew. The reward offered by the Game Department for those who reported poachers and hunters killing game without a permit was large enough to turn the most loyal servant into a hunter's worst enemy. Life or death situations were no excuse. If you killed an animal without a permit, your license would be immediately revoked.

"Perhaps we can remind them that if you're out of work, so are they," Caesar offered.

Big Jim's brow furrowed. "We'll see," he replied, sullenly. He turned to Mary, lying on the ground while Caesar busily nursed her wounds. He barked a command to the wapagazis to tend to the askari lying in pain on the ground, and they ran to him, lifting him and carrying him away from the river so they could nurse his injured leg.

"We'll take care of this and prevent infection," Caesar said, cheerily. "Remember what I told you when we first met? A professional hunter is guide, mechanic, camp manager, story-teller, and sometimes doctor. But most important, we are good at playing cards with a chest full of brandy always on hand."

Mary managed a smile. "Guess I should have listened to you," she said, meekly looking at Big Jim. "Right about now that brandy sounds delicious."

Big Jim stood towering before her, managing a slight smile. "Hurry up and we'll have that spot of lunch," he said, with a touch of humor.

"What are we having?" Caesar asked, observing Mary closely.

"Oh, I believe you'll both enjoy the food," Big Jim said, amused by the inquiry. "We're having catfish caught in the river with a side of yams."

Mary managed another smile. "Sounds delicious."

Big Jim helped Caesar lift Mary to her feet. They started to walk toward the camp when they saw a reed-thin native appear from the ten foot high tall grass.

"Who in hell is this?" Big Jim asked, to no one in particular.

The native wore sandals, a worn-out loincloth, and carried a satchel bag of water made of goatskin strapped over his shoulder and chest with a thin piece of leather rope. He held a near-broken spear as a walking staff to help him keep steady while walking.

"He's either drunk out of his mind or lost," Caesar noted.

The native staggered toward the three whites, stopping a mere ten feet in front of them. "My name is Mashaka," he said, with effort. Then he fell to the ground, unconscious from exhaustion.

Chapter 24

Crocodiles may grow over 20 feet in length. They view people as prey same as they view a gazelle, or Cape buffalo. They fear nothing, and can sprint a short distance up to 35 MPH. Cunning, calculating, and deathly intent on killing for food, these creatures have changed very little over millions of years. Many hunters prefer to forgo tracking a crocodile. But if a paying client wants one...

Big Jim drove the land rover across the grassy *Maasai Steppes* at a steady 30 MPH, quite fast considering the dangers traveling over uneven terrain. One sharp rock, a tire over a hole in the ground burrowed by a warthog or aardvark, or sandy ground and the journey could come to a quick halt.

But time was of the essence.

Caesar and Barake were with him, along with two wapagazis. He left Nyeusii in charge of camp, instructing him to keep close watch on the injured, recovering white lady.

Caesar protested leaving her alone. "At least one of us should remain with her," he suggested.

Big Jim was adamant. "If this *Mnyama* exists I'll need you," he said with finality. "After what the native Mashaka told us, the sooner we bring closure to this matter the better."

When Mashaka collapsed at their camp Big Jim had him carried to a tent where he put his knowledge of bush medicine to work. When on safari a hunter found himself busy nursing wounds of those mauled by leopard or lion, clients sick from fever and exhaustion, or tending to snakebites. Mostly it was tending to heat exhaustion and sore feet. In Mashaka's case the African was dehydrated and near starving.

Big Jim managed to pour a few spoonfuls of water down his throat, not too much for fear of making him cough uncontrollably. A dose of penicillin to control bacterial infections was administered, and when Mashaka opened his eyes Big Jim sat him up on the cot to bring him to consciousness.

"What are you doing here?" Big Jim asked.

Mashaka spoke in broken sentences, but Big Jim and Caesar got the gist of it. The African had sworn to kill the white hunters and destroy his plantation, the *Mbuga za Peponi*, in a demonstration of respect to the *Jabilo*. Apparently this medicine man was angry with the locals for their reliance on the white hunters. Natives turned to them for dealing with troublesome animals instead of seeking help from the *Jabilo*. This damaged his pride and the *Jabilo* summoned a beast, the *Mnyama*, for revenge.

Big Jim and Caesar did not believe in such superstition. "The natives do," Big Jim said, running his fingers through his hair, trying to think this through.

The worst scenario would be for a native uprising. That spelled disaster for their livelihood. Despite years Big Jim and Caesar had devoted to building close relationships with Africans they were still foreigners, employers, the *Bwana* who dictated how they lived.

A stroke of luck came their way when one of the wapagazis burst inside the tent to tell them a *nyati* of immense size was seen in the swamps in the *Maasai Steppes*. It never ceased to amaze Big Jim and Caesar how natives received information so many miles out in the bush veldt. One technique used by natives was to pass word by drum-beating on fallen tree trunks. It was a form of communication only locals understood, and a way of warning tribes of lurking danger.

Not wanting to miss an opportunity when it presented itself, Big Jim and Caesar loaded their heavy double rifles, packed plenty of extra cartridges, food, water, and took off. With luck they would be back in time for dinner.

Driving along the steppes they came across a grove of trees with vultures occupying every branch. "What do you suppose they're up to?" Caesar asked.

Barake pointed in the direction with his *assegais*, the short, heavy weapon with a two-edged blade 6" across its widest part. This spear was not for throwing, but for stabbing and jabbing to keep predators at bay. The *Zulu* warriors made this weapon famous during their battles against the British in the Transvaal in the late 19th century.

"*Fisi kulisha juu ya Kifaru,*" the African said.

Big Jim and Caesar looked closely and saw what Barake saw. At the base of the grove of trees, through the high grass lay a female rhinoceros, a *kifaru*. It had been birthing a calf when a pack of hyena, *fisi*, attacked her. The filthy creatures pulled the calf from between the cow's legs, tearing the baby rhino apart in seconds. While they devoured the calf, two other *fisi* bit into the rhino's head, snapping off the horns, which were actually made of keratin, the same protein making up fingernails and hair. Some cultures believed the horn to contain magical powers, a source of good luck. To the *fisi* the horn was little more than another piece of grub to fulfill their strong desire for food.

"In Africa, nothing is wasted," Big Jim said with reflection.

"Shall we put her out of her misery?" Caesar asked. The inflection of his tone indicated the pity he felt for the *kifaru*.

Big Jim glanced at Barake and the two wapagazis in back of the rover. They had been with him for years, but the reward for reporting hunters shooting game without a permit was valuable. It could feed their family a full year, too much to forgo no matter how much you liked the white hunter employing you.

"No," Big Jim said flatly. "We don't have much daylight left. Let's keep on the move."

Caesar was aghast. "I can't believe you're being so inhumane," he said, hoarsely.

"We nearly lost our licenses with the death of Nigel Stewart," argued Big Jim. "I'm not about to risk losing it permanent by shooting a rhino we have no license for."

"It's the humane thing to do," Caesar said, again hopefully.

"Stop arguing." Big Jim's voice lost its edge of self-control, becoming more dictatorial in tone than usual. "We stand to lose our license as it is with the croc incident. Do you really want to press our luck?"

"If you're worried about the boys, I'll pay them extra to cover the reward they stand to receive."

Big Jim looked at the natives again, who sat stone-still in the back watching the pack of *fisi* eat the nearly dead *kifaru* right before their eyes.

He shook his head disdainfully. "She won't last much longer anyway," he reasoned. "No sense wasting a bullet."

BOOM!

The discharge of the .450 Army and Navy Double Rifle from the back of the land rover caught the white hunters by surprise, and they jolted in their seats. It was a perfect shot, killing the near-dead rhinoceros outright when the .500-grain bullet struck it in the head.

"Barake!" Big Jim shouted. "Have you lost your mind?"

The native lowered the rifle slowly. At 50 yards distance and with a pack of hyena covering the creature, it was a difficult shot. In truth, most askari were superb shots, only they never had the opportunity to demonstrate it on safari. That privilege was left for the paying client and the employing white hunter.

"I'll take responsibility if this is reported," Barake said, solemnly. "Let's leave while there's still light."

Big Jim and the others watched as the hyenas, unphased by the sound of the bullet, continued filling their bellies with fresh meat and blood. Big Jim drove off in a hurry, leaving a trail of dust behind them.

They drove for a full hour and saw great herds of zebra, giraffe, elephant, and lion in the long grass half asleep, half stalking prey. There were even herds of wildebeest by the thousands.

"Are you certain about that report?" asked Caesar.

Big Jim shrugged. "The locals are reliable enough," he reasoned.

"Certainly, but it seems we've seen everything there is to see except for the buffalo."

"Give it a rest, will you?"

A moment later one of the wapagazis shouted, *"Zaidi ya hapo!"* (Over there!)

Big Jim brought the car to a skidding halt, kicking up a cloud of red dust. They looked in the direction the native boy pointed. Sure enough, there was a buffalo standing alone in the swampy tall grass. It stood still, staring back, observing them with seemingly keen interest.

"I never did like the way those creatures look at you," Caesar said, matter-of-factly.

Big Jim agreed. Earlier in the year he met an American author by the name of Robert Ruark, who embarked on a month-long safari with *Ker and Downey Safaris*. His guide was 28 year old Harry Selby, an up-and-coming hunter who learned the tools of the trade from hunting legend, Philip Percival. Ruark wrote a book of his expedition and described the Cape buffalo as the type of beast who *stares at you as though you owe them money.*

Well put, Big Jim thought, reflectively. "And today's payday," he said aloud.

"What's that?" Caesar asked.

"I was thinking about how that American writer said the *buff* stare back at you like you owe them money."

Caesar nodded. "Right. I'd say the chap coined it well."

They disembarked from the car and grabbed their rifles. The wapagazis remained in the vehicle. They had no rifles, only their short spears and long knives. Not the sort of weapons one uses against a *nyati*.

Barake opened the barrel from the stock of his double rifle and removed the spent cartridge used on the rhinoceros. Sliding in a fresh cigar-sized cartridge, he snapped shut the barrel with the stock and waited for the white hunters to give the word to move.

"You'd better wait here Barake," Big Jim said. It was not a suggestion. "Caesar and I will have a go at this." He left no room for debate.

The two moved forward, taking slow steps, holding their double rifles at port arms. Had they farther to walk they would have had to carry the heavy rifles over their shoulders. At 16 lbs. each one could not carry the double rifles at port arms for long.

Big Jim noticed the size of the creature to be larger than normal. "As I recollect," he started with a curious inflection, "They don't grow bigger than six feet in height, right?"

Caesar noticed the incredible size of the creature, too, and did not know what to make of it. "He's mighty big," he noted.

At one hundred yards the two hunters stopped. They were about to take aim when the sudden sound of drums beating took hold of their attention. They looked to and fro, searching for the location of the native musician.

"Do you see him?" Caesar asked, irritably.

Big Jim shook his head. "No."

The drum beating maintained a steady staccato. It sounded like nothing one would hear from a talented drummer. It simply beat over and over and over.

Bahm – bahm – bahm – bahm – bahm.

It could have been a native beating against the hollow trunk of a fallen tree, or that of an actual drum. Whatever the case, it bothered the hell out of the white hunters and they wanted it to stop.

After a few moments Big Jim grabbed hold of himself. "Let's tend to the business at hand," he said with deliberation. "No sense putting off what we have to do."

"I couldn't agree more," Caesar replied. "I find it amazing how far people go to keep their licenses to hunt," he added, with a combination of sarcasm and regret. The regret came from his experiences with the Cape buffalo. They were not easy creatures to kill. Sometimes you could disperse a herd of buffalo with a wave of your arms. Others faced off with you and charged like a locomotive.

They inched forward with caution and did not move more than two steps when they caught sight of a pack of African Wild Dogs appear directly behind the giant buffalo. They were seven in all, sleek, dirty, and big-eared with their hides in patches of black and orange.

The very sight of the wild dogs reminded Big Jim how easily repulsed his clients became at the sight of the dogs tearing apart a Grant Gazelle, or wildebeest, or zebra. The dogs were incredibly fast and intelligent, always working in a team of five or more. They attacked with skill, and utilized tactics to corner their prey before tearing it apart in seconds. To witness them hunting and chasing prey was a rarity. At one point the dogs were nearly wiped out, considered to be a nuisance.

Fortunately the Game Department believed the African Wild Dogs, *Lycaon pictus*, to be a necessity in the balance of wildlife. Socially intelligent, fiercely dependent upon the pack, and quite thorough, the wild dogs feeding on herds of gazelle, wildebeest, and zebra, to name a few, prevented the territories from being over-grazed, thus keeping the land fertile.

"What do you suppose they intend to do?" Caesar asked, incredulous at the sight of them.

Big Jim had no idea. Wild dogs never took on the buffalo. That would have been asking for death. He noticed how the dogs remained behind the buffalo, not appearing as though they were about to attack it. Rather they stood behind the beast like soldiers waiting for orders. It was the damnedest sight they had ever seen.

Big Jim was first to raise his double rifle. Caesar quickly followed. They leveled their aim for the buffalo's chest. If their shot proved clean the 500-grain caliber bullets would pierce the chest cavity and go straight through the heart. For any other animal it would cause instant death.

But the Cape buffalo was no ordinary animal. These creatures were known to continue its charge despite being pummeled with heavy-caliber rounds through the chest, penetrating its entire body length. To have a buffalo charge full speed at nearly 40 MPH over uneven ground was equivalent to facing a runaway train.

Their fingers touched the trigger. They drew a breath, exhaling slow, pausing halfway. They started squeezing the trigger.

The drum beating stopped!

It was enough to force the hunters to lose concentration, and they lowered their rifles, searching for the whereabouts of the drummer.

Big Jim was the first to see him.

Standing atop a green hill dotted with acacias stood an African.

He was an old man, his short curly hair turned white years earlier. He wore only a loincloth and robe strung over his shoulder. His feet were adorned with worn sandals, *and the six foot walking stick he held upright probably was the only thing holding him up*, thought Big Jim.

"Who do you suppose he is?" he asked.

Caesar shook his head. "I have no idea. Never seen the chap before."

The buffalo trudged forward, its heavy-hooves pounding the earth like a jackhammer. The ground beneath their feet trembled, and the vultures perched in the trees flew off in a hurry. Big Jim and Caesar had never seen anything like it before.

They raised their rifles to shoulder level, took aim, gently touched the trigger, inhaled and exhaled halfway, paused, Big Jim closed one eye while Caesar kept both open, and they squeezed the trigger.

Click! Click!

The sound of a misfire was unmistakable. The hunters' eyes practically popped from their sockets. In synchronicity, they switched the release lever, opening the barrels from the stock, and removed the faulty cartridges, tossing them to the ground. They swiftly shoved fresh cigar-sized cartridges in the chambers, and snapped the barrels shut. They instinctively backed away, trying to maintain balance over the uneven ground.

Big Jim was first to lift his rifle again in preparation to shoot. He drew a bead on the beast as it continued its steady march toward them when a shout from Caesar distracted him.

"Blimey!" Caesar shouted.

The English hunter lost balance over a rock and fell to the ground with a thud, his double rifle clattering away on the rocky ground.

"You okay?" Big Jim asked, looking at his longtime friend, then at the buff, and back again at Caesar.

"Forget about me," the Englishman retorted. "Shoot the bloody beast before you muck it up the way I did."

Big Jim took aim again and touched the trigger with the index finger of his left hand. He started to squeeze the trigger.

BOOM!

Big Jim flinched. *What the hell was that?* he wondered. He was certain he had never squeezed the trigger. Sure enough, when he checked he hadn't.

The buffalo bellowed a deep, guttural shriek. Big Jim and Caesar had heard the cry before. It was called the Cape buffalo's *death bellow*. Only this one had a slightly different pitch. It was almost as if the buff cried in anger versus its own dying breath.

The bullet struck the creature squarely in its boss adorning its head the way a crown adorned a king. Catching the giant by surprise, the buff stopped dead in its tracks, shook its head, and scanned the terrain for the source of its pain.

Big Jim was not about to lose this opportunity. He raised his rifle and aimed for the chest like before.

The buff seemed to know it lost the advantage, turned, and quickly disappeared in the long grass.

"What the hell is happening?" Big Jim asked.

"Look," Caesar said. He pointed west of where they stood.

Out of the heavy thickets of dense brush came a single white man. His trousers and khaki shirt were in tatters. His boots looked worn through the soles. And his strikingly bald head was unmistakable.

Big Jim recognized the man in an instant. "Stanley Kowalski." He spoke the name with utter disdain and disgust.

Chapter 25

After years in the bush, professional hunters have been known to lose their sense of judgment, even their nerve. When this occurs they no longer know when to pull the trigger on a charging animal, thus making themselves a threat to their clients and themselves. Still, to give up hunting altogether takes more inner strength than non-hunters can ever realize.

"I expect gratitude for saving your life." Kowalski bragged with deliberate intention of touching Big Jim's nerves. "The *Mnyama* would have busted you in half had it not been for my fine shooting."

Big Jim had no intention of showing the slob, Kowalski, gratitude, but he could not argue. His well-placed shot forced the buffalo known as the beast, or *Mnyama* in Swahili, to stop its charge, and bolt into the long grass.

"If it's gratitude you want," Big Jim said, in a subdued voice, "you'll have to be satisfied with a meal and drink."

When the buffalo disappeared Big Jim and Caesar agreed it was pointless to follow. The long grass was dark and dangerous, making for a bad combination.

When Kowalski reached them he suddenly collapsed from exhaustion. It took all the strength he could muster to make it this far in the bush on his own with no vehicles, no gunbearers, and only able to feed himself with the occasional guineafowl he managed to shoot. Big Jim ordered the askari and wapagazis to carry him back to the land rover.

They returned to camp and Kowalski awakened and demanded

a tent and cot for some rest. Big Jim was not one to take orders from the likes of the Polish hunter, but... *I do owe him for that shot.*

A short while later Kowalski entered the tent Big Jim ordered set up for his new guest. He sat heavily on the cot and grinned, displaying his near-toothless gums. "Have any brandy on hand?" He licked his dry lips and rubbed his stubble chin with his hand, praying his rival would indulge him.

"I'm not about to get you drunk," Big Jim snapped.

Kowalski exhaled. "It'll calm my nerves," he explained. Then he offered, "You want me to tell you what I've learned about this damned beast, don't you?"

Big Jim removed his broad-brimmed hat, scratching the back of his head. *Aw, what harm could there be in a drink?* "First tell me what happened," he said curtly.

Kowalski told him how he and clients, Joachim Strasser and Georg Weismann, encountered the creature. He went over the minute details of having tracked the beast and found it in the swamp. He recalled having dropped the beast with a well-placed shot.

"The creature dropped like a load of bricks, but it rose from the red cloud of dust and charged," he said, recalling with great effort the incident that nearly cost him his life.

Had Big Jim not seen the beast for himself he would have thought Kowalski to be lying.

...But now?

Kowalski finished by telling how a great herd of Cape buffalo came out of nowhere and stampeded his safari. "It were as though they were under the command of this *mnyama*," he said, still shocked over the incident. "They killed my clients and wapagazis," he continued. "I decided the only thing I want from here on is to destroy this creature. Whoever kills it will be a hero to the natives."

Big Jim agreed with him there. The natives were a superstitious people and believed a hunter's greatness came from the animals they tracked and killed. The more dangerous the animal proved to be, the greater the hunter to be admired.

We're a vain lot, Big Jim admitted silently.

He waved a hand to a group of natives in the kitchen tent. One of the *M'pishis* (cooks) brought a plate of Guineafowl *(Numida meleagris)* a seed and insect-eating bird resembling partridges, only with featherless heads. Very tasty and considered a delicacy by most clients when on safari. There were also corn ears and beans on the side. Much to Kowalski's delight the tray included a half bottle of imported Canadian whiskey.

Starving as he was, Kowalski reached for the bottle, tossing aside the glass, and took a long swig of whiskey.

Big Jim winced at the thought of the hard liquor stinging his throat. He liked a drink after a good day of hunting, same as anyone else, but this? "Better get some food in you and rest," he said in a subdued voice. "We'll talk later."

He started to leave when Kowalski shouted, "You're taking me with you, you *bastard*!" He spat the words like a spitting cobra.

Big Jim stopped, and turned to face the shallow man. "We'll talk later," he repeated. And then he left the tent, closing the double fly behind him.

Caesar closely followed him. "What do you think?" he asked, observing him keenly.

Big Jim decided to do something he had long-ago given up. He reached in his shirt pocket and pulled out a pack of *Lucky Strike* cigarettes. "We'll see," he said non-committedly.

"I think we should bring him along," Caesar said.

Big Jim looked at him irritated. "Not you, too?"

"What the hell choice do we have?" Caesar challenged. "The man's been tracking the beast for days, against impossible odds. I don't like the bastard any more than you, but he knows what we're up against better than either of us. It would be foolish not to bring him along."

Big Jim mulled over the decision like a man who could not decide what to order for dinner at the *Norfolk Hotel* in Nairobi. He could not argue Caesar's point. The mere fact Kowalski had made it this far in the bush on his own proved his will and determination.

"Not to mention a lack of brains," he said, aloud.

"What was that?" Caesar asked.

"Never mind," he said, waving off the question. He drew from the cigarette and winced. His chest swelled and he coughed heavily twice. "Damn things are made to kill you," he swore. He dropped the cigarette and buried it in the ground with the toe of his boot.

Caesar laughed.

"What's so funny?" Big Jim snapped. "That pipe of yours isn't adding years to your life either, you know." He sounded like a kid trying not to be bested on a playground.

Caesar grinned back. "Your idea of what's meant to kill you strikes me as odd considering your livelihood isn't exactly a safe occupation."

Big Jim got the point, and the life expectancy of a professional hunter came to mind. "If you were smart you'd quit too." He pointed at Caesar's pipe.

"It takes guts to quit something one enjoys."

Big Jim grinned. "Same as hunting, right?" He was about to say something else when Barake approached.

"We're running low on meat," he said. "I'll go and get some." He shouldered his rifle and started to leave.

"No," Big Jim said, "I'll go."

"Why?" Caesar asked.

"Because I need to," Big Jim replied.

"What's all the commotion?" It was Mary. She had kept away from Kowalski's tent as told, but her journalistic instinct had got the better of her. "Where are you going?"

"To get some meat," Big Jim said.

"May I join you? I'd like to see you on a hunt. I might get some good photographs with my *Brownie*." She looked and acted like a cheerleader.

Before Big Jim could tell her no, a high-pitched scream came from the large double-fly tent used for cooking. Big Jim and the others ran to it. When they got there they found three *M'pishis* swinging meat cleavers at a long black mamba snake. It was a futile move on their part, for none dared to get close enough to strike the snake. One of the cooks lay on the ground holding his leg, apparently bitten, and writhing in pain.

The mamba reared nearly half its six-foot length, hissing like a busted overheated radiator hose, and flared its neck much like the cobra, only not as wide. Still, the black mamba (*Dendroaspis polylepis)* one of the deadliest snakes in Africa, looked as frightening as its reputation.

Big Jim reached for a machete. He pushed the frightened natives aside and in a single stroke severed the mamba's head. The headless portion of the snake constricted and flopped around for about five seconds before it lay still. Big Jim ordered the natives to lift the bitten cook onto the table.

"Get the antivenin kit," he said quickly.

Barake handed it to him and he quickly went to work on the native.

Mary stood close to Caesar, holding his arm. The scene was more than she could have imagined. "What's he doing?" she asked.

Caesar loosened her grip on his arm. "Do you mind, ma'am? You're cutting the circulation."

"Sorry," she said, embarrassed by her behavior. "Is the boy in danger?"

Caesar nodded. "Black mambas are probably the deadliest snakes alive."

"How deadly?" she asked with a touch of curiosity overshadowing any concern for the native boy.

Caesar looked at her with bemusement. He'd mastered the art of determining when a person actually cared about an injured African, or their trophy, or in Mary's case, information. "Their bite is extremely toxic," he began in a quiet voice. "The venom attacks the *vagus nerve*, increasing the heartbeat of the victim and making it difficult to breath." He paused, looking on with concern. "He stands a chance with the antivenin if it's administered in time."

Mary watched Big Jim at work with fear and curiosity. "How long before we know?" she asked.

Caesar checked his watch. "About half an hour."

Everyone looked on while Big Jim displayed his talents as a field doctor.

Mary was reminded of what Caesar had told her earlier on. 'A hunter is a guide, mechanic, a gentleman, good with the jokes, and good at playing cards. He's also a field doctor should the need arise.'

The mood in the camp was subdued. Mambas always put the fear of God in people, and the black mamba most of all. Caesar explained to Mary how the black species was deadlier than its twin, the green mamba. They were extremely territorial, fast-moving, and looked as scary as hell. Their ability to rear high accounted for many facial bites, not to mention adding terror at the sight of such a creature lurching before you.

Thirty minutes passed before Big Jim came out of the kitchen tent. He looked exhausted, standing there with his sleeves rolled up, perspiration rolling down his forehead, and the armpits of his shirt stained with sweat.

Caesar approached him. "Well?"

Big Jim nodded. "He'll make it," he said. "But he won't be climbing trees any time soon. He'll be of no good to us on the remainder of this venture. We'll have him driven to town in the lorry. Two of the boys should do."

Caesar offered him his flask. "Here, have a belt of man's best friend."

Right then the steady beating of a distant drum caught their attention. It was the same dull, rhythmic tune they heard when facing the buffalo earlier. The sound frightened off birds, made wildebeest scurry away, and even the crocodiles scrambled off the shore and into the river.

"What the deuces is that?" Caesar asked.

Big Jim noticed the wapagazis trembling with fear. "Kubakia shwari!" (Remain calm!) he ordered. It would be difficult, he knew, to keep the natives in control. Superstition was very much alive and well in Africa, even in the mid-twentieth century.

"Look!" Mary pointed to a hill in the distance. Standing atop the hill was a man.

"That's the same bloke as before," Caesar pointed out. "Who do you suppose he is?"

Big Jim had no idea, but something told him the old native was the cause of all this brouhaha.

Chapter 26

In rural African villages natives believe they have been cursed when things take a turn for the worse. When crops fail, animals die, and children become sick they seek help from the Jabilo. It is believed through the Jabilo's witchcraft that the curse may be lifted. And yet this same Jabilo is feared for unleashing a terrible wrath of revenge, which could be provoked by the desire to demonstrate power.

Mokonzi sat cross-legged in front of the fire, watching the guineafowl cook. He liked this bird any time of day. It tasted more agreeable than the *posho* common among natives. The dough-like maize of mixed meat and vegetables was good for some, but not him.

I am a Jabilo *and deserve better*, he told himself. And the guineafowl would more than suffice.

Thus far he was happy with the string of events. His magic summoned the *Mnyama* and it wreaked havoc across the territory. Other animals played their part, too. The *chui* killed the game warden, and the *Mnyama* attacked the village. Now the black mamba added fear, as if it were possible considering the natives were already as fear-stricken as humanly possible. Word was sure to spread to the nearby villages. It always did.

And my power will be unquestioned, Mokonzi said silently.

The sun was setting fast, and caught the attention of the old man. He watched it fall behind the horizon; lighting up the wide open steppes with Grant Gazelle, wildebeest, zebra, elephant, and giraffe numbering in the thousands, grazing peacefully as the dark orange light of dusk slowly vanished. Moments later the territory was plunged into darkness.

Good, Mokonzi thought. *The* Mnyama *works best in the dark.*

He removed the leather satchel from across his shoulder and opened it. Drawing out a small pouch made from goatskin, he poured the contents into the fire. To anyone else the act would have been meaningless. To the *Jabilo* it was precisely what he needed to summon the beast.

When the guineafowl was ready to be eaten Mokonzi removed it from the stick holding it over the fire. He pulled off a leg with his filthy hands. Cleanliness was not always an option in the bush, and he bit into it with the left side of his mouth. He had to, for the front teeth in the right side of his mouth fell out from decay long ago.

He removed the plug in the canteen of water made from the stomach of a goat, and covered in goatskin for protection, and put the opening to his mouth. Before he drank the deep, guttural bellow of the Cape buffalo caught his attention.

It is close.

Mokonzi took a drink and put the plug back in. Rising to his feet, he waited.

A few moments passed when the steady sound of hooves pounding the earth reached his ears.

It comes. Mokonzi stood firm, unafraid and anxious. The pounding hooves grew louder as the beast came nearer and nearer. The old man could not keep the corners of his mouth from pursing into a malicious grin. He had too much to be thankful for.

There it is!

Looming before him was the enormous shadow of the beast. It was much larger than the ordinary Cape buffalo, and certainly evil-looking. Its dark hide oozed a crimson-colored liquid from its skin beneath its hair. And the beast emitted an awful stench.

The smell of death, Mokonzi thought.

The creature's bloodshot eyes narrowed. The boss adorning its head was the largest set of horns crowning any beast the old man ever saw.

"They are here," he said. A moment later he added, *"Kurejesha heshima yangu."* (Restore my honor)

The *Mnyama* snorted and grunted, and then turned and disappeared.

The malicious grin returned to Mokonzi's face. *My time has come.* And he started to eat with a hearty appetite. He stopped chewing momentarily and stared at the drumstick. *This will be the last time I cook for myself. Other Jabilo's are treated like kings in the villages they live. And so it will be the same for me.*

They spent their days curing the sick with spells and bringing rain so that crops thrived. The return was to live out their days in relaxation, and grow fat off food hunted by the strong warriors.

I will have a hut for my own, and it will be the largest in any village!

Mokonzi indeed had grand plans for his future.

And the Mnyama will make them true.

Chapter 27

If African officials made public the number of human deaths by man-eaters each year or the number of people killed by snakebite, there are those who believe the tourist industry would collapse. However, the bold adventurous types steadfastly disagree. For them the thrill of danger is reason enough for some to venture in the African bush.

The cry stirred everyone in the camp.

"What is it?" Mary asked. She practically jumped from her chair at the dining table.

Big Jim thought best they should have dinner outside of the tent and enjoy the dusk. After the mamba incident in the cooking tent he was certain no one would disagree.

"Sounds like a *death bellow,*" Caesar said, staring in the distance.

"No," Big Jim said. "The pitch was too high. It was close to a roar, but not quite."

"A lion?" Mary asked.

"No," replied Big Jim. "Could be a *shamba* fighting another male for control of a herd."

"*Shamba*? What's that?"

Big Jim glanced at Mary apologetically. "Sorry. It's a rogue elephant that raids crops. They're known to fight it out with other bulls for food and mates."

A native askari came running into the camp. He wore a red six inch tall Fez hat with back-flap, khaki shorts, and a white jersey shirt with sleeves rolled up to his elbow. He carried a .350 Mauser repeater slung over his shoulder by the leather strap. He went straight to Big Jim and Caesar and began talking in a loud, nervous voice.

The two white hunters walked a short distance from the table with the askari while Mary looked on with much curiosity. She could see Big Jim and Caesar understood what the native said in Swahili, and his words had a harrowing effect on the other natives. The wapagazis began chatting amongst themselves in nervous, hushed tones, looking over their shoulders in the same manner a person in fear of being followed would.

And they say women gossip, she thought to herself.

Big Jim spoke in a raised voice, quieting them down, and then turned to speak in private with Caesar. Mary strained to listen, but they were too far and she did not want them to notice. A moment later Big Jim walked off to his tent, and Caesar approached her.

"What's going on?" she asked, anxious.

"The native claims local villagers saw what they believe to be the creature not far from here." Caesar sounded uncertain. "The cry we heard earlier is supposedly a challenge for us to track it and settle matters."

"An animal challenging you—you don't believe so do you?" Mary was astonished by the notion of animals challenging people.

"Animals are known to challenge people, yes," Caesar admitted. "They're as territorial as we are and stop at nothing to protect their herd, or pride, and their feeding ground." He scratched his head. "In any case, it doesn't matter whether I believe it or not. The natives do and if we don't find this creature and kill it, Big Jim and I lose face. And this is the most important asset a professional hunter can't afford to lose."

Mary nodded understandingly. "What are you going to do?"

"We're going to collect our bush gear and have a go with whatever is out there," he said, in a flat, toneless voice.

"Is that wise in the dark?" Mary already knew the answer. Big Jim explained earlier how traveling by car or lorry at night was discouraged. There were no maintained roads and a bad turn over a boulder or ditch could leave you stranded in unfriendly territory.

"We don't have much choice," Caesar said, with regret laced

in his tone. "The natives are worked up about this evil creature conjured up by a witch doctor."

"They refer to the creature as the *Mnyama* and they call witch doctors a *Jabilo*, right?"

Caesar managed a smile. "Yes. You have good memory." He felt appreciated when clients took in what he told them over the course of a safari. "Anyway, we must go through the motions of doing something constructive now, or risk losing the wapagazis for good. They need to believe James and I will destroy this beast." He shook his head, reflecting over the superstitious nonsense that seemed to be turning their lives inside out. He added with a touch of humor, "It's probably an elephant drunk from having too much *marula*."

"What's *marula*?"

Caesar needed to collect his bush gear too, and did not wish to spend idle time educating a westerner. However, he liked Mary and enjoyed her enthusiasm. "It's a tree with fruit which elephants eat. African lore holds that fermented fruit rotting on the ground is eaten by elephants, which turns them into drunkards for a short period."

"Drunk, is that possible?" She was highly surprised.

"Yes, when you consider the digestive system of an elephant is slow, it takes between 24 and 48 hours for foods to pass through it. During this period an elephant can grow mad as a hatter." He started to walk to his tent before turning to face her once more. "Of course there's no scientific proof any of this is true," he added, non-committal.

Mary smiled. "But they believe it, and that's all there is to it," she said.

Caesar grinned. "By Jove, you're learning."

Caesar started to turn when Mary took hold of his arm. "Caesar, what do you suppose it is, this creature?"

Caesar sighed exhaustively. "I bloody hell wish I knew," he confessed. "By all accounts it looks to be a larger than life Cape buffalo, but they don't grow as big as this one."

"Then what is it?" Mary was not about to drop the matter. She wanted to know all the details about this creature terrorizing the local villagers.

Caesar shook his head in thought. "I'm not sure, but one thing I am certain of is that before we're through with this safari you'll have one helluva story."

Chapter 28

Obsession to hunt can be overwhelming—and dangerous—for the hunter who does not put safety before his desire to pull the trigger. It is for this reason one must know when to call it a day and live to hunt another day.

"**I**'m coming with you!" shouted Kowalski. He spat the words like a drunk cursing his wife for failing to refill the liquor cabinet. "I've been tracking this beast for days and I'm not about to give you the opportunity of besting me."

Right then Big Jim could not help but wonder if it were possible to dislike the man any more than he already did. *Probably not,* he thought. "Listen, pardner," he said, speaking like an American cowboy sheriff to the town drunk, "You're lucky I don't turn you over to the Game Department for not reporting the deaths of your clients. You'd not only lose your license, you'd probably get deported."

Kowalski flashed a scalding glare. He wanted to leap at *Kubwa Jim* and rip out his throat!

Big Jim, the man, the myth, the dashing handsome Great White Hunter who commanded the natives in the manner of Edgar Rice Burroughs' Tarzan, the Ape Man. The hunter so infallible he could trek the length, width, and breadth of the Dark Continent in search of the most difficult game to hunt, and aim true enough to hit his mark. Well, Stanley Kowalski was having none of it!

"I may not be pretty, but I'm going to do what I want. And you're not going to stop me," he blurted.

Big Jim reached the edge of patience. He moved a step forward to lay into Kowalski when Caesar called out to him. "James!"

Big Jim stopped and stood still, fists clenched tightly, eyes glaring. He looked at his longtime British friend, and took a deep breath. He thought about how good it would make him feel to teach the bastard Kowalski a lesson, but then thought better of it.

"You've got a big mouth," he said with disgust.

Kowalski displayed an evil grin. "Tell me something I don't know."

A tense moment passed when Big Jim's good judgment got the better of him. "I'm bringing you along not because you say so, but because I don't want you here alone with my men."

Kowalski's grin broadened. "Or the girl, you mean."

He's smarter than I thought. "You better believe it."

Big Jim went to his tent for his rifle and gear with Caesar and Barake in tow.

"You think it's a good idea to have him along?" Caesar asked.

Big Jim walked out of the tent and looked up at the sky. A slight sliver of moon lit their path. "No," he said sharply. "It's a lousy idea. But I want that bastard close. He's more dangerous out of sight than standing among us."

Caesar agreed. "We have good vehicles, enough cartridges, and a good knowledge of the territory," he said, with a positive tone. "We should be able to wallop this creature by mid-afternoon tomorrow."

Big Jim wanted to believe him. He instructed Barake to get things ready. "We'll take one car," he said. "You and Taabu will come along. Let Davu know he's to remain with the men here and will be in charge until we return."

Barake agreed. Davu was a wapagazi, but a good shot with a rifle, and the others respected him.

"When do we leave?" Caesar asked.

"Now."

"Where are we going?" It was Mary. She appeared from nowhere. "I heard shouting between you and Mr. Kowalski. I take it you're not the best of friends."

Big Jim did not appreciate the sarcasm. "You're a good judge of people, aren't you?"

"I'm afraid you won't be joining us, my dear," Caesar told her. He noted her look of disappointment. "Traveling by night isn't advised, and we're only doing so to bring closure to this episode before word spreads to the nearby villages. You see, the natives are superstitious beyond belief."

"What is it they're afraid of?" she asked, her curiosity more than piqued. In truth she already knew, but wanted the hunters to explain again in case she had missed anything in her notes.

Caesar, being ever the English gentleman, was more than happy to explain. "A *Jabilo*, or witch doctor as you Americans probably know them by, is believed to have summoned a *Mnyama* to lash out against the locals for no longer respecting his magic."

"What's a *Mnyama*?" Again, Mary asked a question she already knew the answer to, but a professional journalist once told her, 'A good journalist always makes certain their information is correct before publication.' *And I'm not going to let it be said that I wrote without doing my proper research,* she said silently.

"It means, Beast," answered Big Jim. "Everyone believes the animal to be an evil creature seeking vengeance for the witch doctor." Big Jim spoke curtly and with a cold edge in his voice. He was obviously exhausted over this episode and anxious to bring closure to it.

"You can't be serious," Mary said, looking bemused.

"I'm not," Big Jim said, quickly. "The natives are."

The hunters prepared to leave, but Mary wanted more information for her notes.

Think fast! "Wait!" she shouted.

The group of five stopped and turned to face her right as they were about to board the land rover. Mary froze, unable to find the words.

"Well what is it?" Big Jim asked, impatiently.

The question snapped Mary from her momentary trance. "I mean—you speak as though we live in the dark ages," she managed to say at last. "After all, we live in the twentieth century. Surely the people in Africa cannot be naïve enough to believe in witchcraft?"

It was a baited question only a journalist could ask, one designed to retrieve information from the person being spoken to, Big Jim knew. He had been on enough safaris to know when a person asked questions because they truly did not know and had the curiosity of a child. He also knew when persons put their questions to him to test his knowledge and experience as well as get him to divulge information.

Journalists come in all shapes and sizes, he told himself with a sigh. He stood before her looking all business. "I need you to listen." Big Jim paused, deliberately. "Look around you," he said, motioning with a sweep of his arm. "Is there anything modern about our surroundings, which remind you of home?"

Mary looked to Caesar, who stared back and offered no hint as to what crossed his mind, and then she turned back to Big Jim. "I only meant to inquire as to the reason for your desperation," she managed to say, shrugging her shoulders like a schoolgirl giving in to the classroom teacher.

Big Jim would have none of it. "Don't lie to me," he snapped back. "I understand your profession and reason for asking questions. But this is no simple story. People have already been killed by whatever is out there, and if we don't stop it more people will die."

Mary was startled. She had not expected her handsome adventurer to turn on her so suddenly. "I only wish to make certain I write the facts as they are," she said, in a rather limp tone.

Big Jim nodded. "I suppose we'll have to wait for the book to find out if you paid attention."

The hunters and natives climbed into the land rover with Big Jim at the wheel, Caesar sitting beside him, and Kowalski and the natives in back. He started the engine, gunning the motor to a high pitch, switched gears from park to drive and sped off rather fast considering the rough terrain.

Mary watched them until they were out of sight. She stared into the darkness for a few moments before Davu approached her.

He touched her shoulder, bringing her back to attention. "Are you all right, Miss?" he asked, in broken English.

"Yes, yes I'm all right," she stuttered. Then she turned and walked straight for her tent. *I have a lot of note-writing to do.*

Chapter 29

Villagers often sought the help of white hunters to shoot troublesome animals in order to protect their crops and tribe. This reliance on the men with 'fire sticks' strained relations with the Jabilos, who viewed their interference an insult. Thus, the Jabilo placed curses and spells on villages to keep the people in line and remind them to respect their magic. The white hunters regarded this as silly superstition, but respected the fact that natives believed.

Big Jim drove the land rover as usual. It was not that he did not trust Caesar or the askari. More so because it demonstrated to natives that *he* was the man in charge. The *B'wana*, boss-man.

Thank God no one calls me that, Big Jim said silently.

European landowners had a terrible reputation with natives. They took over land belonging to locals for thousands of years, forcing them to relocate to less hospitable territory more difficult to raise crops and find water, and more dangerous to live. The farther out in the bush the tribes moved their villages meant encroaching on territory belonging to *simba*, *chui*, *tembo*, and *nyati*, to name a few.

This clash of man and beast brought on a terrible toll of death for the natives. They did not have the fire-sticks like the white hunters, who enjoyed marching in the bush for the sole purpose of shooting game. Thus, their reliance on white hunters grew ever more. European landowners, cattle ranchers, and farmers couldn't have cared less about the difficulties the natives faced. They simply wanted the land.

And they took it, quite legally too, and without regret.

These people were called *B'wana* by the natives who worked the fields, herded the cattle and other animals, served as coolies, and forced by the government to pay high taxes to live on their property, or risk imprisonment. What took place in Africa reminded Big Jim of how early Americans took the land from the Native American Indians.

I suppose people are alike all over, he reflected.

Big Jim wanted nothing to do with the name *B'wana*. And so he made certain the wapagazis and askaris who worked for him refrained from calling him that. But their respect for him required him to be ordained with a name fitting of his character.

Kubwa Jim seemed fitting. He always found the biggest game, walloping elephants and buffalo like he was born with a .577 Westley-Richards Double Rifle in his crib. He respected the village chieftains, and the people. He opened up a school on his property, which miffed his European neighbors, but endeared him to the children. And he did not charge them outrageous prices to keep their mud huts on his property.

Indeed, in the eyes of those close to him, the name *Kubwa Jim* was appropriate.

It was dusk when they left camp, and not long before near total darkness made the journey more difficult. The road they travelled was little more than a game trail made by wildebeest or zebra, and the long grass was likely to be infested with *simbas* lying in wait for unsuspecting prey. They had to be extra aware for it was not uncommon for a lion to strike, dragging off an unfortunate passenger out of a car to feed on.

Big Jim kept the speed at no more than 10 miles per hour. The trail was so bumpy and treacherous he dared not risk traveling faster.

"When did you become so gutless," Kowalski said, bitterly.

Big Jim could not take his eyes off the trail to address the slob sitting in back with Barake and Taabu. It was so dark the headlights were practically useless and he could not risk striking a boulder or driving into a pothole.

Caesar handed Kowalski his flask. "Here," he said, "have a belt of man's best friend."

Kowalski reached for the flask, which was quite a chore in the bouncing vehicle. He took the flask and grinned condescendingly at the back of Big Jim's head. Only a person like Kowalski saw this as a small but enjoyable victory over his nemesis.

He put the flask to his mouth when the vehicle suddenly jolted. "What the bloody hell?" Kowalski barked. The opening of the flask struck him hard on his upper lip, spilling some of its contents on his shirt. "You did that on purpose!" he shouted.

The vehicle came to a halt, and Big Jim pivoted in his seat to face Kowalski. "I suggest you keep quiet for the remainder of this trip," he said.

Kowalski stiffened. *I take orders from no man.* "Or you'll do what?" he snapped.

Big Jim stared coldly. "I'm not playing poker here." He paused to let his meaning sink in, and saw that Kowalski understood.

"We all need to keep our mind on the business at hand," Caesar added. "Only together will we bring closure to this madness."

Big Jim always admired how his English friend knew when to contribute. He turned back to his front, grinning and shaking his head, and then started driving once more.

Caesar noted the look on his face. "I recall you smiling similarly when I showed you a photograph of Betty Grable displaying her backside."

They drove on another hour, bouncing and jolting in the car. On more than one occasion each felt like their teeth were going to pop out of their mouth, but Big Jim managed to keep the land rover on the trail. A breakdown at this point would be dangerous so far from camp. Like all professional hunters, Big Jim and Caesar had become quite good at improving their mechanical knowledge of vehicles out of necessity. But traveling so far in the bush, and at night, would make any work on the land rover difficult.

At night with no moon to illuminate the territory they could not appreciate the beauty of the steppes, or the lush jungle, the wide open terrain studded with Ficus, Acacia, Msasa, and Baobab trees thriving in their respective environments. It was unusual to see so many species in close proximity.

"That's Africa for you," Big Jim used to say. "It's full of surprises."

When they came to a patch of trees Big Jim stopped the car. Running water caught their attention.

"We're near a river or stream," Caesar noted.

They listened. They waited. Wind rustling through the long grass and trees reached their ears, but nothing more. A moment later their noses were upturned by a most dreadful stench.

"Baboons!" Kowalski cried.

Even Big Jim and Caesar had to put their handkerchiefs to their nose. Baboons were dirty, filthy creatures with a stench strong enough to upturn a corpse.

A moment later the high-pitched screeching familiar with large packs of baboon filled the air. A large family of them had taken refuge in the trees here for the night, safe from the dangers lurking on the ground. A lion roared in defiance, apparently awakened by the baboons. African Wild Dogs started barking, and the hideous laugh of nearby hyenas added to the cacophony of the baboons' endless screeching.

"Let's get out of here!" Kowalski screamed.

"Shut the hell up!" Big Jim snapped.

Caesar turned to Big Jim. "I hate to agree, but perhaps we should travel a way further. We'll never be able to track the buff with such an audience giving away our position."

Big Jim looked irritated, but knew Caesar was right. The buffalo was an intelligent animal and the baboons had given away their position. He started the car and slowly continued driving along the river bank another half hour before reaching another patch of trees.

They waited and listened, and this time they were not met with a chorus of wildlife.

Good, Big Jim thought. "We wait here for sunrise."

Only Kowalski managed sleep. When dawn came the chilly night air was replaced with sudden warmth from the bright sun rising across the steppes and mountains in the east. It was a beautiful sight, but they failed to appreciate it considering their current task to be dealt with.

Big Jim thought about Mary Watkins. He felt good about his decision not to bring her along. This was no game they played. But the way she looked at him when they left her in the care of Davu disturbed him. He had seen that look before from female clients taking a liking to his company. Too often women on such a journey grew sentimental and became drawn to the *Great White Hunter*.

I suppose we have Hollywood to thank for that, he thought.

He appreciated female attention the same as any man, only on safari having an affair could be more dangerous than stalking a lion in the long grass. "Did she think we were married," Big Jim said aloud, and to no one in particular.

"How's that?" asked Caesar.

Big Jim realized he had been thinking out loud. "Never mind," he said, looking irritated.

Caesar looked on quizzically. "Nasty habit of yours," he said, in a hushed voice so the others would not hear.

Big Jim turned and faced him. "How's that?" he asked, pretending not to know what he meant.

Caesar grinned in such a way that embarrassed Big Jim. "Talking to yourself when you've got such interesting company to keep you entertained," he said, stifling a laugh.

Big Jim heaved a sigh. He disliked people catching him doing that, but it was a moot point for now. *Why argue.*

They got their gear from the back of the land rover. Extra cartridges were placed in the loop holes of their shirts and vests. Each carried a leather satchel of food, water, and medical kit. They laced up their boots and rolled down their sleeves to protect their arms from the blades of long grass they would be forging through.

Kowalski noted how Barake and Taabu wore traditional native garb of sandals, loincloth, a rolled robe over their shoulders, and a leather pouch of *posho* containing their rations. They armed themselves each with an *assegais* spear and a *panga* throwing knife.

The *assegais* were a common enough weapon, but the *panga* seemed a bit much. It weighed close to two pounds and reminded westerners of the famed *Bowie* knife. White hunters called them bush knives.

"What do you think you're going to do with those?" Kowalski challenged. "We're going after a *nyati*, and you'll never help bring it down with those Zulu weapons."

Barake and Taabu stared back stoically.

"And why aren't you wearing boots?" Kowalski continued. "Your ankles are going to be skinned in the long grass with sandals."

"Back off," Big Jim said, sharply.

But Kowalski persisted. "I note your other boys wear jerseys and khaki shorts. What makes these blokes special?"

"Shut that hole in your face!" Caesar shouted. "It's far too early to argue and your breath reminds me of the baboons' stench."

Kowalski started to say something when a high-pitched shriek filled the air.

"Elephant," Big Jim said.

It was close, too, and in the long grass coming their way. They could hear its heavy hooves trampling through the brush. They spread out ten paces abreast, eyes front and rifles held at port arms. The three white hunters pulled back the hammers to their double rifles. They were ready. For a fleeting moment Big Jim thought about what Kowalski had said. He was right how Barake and Taabu should have armed themselves with rifles. They certainly were good enough shots. For some reason they chose to fight the *nyati* with traditional weapons.

Big Jim was not about to interfere with their native beliefs. *If they want to take on the beast on their own terms, who am I to argue?*

The elephant shrieked again.

"Sounds like it's in a fit," Caesar noted.

Big Jim agreed. "Get ready," he said, in a calm and steady voice.

A second later the elephant burst through the long grass and brush, charging full speed across the stream. Its intent was obvious. The three hunters raised their rifles and pulled the triggers.

The double rifles exploded! Long orange balls of flame breathed from the barrels of the rifles. They heard the smacking sound of the bullets striking the elephant, but with no apparent effect. This came as no surprise to Big Jim and Caesar. To bring down an elephant one had to strike its brain, or at the very least numb it. The problem lay in the size of an elephant's brain being no larger than a human fist. Smashing it to jelly as the world's largest land animal charged took more than being a good shot. One had to have a good share of luck, too, they all knew.

They fired a second volley and saw the bloom of flower-sized marks appear on the elephant's head. They were definitely hitting the *tembo*, but not in the right spot.

Big Jim unsnapped the gun barrel release lever, removed the spent cartridges, and quickly reloaded. He had just snapped shut the barrels into the receiver and started lifting his rifle when the elephant reached them.

Taabu was closest to the elephant. He had his spear ready to throw and stood stiffly in place, waiting for the right moment.

"Taabu!" Big Jim called out to him, but the native did not respond.

A moment later he threw his spear, striking the elephant above the trunk. The blade hit bone, dangled a bit, and then fell to the ground.

The elephant raised its trunk and slapped it against Taabu, tossing him to the ground like a rag doll. It reached the land rover, reared on its hind legs and came down hard, crushing the hood of the car. The sound of the chassis cracking, tires deflating, and metal being crushed under the tremendous weight of the bull was deafening.

The elephant swung around and with incredible speed returned to where Taabu lay. It wrapped him in its trunk and lifted him, throwing him 20 feet in the air. The native fell hard against the rocks, lying still with blood smeared on his head and face. The breath must have been knocked out of the African when the elephant first struck him, because he never let out a cry.

Big Jim and Caesar fired a round each. The boom from their rifles did more to catch the elephant's attention than the smacking of its hide when the 750-grain bullets struck it. The elephant seemed unimpressed. It stared at the two white hunters with a look that would have turned most men into retreating cowards.

But the *tembo* did not charge. Instead it lifted its trunk and shrieked a high-pitched fit of anger.

Kowalski lowered his rifle, disturbed by how the elephant continued to defy them.

Big Jim and Caesar lifted their rifles and fired simultaneously. A split second later the elephant fell, pole-axed by a frontal brain shot. A cloud of dust rose from where the elephant laid dying. Big Jim ran up close to the elephant, aimed point blank at the side of the bull's head and pulled the second trigger for good measure.

BOOM!

Chapter 30

Tracking an animal's trail through the long grass was dangerous, but at times necessary. In some places the grass proved thick enough to conceal a herd of elephants, or a pack of lion waiting to pounce on unsuspecting prey. When a client failed to kill his game and the beast sought refuge in the long grass, it was up to the professional hunter to go after it and finish the job. Leaving the animal to suffer from injury was not considered sportsman, and could cost the hunter his license and reputation.

"Looks like we walk back," Kowalski grumbled.

He stared with disgust at the wrecked car while the others ran over to Taabu. His body looked as though every bone had been smashed. His eyes bulged wide from apparent fear and the inability to breathe after having been swatted aside in the manner of a person swatting a fly. And his body was smeared in blood.

"Do we bury him now?" Caesar asked.

Big Jim looked at Barake. Taabu had been like a brother to him. Now he was gone, all in the blink of an eye.

"I don't want to lose the light," Big Jim said with restraint.

Barake knelt beside Taabu for a few moments, and then slowly rose. He stared blankly at the white hunters. "Sisi lazima hoja sasa," (We must move now) he said, hiding emotion. He was a warrior and knew there was work to be done.

They lifted Taabu's body and carried him back to what was left of the land rover. Then they wrapped his body in a blanket and tarp and put him in the back of the car.

"Damn hyenas may catch his scent and come after him," Caesar noted, with disdain.

This was true, Big Jim knew. Hyenas had an incredible sense of smell, able to catch scent over two miles away. The *fisi* tracked, hunted, and killed prey up to 80 percent of what they ate. An impressive ratio compared to the lion, which actually scavenged for food more than the hyena, much to everyone's surprise. They heard the hideous laugh of a pack of *fisi* nearby, and it was likely they would come and feed off Taabu's corpse.

Big Jim hated the idea of leaving him. "We have no choice," he said, flatly. "We have maybe six hours to track the buffalo before we must make way back to camp if we're to return before dark."

Caesar pondered that. "This is a lot of territory to cover in six hours," he said, sweeping the terrain with his arm.

"I know," Big Jim replied.

It was now or never. News of the *Mnyama* being near was a good thing. It meant taking care of business now instead of much later. The longer this fight dragged on between hunter and beast, the more fear the natives would suffer. At some point they would lose confidence in the white hunters, possibly uprising against them for failing to kill the creature. Not to forget how this would shift their loyalty back to the *jabilo*.

Big Jim disliked the superstition among the natives he lived with for so many years. After all they had been through together everything was at risk because they believed a witch doctor summoned an evil beast to wreak havoc on them for doubting his magic over the white hunters' rifles.

Times like this made Big Jim wonder if his chosen trade was worth it. *Or should I pack up and return to America?*

He recalled his first hunt after the war. He had travelled to the Colony of Kenya after his discharge from the army and was hired by the Game Department to 'crop' elephants in the Yatta Plateau north of Tsavo. This territory was known for harboring large herds of elephant, and the government needed to reduce their numbers. Big Jim had no professional hunting experience up until then, but the government was in need of people who could shoot. His military background was credential enough and after his first 'cropping' experience he decided to learn how to track and hunt game, which was more sporting than the cropping of herds. After his first safari the man was hooked for good.

Don't kid yourself, he told himself. *It's dangerous and not as glamorous as people are led to believe. Still, it's damned more exciting than most professions. Besides, life without excitement is no life.*

They walked over to where the elephant laid.

"Strange to find it here this time of year," Big Jim noted. "Most elephant migrate south and there are no nearby villages for them to raid crops."

Kowalski stared at the land giant, mesmerized by the size of its tusks. He recalled how terrifying the bull looked when it attacked them. It moved with incredible speed, flapping its ears back, trunk raised high, and screeching a loud piercing shriek.

"They truly are the *King of Beasts,*" he said.

Big Jim agreed.

"What about the tusks?" Kowalski asked quickly.

Everyone stopped. They were all taken aback by such indifference.

Big Jim looked at Kowalski with a menacing stare that would have made Heavyweight Boxing Champion, Rocky Marciano, shrink. He never thought he could dislike Kowalski more than he already did, but the man had proved him wrong once more.

"Why are you surprised?" Kowalski spat. "They must be five footers, weighing at least 85 pounds each!"

Kowalski was right. They were big tusks and guaranteed a hefty price in the ivory trade. *Why this guy has all the luck,* he wondered.

One of the tusks was a tad shorter than the other, probably from the elephant using it more often than the other for scraping against the side of trees to knock down fruit, or digging up dirt around crops to make it easier to pull them up. Elephants often favored using one tusk over another in this way.

Kowalski stared back at Big Jim. "What? You don't approve?" he said, challengingly.

"Too damned right we don't approve!" Caesar intervened. His face turned red with anger.

Kowalski sneered. "I can guess *Big Jim* doesn't, but what about the *kaffir?*"

Barake stiffened. No one called him that!

"You're overstepping it, man," Big Jim warned. He stepped forward a few steps facing off with Kowalski, who did not back down. "We have pressing work to tend to, but if you prefer we can settle this now."

Barake did not like others to do his fighting for him, and touched Big Jim's shoulder. He nodded and stepped aside for the native.

Kowalski barked a derisive laugh. "You think you can handle me?"

Barake had no doubt he could. They stood at roughly the same height. Barake was lean and fit, whereas Kowalski was fat, strong, but slow.

And stupid, thought Big Jim and Caesar.

Right then the same familiar drum-beating began.

A lion roared.

Then the hyenas laughed.

The African Wild dogs barked.

And a leopard growled.

"This is not right," Big Jim pointed out. "They don't gather in such close proximity with each other."

"These do," Kowalski said. "Why are you so interested in killing this buffalo?" he asked, point blank. "I told you both before, it's mine."

Big Jim stared off in the field of long grass, trying to catch a glimpse of the animals awaiting them. "You're not capable of taking care of this matter, Stanley," he said, speaking like a foreman to a layman. "You're only along because I don't want to leave you alone back at camp."

Kowalski laughed again. "Because you're afraid I might have my way with that pretty little tart?" He started to laugh again when a sharp pain on the left side of his face knocked him off balance. Kowalski lost his footing on a rock and fell back on his haunches. He shook his head, clearing the cobwebs, and spat out the blood in his mouth.

He looked up and saw Barake looming over him. He no longer looked the same. The native appeared menacing instead of the peaceful, tranquil quiet man who always seemed to be where he was needed.

Kowalski stumbled to his feet. "No one cold cocks me!" he shouted.

Right when he started to lunge at the African a long, deep-throated bellow filled the air. Its sound was so striking that all other animals quieted down and the steady staccato of drum-beating ceased.

"There it is," Big Jim said.

Chapter 31

During a professional hunt death lurks around every tree, every river crossing, in the long grass, and in the bush. It will consume you once you disrespect the dangers you face. Thus, it is better to be sure you want to hunt before making the journey.

They marched with more caution than usual for good reason. The group of animals they faced did not live peacefully amongst each other. Leopards spent their day sleeping in trees, not in the long grass. From above they pounced on humans and animals alike. The long grass was where the lion reigned. Here they blended easily like the chameleon. Hyenas preferred wooded and open terrain in their all-consuming search for food. The African Wild Dogs followed the great herds of wildebeest and gazelle on the open steppes and veldt. In packs of six to ten they worked as a tight-knit team, cornering their prey before ripping it apart. They worked so well together a United States Marine drill sergeant would drool with jealousy.

The buffalo was expected to be here, but not the elephant. That had caught them by surprise.

"Did you wonder why it went after the land rover first?" Big Jim asked, while they marched into the field. He had found the buff's tracks and led the way.

"What do you mean? It went after Taabu first."

"No. Taabu was in its way. It knocked him aside and went straight for the car, with purpose even."

Caesar reflected for a moment. In fact, it did appear that the elephant's main target was the land rover. He thought nothing of it at first. Quite often elephants chased after cars when they invaded their territory. So long as one got away, the scene could be exhilarating—unless it caught up with you.

He looked at his watch and shook his head. "We aren't making good time."

"Will you two be quiet?" Kowalski growled. "You're giving away our position."

Big Jim and Caesar hated to admit it, but the slob was right. Stealth could not be abandoned at any time, especially when one faced off with a Cape buffalo.

Barake made a sound similar to the small white-headed Buffalo Weaver birds (*Dinemellia dine melli*), and caught Big Jim's attention. These little birds followed buffalo everywhere and by whistling a tune similar to the little creature he would not give away their position.

He looked at Barake, who motioned with a halting hand for everyone to be still.

They listened.

The wind rustled through the grass. The sound of the animals they heard earlier had fallen silent.

Then they heard it.

Something large was trampling through the grass. They could not determine its path, nor could they see it through the thick blades of grass. This reminded Big Jim how easily large animals could remain hidden in the thick brush and long grass. Amateur hunters dismissed this, claiming how any large animal was an easy target.

That's why they're called amateurs, Big Jim thought. *They always underestimate what they hunt.*

They picked up their march and followed the path. At some point they would find an opening, and with luck the buff that created so much disruption in their lives would be seen and brought down.

Marching over the rough terrain, Big Jim noted how even good pair of boots doesn't hold up well for long. *Not in Africa,* he told himself. The rocks, and pot holes, and uneven ground cause you to trip, fall, sprain an ankle, or worse, break a leg.

By mid-morning they could see it was going to be an unbearably hot day. The cool of the night and early morning breeze dissipated, giving way to the broiling sun beating down on them like a child with his first set of drums. Perspiration rolled down their foreheads, stinging their eyes. Their shirts clung to their chest as they soaked up sweat bubbling from their pores.

Kowalski felt the beginning of a rash between his thighs where skin scraped against skin. *Damn chafing!*

Big Jim turned around to see what the commotion was about. He hated having Kowalski behind him, and armed to boot!

Better him than a client, he thought.

He recalled on one particular safari a client wanted to follow Big Jim on the march rather than walking by his side. This went against Big Jim's better judgment. Clients were amateurs regardless of how long they hunted. They made mistakes that cost lives. This one insisted to the point of balling like a kid refusing to have a bath.

Big Jim acquiesced, but firmly told the man to keep his rifle unloaded.

"What if game presents itself?" the man asked.

"There'll be time enough for that later," Big Jim replied. "But if you must walk behind me, keep your rifle unloaded and the safety on."

Ten minutes further in their march the client fell over uneven ground, dropping his rifle. When it struck the rocks the hammer fell. A loud crack rang out as the 30.06 caliber rifle discharged. The bullet passed harmlessly into the ground, but Big Jim scolded the client like a father would a child for refusing to listen to his mother.

Kowalski knelt on one knee. He needed rest. The trail was rough-going, and the heat made it no easier. He reached for his canteen and took a long drink.

Big Jim shook his head. "He runs out of water, he better not expect a drop from me."

Caesar felt the same. "He can drink murky swamp water for all I care."

Barake walked over to Kowalski and snatched the canteen free from his hands.

"What the deuces do you think you're doing?" he screamed.

"Our water isn't indispensable, you know," the native replied.

Kowalski started to say something when a blurred spotted figure broke through the long grass and leapt high in the air. Kowalski fired his double rifle at the figure and was sure he hit it, but the big cat toppled Barake and went straight for his throat. The native had been taken completely off guard, dropping his *panga* and *assegais* in a desperate attempt to keep the cat at bay.

The leopard had been tracking the two-legged animals from the moment they entered the field. It moved stealthily parallel with them, never making a sound, and waited for the moment to strike when they least expected it. These felines had a reputation for being the quietest killers, never falling from a single shot, and always going for the face and throat.

Barake screamed in pain as the leopard bit hard into his face. The big cat's claws dug deep into his torso, tearing apart flesh and spilling out Barake's organs. Blood spurted from Barake like an over-worked fountain, staining the spotted leopard's coat and grass. The big cat growled fiercely, biting and chomping down on Barake's head.

Kowalski aimed and squeezed the trigger, but not before Big Jim knocked him out of the way, causing his shot to go wide.

"What the blazes is wrong with you!" Kowalski roared.

"Don't be a fool, you bastard!" Big Jim shouted, with equal ferocity. "You'll kill Barake before the leopard does."

Big Jim and Caesar ran over to Barake, but dared not fire for fear of hitting the African. They saw Barake's *assegais* and *panga* lying nearby and picked up the weapons. Big Jim thrust the blade of the spear into the cat's upper body, and the leopard snarled. Its jaws locked onto Barake's skull, determined to tear him apart.

Barake screamed a high-pitched shriek of terror, pain, and anger. He punched the cat in the stomach and the leopard released its grip and clamped down on his forearm, sinking its teeth deep and crushing bone and vein. Blood poured everywhere, and the melee grew worse with the screaming from Barake, who seemed to know he was about to die.

Caesar slashed at the leopard's head with the *panga*, forcing it to release its mouth-hold on Barake's arm. The cat growled and hissed. Its amber eyes glowed with hatred. It swatted its paws at them in an attempt to drive them away, but they would not leave their friend to become a meal for the leopard.

Big Jim thrust the spear's blade into the cat over and over. The leopard grew weak with each insertion from the blade, but angrier still at the pair of two-legged creatures depriving it of its kill. Its growling became less threatening, and its own blood mixed with Barake's. It could not find the strength to leap at the pair standing over it, though it instinctively tried.

Caesar slashed the cat's head three times and Big Jim stabbed it deep in the chest, twisting the blade with each thrust. The leopard screeched a high-pitched wail that made everyone cringe.

Finally, the cat fell over.

Chapter 32

Even the most dedicated hunter must know when to call it a day.

***It's** not even noon and I've lost my two best askari*, Big Jim reflected, somberly.

The leopard was the biggest he'd seen. It was seven feet long, a full grown adult, easily weighing up to two hundred pounds.

What was it doing here?

Caesar tended to Barake, trying to resuscitate him, but he was dead before the cat had been killed.

The drum beating started once more.

"We've got to get out of this field," Big Jim said. "It's no good here."

They hated to leave Barake's body. He deserved a proper burial. No one said anything about it. They had not the time, nor were this the place for such a ceremony.

They pushed on with Big Jim in the lead, Kowalski in the middle, and Caesar picking up the rear. Kowalski wisely removed Barake's canteen of water and leather pouch of *posho*. The way he went through his own, he would need it.

Big Jim heard movement to his front and motioned with a raised hand for everyone to stop.

They listened.

Something indeed was to their front.

Big Jim lifted his double rifle to shoulder level and fired a shot in the air. The field erupted with a flock of the white-headed Buffalo Weavers. The small finches-like bird were known for following buffalo and feeding on insects disturbed by buffalos trampling through fields. Hundreds of the small birds filled the air.

I know you're here, Big Jim said to himself.

The buffalo let loose a long low-pitched bellow, the same one referred to as the *death bellow*, only the pitch was slightly higher than usual.

Big Jim cracked open his rifle and pulled out the spent cartridge. He reloaded and snapped shut the barrels with the receiver. *Always reload after firing*, he told himself. *Never go in with your rifle half spent. Ignore your exhaustion. Ignore the heat. Stay loose and at the ready or you'll be dead.*

The ground suddenly moved beneath their feet. It was as though they experienced an earthquake.

"What the bloody hell?" Caesar screamed.

Big Jim knew it was the buffalo on the move. It was coming toward them. For the first time he saw the long grass part. Right when he spotted the buffalo it charged. The bull lowered its heavily-bossed adorned head and bellowed a low-pitched fit of anger.

Big Jim raised his double rifle and fired. To his consternation the buffalo did not flinch. There was no time to crack open the barrels for reloading. Big Jim dove to his right. He never considered himself an athlete, but at that moment he would have bet he could compete in the World Olympics, for he sailed farther in the air than he would have believed humanly possible.

Caesar, too, dove to the left and out of the path of the buffalo.

Stanley Kowalski did no such thing. He shot the buff dead-on. The creature flinched when the 500-grain bullet slammed into its thick boss. At 2,050 feet per second, the muzzle velocity of the .470 Rigby Double Rifle was like a two-ton lorry crashing into it at 60 miles per hour. Bits and pieces of the boss flew off like wood chips spewed by an axe. The buffalo halted, and with incredible speed took off to its right, forging a new trail through the grass.

"My God!" Caesar shouted. "Have you ever seen a buffalo so huge?"

"No," Big Jim said, still a bit startled over how fast the buff's attack had been. He took in their surroundings.

Caesar thought he looked confused. "Shall we go after it?"

Big Jim shook his head. "No. Let's follow its trail from where it came. It'll likely lead to an opening on the other side of the field. We'll make our stand against it there."

They started to move, but noticed Kowalski stood staring in the direction from which the buffalo disappeared.

"Kowalski!" Big Jim roared.

Kowalski did not move. He remained standing still, holding his rifle in the direction of where he last saw the buffalo.

"Are you all right?" Caesar asked, and touched Kowalski's shoulder.

"What do you want?" Kowalski growled.

"We have to leave," Caesar replied. "It's not safe to fight the beast here."

Kowalski switched the release lever on his rifle to one side, cracking open the double barrels from the stock. He pulled out the spent cartridges and tossed them to the ground. Then he inserted two fresh cigar-sized cartridges.

"What do you think you're doing?" Big Jim asked.

Kowalski scowled. "I told you from the start. This animal belongs to me." He snapped shut the barrels and marched after it.

Caesar walked a few steps after him. "Don't be a bloody fool, Stanley! You stand no chance against it in there, and by yourself."

Kowalski's mind was made up. A moment later he disappeared in the long grass, chasing after the largest buffalo any of them had ever seen.

Caesar turned to Big Jim. "What do we do?"

"Leave him," Big Jim mumbled.

Caesar shrugged with resignation. "God help him."

Big Jim quickly added, "Yes, because I won't."

Chapter 33

When determination consumes the hunter, safety and good judgment are often abandoned. However, there comes a time when one cannot turn back. It is known as a point of no return, and during this period anything can happen—and often does.

The Cape buffalo moved with amazing speed, agility, and stealth considering its incredible bulk. The long grass grew higher than 15 feet in places, barely enough height to conceal the beast. But the field would serve the buff's purpose, and its purpose was clear. Its master had given instructions, and they must be obeyed.

Destroy the white hunters!

Only then could the beast return to the fiery hell from which it came.

The drum beating started once more, and the beast halted in the middle of the field. Its ears perked. It listened. Its bloodshot eyes strained to see its master, but the grass proved too thick. An instant later the image of its master appeared in its mind.

The *Jabilo.*

Their eyes met and their silent form of communication commenced. Several moments passed while the *Jabilo* gave his instructions. No words needed to be spoken. It was unnecessary. Then the *Jabilo's* image disappeared from the creature's vision and the drum beating stopped.

The beast understood. Today was the final day. There would be no further stalking villages and killing the puny two-legged animals existing in filthy mud huts. The purpose of that mission had been fulfilled. *Create fear!*

Today the reckoning with the white hunter, the *white wawindaji*, would reach a conclusion. And then the beast would return to its hell in triumph, its power and strength never to be questioned.

And so it would be with the *Jabilo*. His magic, his medicine, would never be doubted by his people. His reign would be supreme for the remainder of his life. And this was as he wished it to be.

Kowalski stumbled after the buffalo, following its trail.

"I've got you now," he bellowed furiously. "No escape. I saw you flinch. I saw you hurt by me. Now I'm going to finish the job."

Kowalski fell over the loose terrain, picked himself up, and stumbled again and again. The sharp blades of the long grass sliced his face and exposed hands, but he pressed on. The ground became sloshy as he found himself walking through mud, but he knew he was near the beast when his nose caught wind of the nauseating stench of the buffalo.

"I knew I'd find you," he said, grinning evilly.

And he pressed on.

Just then a very deep groan forced him to instantly freeze. Kowalski slowly turned in the direction it came and his color turned pale.

Standing to his right was the shadowy form of the buffalo, partially hidden by the long grass, but visible enough to see it was there. Much to Kowalski's dismay were the other figures standing beside the beast. They were six in all, smaller than a lion, but larger than a cheetah.

Kowalski had never seen anything like it. The buffalo made friends with no animals other than its own kind. And this buff was unlike others he'd seen. It was larger, blacker, and spoored a trail of blood. And its eyes!

Those eyes, Kowalski remembered. It was as though he stared into the devil's very own eyes.

The smaller animals barked a laugh. It was a sound Kowalski

knew.

Hyenas!

They moved forward, breaking through the long grass and stood before Kowalski in all their menacing form.

Kowalski was at a loss. His rifle held two rounds in the barrels. There were six hyenas and one buffalo. No way would he be able to fire and reload in time before they reached him. He found himself wishing he had listened to Big Jim for the first time in his life.

Then the buffalo inched forward and came into complete view.

Kowalski stared back at the evil creature.

The buff grunted.

Then the hyenas charged.

Kowalski quickly raised his rifle and took aim. His fingers touched the double triggers and squeezed one after the other.

BOOM! BOOM!

Chapter 34

Hunters press on for the thrill of the hunt. Nothing else in the world matters more than tracking a wild animal and bringing it down. Our ancestors hunted for survival, and people still do today.

"Did you hear that?" Caesar asked.

"Of course," Big Jim replied. "I'm not deaf."

When the echo from the gunshots faded they strained to hear the sounds of a man screaming in pain. It was faint, but audible enough.

"My God," said Caesar. "What is it doing to him?"

Big Jim listened, bewildered. Kowalski screamed like a man being eaten alive. He'd seen how men reacted when trampled and gored by the buffalo. They screamed, yes. They hollered, yes. But Kowalski sounded like…

Then the screaming ceased.

Big Jim turned to Caesar. "Well, he wanted to face off alone with the beast. Looks like he got what he wanted."

The steady cacophony of the drum beating started and this time they saw the *Jabilo* standing atop a hill. It was the same black man, dressed in sandals, loincloth, a robe thrown over his shoulder, and his head adorned with the plumes of white ostrich feathers. He stood resting on the staff, staring down at them.

"Who do you suppose is doing the drum beating?" Caesar asked.

That was hardly a concern of Big Jim. In a way he was grateful for the odd music. It told them they were near the beast.

After they separated with Kowalski they marched another six

hundred feet when they reached the clearing. A dirty pond of water was nearby, surrounded by ficus trees. Hills and mountains were to the north, and to the south was the outline of the lush jungle. In the east were the vast open steppes with tall peaks jutted skyward at the opposite end.

"This is where we end this," Big Jim said with finality. "We're not going after it in there. We're going to face off with it here."

"How do you know it'll even come after us?" Caesar asked, doubtfully.

"I just know."

The buffalo cried a deep-throated bellow confirming what Big Jim said.

They checked their rifles and spare cartridges. "Let's get under some shade," Big Jim suggested. "I feel like I'm going to melt."

Two hours passed and nothing happened. The drum beating continued, and the *Jabilo* remained standing on the hilltop, never moving, and watching them carefully. The hunters ate and drank to keep up their strength…and waited.

And waited.

Then they heard it.

The buffalo was on the move. Its heavy hooves pounded the earth as it trampled its way through the long grass.

"Makes more noise than a freight train," Big Jim quickly pointed out.

"I like the advantage," Caesar noted with a tinge of satisfaction.

The buffalo exploded from the field and stopped at its edge.

"Damned thing is big!" Big Jim observed.

"I don't like this," Caesar mumbled.

Big Jim glanced at his friend. "There's never been anything to like," he replied, sharply. "We've got to finish this in order to keep the locals from falling prey to that witch doctor." He called him witch doctor with a contemptuous tone.

"Witch doctor or not, that's no ordinary buffalo out there and you know it."

Big Jim agreed. The damned creature looked to be the size of an elephant, which was impossible. *They never grow taller than six foot tops.* "All I know is it can be killed. We both saw it flinch when Kowalski hit it."

"Yes, but what's become of Kowalski now?"

To that, Big Jim had no answer.

They observed the buffalo for an interminably long time, but it made no move to charge. It simply stared, intently observing them. Then without warning, the beast spun around and disappeared in the field.

The hunters raised their rifles and squeezed off a round each. Their rifles boomed!

Too late. The buff had disappeared in the long grass from whence it came.

"Bloody hell!" cried Caesar.

"I don't believe this," Big Jim said, between clenched teeth.

They looked at each other with resignation. Without speaking a word, they discharged the spent cartridges, dropping them on the ground, and reloaded. They snapped the barrels in place with the stock and cocked the hammers back.

"I thought we weren't going after it in the long grass," Caesar pointed out with distaste.

"I thought so too," Big Jim said with disappointment laced in his words.

Then they simultaneously said, "But nothing ever goes according to plan."

And then they marched forward.

The heat, the sun, the sound of the tall grass rustling in the wind, and the stench of the buffalo lying in wait made Big Jim and Caesar's position tense. Going in the field was not a smart move, but it was the only move they could make. Buffalos were smart, known for drawing their attackers deep into the bush, and then doubling back for an oblique attack when they least expected it.

The fact that Big Jim and Caesar knew this was an advantage for them meant they were prepared for the unexpected. Still, both hunters would have preferred to take on the creature out in the open, but that would have been too easy.

Such is the way with hunting, Big Jim reminded himself.

They approached the field with caution, and then followed the buff's trail. They heard the beast moving first to their front, then to their right, and then to their left. They were being taunted. The buffalo was taunting them and they knew it.

The beast moved through the long grass with the grace of a gazelle in open territory. This was quite a feat considering the ground was uneven with mud, water, rocks, and dead wood. The animal stopped, listened, snorted, and went on the move again.

Big Jim heard the beast moving slow at first, then picking up its pace. *Where in the hell are you?* He thought it might be to their front, but he had been wrong before, he remembered.

They continued marching through the field and saw the thick density of the long grass give way to an open area about 50 feet in diameter. *Good*, they thought. *At least we can see what's coming*, they hoped.

Right then the buffalo burst through the grass to their front charging full speed.

The hunters did not immediately fire. They waited. When the beast was at close quarters, 20 feet, they fired.

The 750-grain bullets smacked the beast squarely with the impact of 5,000 pounds of solid cartridge traveling at 2,050 feet-per-second. The animal shrieked a cry of defiance.

Big Jim was certain he hit the buffalo high between the shoulder blades. If so the bullet would have torn through the animal's lungs, causing it to choke on its own blood. But the beast continued to charge with no apparent injury. Its head was low to the ground, preparing to hook them with its long, sharp horns.

Their rifles roared when they fired a second volley and the bullets struck the beast between the shoulder blades. Large red flowers bloomed where the bullets struck the buff's hide, but the creature never lost its stride.

The beast slammed into Caesar, knocking him ten feet back. The thick dense grass broke his fall and the Englishman miraculously managed to hold onto his rifle. He quickly got to his feet and started to reload when his strength suddenly left him. Caesar was feeling the after effects of being struck by the beast, and he fell to the ground like a limp rag doll.

A moment later Caesar felt a surge of strength through his body and he quickly got to his feet. Although he had no way of knowing, the sight of the buffalo charging for what surely spelled his end provided him with the strength needed to react. But there was no time to reload his rifle. And so he turned and started to run for dear life.

By this time Big Jim had reloaded and was bringing his double rifle to bear when the creature reached Caesar.

BOOM! BOOM!

Chapter 35

Death in the bush can be fast or slow. Most persons would say they prefer a quick death as opposed to a slow torturous one. But in the African bush one cannot always choose how one dies.

Caesar felt a sharp pain in the middle of his back and the next thing he knew he was sailing through the air. He flew between the blades of thick grass, which helped break his fall before landing with a thud. His body went numb when the buffalo struck him and when he lost control of his hands his rifle flew from his grip.

Oh no! he cried, silently.

The buffalo came after him and struck him again, smashing his body against the ground. Caesar felt like a kid being pummeled by the schoolyard bully in the playground. The air drained from his lungs. He knew the buffalo was attempting to trample him to death, so he rolled to his left, and then to his right, repeating this maneuver over and over in desperate attempt to avoid being crushed to death.

He somehow managed to grab hold of the buffalo's horns and he held on for dear life. It was the only thing keeping him from being hooked. But the move fared him no better, for the beast slammed his body to the ground like a farmer plowing a field. Caesar lost control of his grip and the animal pummeled him over and over, crushing bone and flesh. Caesar cried out in agony and found himself choking on his own blood creeping up through his throat.

The buffalo then reared on its hind legs and came down with a crashing thud, crushing Caesar's chest and stomach. Blood came up through his mouth like an open spigot, and his eyes practically popped from their sockets. The last thing Caesar remembered seeing were the bright red eyes of hatred glaring from the creature.

Big Jim reloaded and ran after the buffalo with a speed he never knew he possessed. He was midway in the field when he was stopped by the piercing, deep-throated guttural bellow the buffalo were known to make. It was a sound he would never forget.

When the cry faded Big Jim listened carefully for the creature. There was only silence.

Then the sound of the wind rustling through the grass reached his ears. Big Jim moved forward with caution. He came to a halt midway when he thought he saw something lying in the mud.

The crushed body of his longtime friend lay still in the muddy field. Big Jim knelt by Caesar and removed his broad-brimmed hat. Never in all his life did he think he would see his friend like this. They faced danger every day. They survived the battlefields of North Africa during the Second World War. Each believed they were exempt from death.

How could I have been such a fool?

He removed Caesar's partially crushed flask from his shirt pocket and slid it in his own. Caesar carried this everywhere. It would remind Big Jim of their friendship. Then he took the spare cartridges from Caesar's vest and put them in his vest pocket. He may have need for them, he knew.

He started to rise when Caesar gurgled a mouthful of blood.

My God! He's alive! "Caesar, can you hear me?" Big Jim put his ear close to his mouth.

Caesar's eyes opened slowly. They were bloodshot, and he had difficulty breathing with cracked ribs and a broken chest.

Big Jim removed the medical kit from the satchel he carried and bandaged the open cuts. He took Caesar's handkerchief from his breast pocket and used it to wipe the blood from his face.

"As you once said, a gentleman never goes hunting without a handkerchief."

Caesar managed a slight, painful smile. "You have a good memory," he said, slowly between gasps. "However, your timing for humor is terrible."

"Don't talk."

Big Jim lifted Caesar's upper body to a sitting position and dragged him to a log where he rested his back against it. He removed Caesar's shirt and wrapped a bandage around his chest and stomach.

"We've got to stabilize your ribs. They're probably broken and I can't take you back to camp until I've finished off this buff."

The buffalo bellowed again, and Big Jim was snapped back to the task at hand. He looked down at Caesar.

"Go," the Englishman said with great effort.

Big Jim stared in the direction of the beast's cry. "Okay, you bastard!" he shouted. "Let's finish this."

He checked his rifle. It was loaded. The weight of the rifle was slippery in the palm of his sweaty hands. One by one he wiped his palms against the side of his pants to dry them.

Let's do this.

The damned drum beating picked up again, and Big Jim swore the first thing he'd do after killing the creature would be to shoot the *Jabilo*. He marched on through the muddy long grass. He could not see the beast, but this time he found himself grateful for the dense cover the field gave him.

If I can't see you, you can't see me, he reasoned.

He smelled the stench of the buffalo. It was close. Very close. He heard the beast bellow again.

Damned thing is taunting me!

Then he thought better to leave the field and take on the beast in the open terrain. *No sense pushing my luck,* he thought. He looked up at the sky and determined which way to head back to the land rover, and started making his way back.

He did not get far when he came across the remains of Stanley Kowalski. There was hardly anything left. Big Jim knew whatever it was that finished off Kowalski was not the buffalo. *They do not eat meat.* This was the work of a pack of animals. Blood was everywhere, but only parts of Kowalski's rifle, boots and clothing remained. There were no bones, no organs, or anything left of the human body. Whatever it was that finished him had eaten him whole.

Looks like the work of Wild Dogs or Hyenas. That's what he thought they heard earlier.

Big Jim felt no emotion. Kowalski had been an embarrassment to the profession. *Better for all of us that you're dead.*

He continued his trek, but after 15 minutes of marching realized he was going in circles. The beast was nowhere in sight. *No sound either, only its horrid stench.* He heard the drums rhythmic beating in the distance.

*Blasted drum beating! If I never hear another drummer I'll—*He did not bother finishing his sentence.

The creature breathed heavily. Something was not right. For the first time it could not move as swiftly as before. It wheezed heavily and blood bubbled through its nostrils. Something did not feel right, but it knew not the cause.

The command to strike had been given. The drums continued. It would finish off the two-legged animal once and for all. And then the prophecy would be fulfilled. Of course the buffalo knew nothing about a prophecy. This was conjured by the *Jabilo*. He was another two-legged creature seeking to maintain authority over his people. Killing the white hunters would prove to the natives their fire sticks were no match for his magic.

The creature lifted its head to smell its prey, but blood clogging its nostrils prevented it from doing so. It strained its ears, but the drum-beating interfered. It had no way of reasoning, but victory was no longer self-assured for it. In a fit of anger the creature let loose a long deep bellow, which sounded like a cry of defiance.

Big Jim moved slowly through the field when he heard the cry and stopped mid-stride. *Damned thing is close.* A few tense moments passed before he started moving again ever so quietly so as not to give away his position. Buffalos had a keen sense of smell and hearing and he could not afford to give the beast more advantage.

You've already got me searching for you in the long grass; I'll not make this mistake any easier by giving away my position. If you want me, you'll have to come and get me the way I do for you.

He clenched his rifle. Not too tight, he said silently. *Stay loose. Once you finish the creature you've got to get Caesar out of the field and back to camp. He's got less than a day without proper treatment.*

He marched forward another five minutes before the drum beating ceased.

And then there was silence.

Now what?

He heard movement to his right and swirled in the direction from which it came, rifle ready, finger touching the trigger, but only gently. He did not want to risk firing a shot by accident. *Be cold and calculating.*

Then movement came from his left and he swirled to face it.

Nothing.

What's going on here?

The buffalo moved forward, one leg at a time, and with each movement the earth trembled.

And Big Jim felt it. *But from whence does it come?*

He moved in a three hundred and sixty degree turn and saw nothing, but knew the animal was making its way toward him. Then he saw the grass break ever so slightly. The dark looming figure of the buffalo's head was first to appear. It pushed through the long grass until it stood fully exposed before him.

Big Jim faced off with the creature not more than 20 paces to his front. He saw the blood bubbling from its nostrils and noted its chest heaving with each breath.

"So, I did strike you where it counts," he said aloud. And then he added, "And now I'm going to finish you."

The buffalo charged!

Big Jim squeezed both triggers one after the other!

Click! Click!

"NO!" he screamed. His rifle misfired.

Chapter 36

Even in victory, one cannot help feel a sense of emptiness and shame.

The buffalo lowered its head and struck Big Jim in the stomach, tossing him high in the air. Big Jim held tightly to his rifle. Losing it would be a deadly mistake. He hit the ground hard, but kept his wits about him. The thick blades of long grass broke his fall, preventing him from further injury.

The buffalo chased after him and Big Jim rolled to the right, an act which kept him from being trampled by the buff's giant hooves. But the creature swirled and with the flick of its head knocked Big Jim down just as he was getting to his feet.

The creature started pummeling Big Jim, smashing his body against the ground with its massive head. Big Jim had difficulty breathing, and everything happened so fast he had difficulty maintaining a clear line of vision. His fingers loosened the grip on his rifle and a moment later it was gone, so he did the only thing he could. He held on to the buff's head for dear life.

The creature bellowed long and loud, swinging its head left and right, angrily trying to throw the hunter off it. Only when Big Jim could no longer maintain his grip, he found himself sailing through the air and crashing into the long grass.

The creature charged after its intended victim and abruptly skidded to a halt, kicking up mud and dirt that showered Big Jim. The beast breathed heavily, staring at the hunter with its bloodshot eyes angrily giving away its intentions.

Big Jim caught his breath. His vision cleared and he saw the creature standing before him not more than 20 paces away.

Where's my rifle? If only I had my rifle!

He moved to get up when his hand felt something familiar. He looked and saw it was Caesar's Rigby .470 Double rifle.

He looked at the beast and saw its eyes narrow. It practically challenged him to try and reach for it.

"You're damned right I'm going to!" Big Jim shouted in defiance.

In the blink of an eye he cracked open the rifle and loaded two fresh 500-grain caliber cartridges in the chamber.

Also in the blink of an eye, the beast charged ahead at full speed, shrieking its familiar deep guttural bellow. Its insatiable fury was unlike anything Big Jim had ever seen in an animal.

Big Jim locked the barrels with the receiver and cocked back the hammers. "Go back to hell where you came from!" he cried, and then squeezed both triggers simultaneously.

BOOM! BOOM!

The rifle roared and kicked violently in Big Jim's hands.

Both shots struck the beast in the throat while it was mid-stride in its charge, and exploded out the back of its neck. The creature lost all sense of awareness and crashed to the ground with a thud, rolling over and over through the long grass before skidding to a halt. Big Jim barely had enough time to roll out of its way and keep from being crushed beneath its immense weight.

The sound of the buffalo bellowing combined with the gunshots frightened animals near and afar. Great flocks of bird took to the sky, herds of wildebeest, zebra, giraffe, and elephant scurried away, anxious to be nowhere near this territory. Not after what had happened between the hunter and the beast.

Big Jim got to his feet and quickly reloaded. Even at this stage he took no chances. He ran up to the creature, stumbling part of the way due to an injured leg, and looked into its dark-red eyes. The creature blankly stared back, never understanding why it could no longer move.

Without further hesitation Big Jim thrust his rifle at the side of the animal's head and fired both barrels point blank range.

BOOM! BOOM!

The creature jerked and went still.

Big Jim stepped back. He took a deep breath, filling his lungs with much-needed air. His chest pounded from excitement and fear, and his heartbeat had yet to come down to normalcy. When he managed to calm himself he stepped closer to the beast for survey.

It was unlike any buffalo he had seen before. It certainly was the largest, too. Its hide was blacker than most other buffalo, and those bloodshot eyes were now a dull black. Parts of its hide were caked with mud from rolling in ponds and rivers, as was the buffalo's trait. Large ticks clung to it, sucking as much of the crimson ooze seething from its hide like an open sieve. And the stench was horrible. It was all Big Jim could do to keep from coughing up his guts.

Closer examination displayed dark holes in its hide where the beast had been struck by large caliber bullets. Any other animal, Big Jim knew, would have been felled from such physical damage.

Then again, you aren't ordinary.

The drum beating started up again, only this time its tune played differently. Before the music was a steady cacophony of a dreadful tune, one that brought back memories of watching a horror film in the cinema. This new tune of drums sounded lively, expressing relief and conclusion of this drama.

Big Jim pulled out his knife from the sheath, walked up to the buffalo and sliced off its ears and tail, trophies and reminders of this ordeal. Also proof for the natives that they no longer had to fear what they called the *Mnyama*. He stuffed them in his sack and marched out of the field. When he reached the open he looked back at the hilltop where the *Jabilo* stood.

The old man stared down at the hunter, only he did not appear as mesmerizing as before. "Now you're just as ordinary as you've always been," Big Jim said aloud.

Although the *Jabilo* was too far to hear, he turned his back to Big Jim as though he knew what he said, and slowly walked away disappearing from sight.

Big Jim looked back at the field from where he came. In there laid the beast, Stanley Kowalski, Barake, and his close friend Caesar Wilde. He was victorious against the creature, but felt no joy. Somehow he felt his life would never be the same.

My God! Caesar—I've got to get to him!

He ran as fast as he could through the long grass, ignoring the sharp blades cutting his face and hands. When he reached the place where he left his friend he was surprised to find him gone.

What the hell! "Caesar!" he shouted. "Caesar, where are you?!"

BOOM!

It was the familiar sound of a double rifle being fired in the direction where they left the land rover. *That has to be Caesar*, he reasoned.

Big Jim ran through the field and when he broke through its edge he found Caesar sitting against the side of the car. He ran up to him and handed him a canteen of water.

"You bloody fool. How in hell did you manage to crawl this far in your condition?"

Caesar took the canteen and drank carefully, for his chest strained from each swallow. "You'd be surprised what one can do when one has the desire to survive," he said, wiping his mouth dry.

Big Jim smiled. "No, I wouldn't."

Chapter 37

In Africa, the strong always prevail.

The next morning Mary Watkins awakened with a start. She had a terrible dream. It was of the buffalo that had created so much havoc for Big Jim and Caesar. The natives called it the *Mnyama*, she remembered.

Mashaka came to her tent to tell her that Big Jim had returned. Mashaka had been in her dream, too. He was angry over not being permitted to travel with Big Jim and Caesar to kill the *Mnyama*.

Big Jim had been adamant. "A large party isn't the way to take on this challenge," he said. He ordered Mashaka to remain in the camp with Davu and the other wapagazis. Besides, the native was not physically up for the challenge after such a long journey.

"Where is he?" she asked, with relief.

"By the river bathing," he replied.

Mary slipped into her pants and boots, threw on her blouse, and ran outside. When she reached the river she saw him.

Big Jim washed himself in the crude canvas sink supported by a wooden tripod. A pair of wapagazis stood by him holding towels. He was shirtless, but still had on his trousers and boots.

Mary ran up to him. "Are you all right?" Her voice was laced with concern.

"I'm as right as anyone can be," he answered, exhausted from the long march back.

She saw the scars on his body, the ones he had received from the lion attack, and she recalled what Caesar had told her. He never liked discussing how he had received those injuries.

"Where are Caesar and the others?" she asked with deep concern.

Big Jim pointed to a nearby tree where a group of wapagazis tended to Caesar's injuries. She ran hurriedly over to the Englishman, kneeling beside his body lying on a blanket.

"My God, you look a frightful sight," she said, fighting to hold back tears.

Caesar grinned. "I've never felt better," he said, weakly.

Not far away she saw the litter Big Jim made of two wooden poles roughly the same length of a man's body, tied together with rope and thick strands of vine and long grass. It reminded Mary of the type of litters made by Native Americans during the Old West period.

"James carried you here on that?" she asked, with surprise.

Caesar nodded. "No problem for a big boy like him."

She touched his forehead. "Are you going to be all right?"

Caesar nodded. "If I can survive a pummeling such as the one I did back there in the long grass, I can survive anything." He motioned with a nod to his satchel nearby. "Be a dear and hand me my flask, will you? I've been longing for a belt of gin all morning."

On a wooden chair was Big Jim's shirt and satchel. On the seat was a pair of large buffalo ears and a long tail. The natives looked at them and grinned with relief. They mumbled in Swahili about the trophies and a few ran off, wild with excitement. They were going to inform the villagers that the terror was over.

Mary went to the chair and stared at the items, too. She looked thoroughly confused. "I don't understand," she said, frustrated. "What does this mean?"

Big Jim dried his face and hair off with a towel. Then he handed the towel to one of the wapagazis and turned to face her. "It means life goes on as we know it," he said, with relief and finality. "The curse is over. The beast is dead."

Mary paused, still looking confused. "Just like that?"

Big Jim shrugged. "Yeah, just like that."

He walked over to where Caesar laid and knelt beside him. "How are you feeling?"

Caesar took a drink from his flask. "Never better, old boy."

Big Jim reached into his pocket, took Caesar's hand, and placed a familiar item in his palm. "Here, I thought you might need this and continue practicing."

Caesar looked at his palm and his eyes brightened. "My harmonica! Where on earth did you get it?"

"One of the wapagazis in the lorry stopped and picked it up. He gave it to me and asked not to give it back to you until this safari was over."

"Why's that?"

Big Jim smiled. "He said your blasted playing kept them from thinking straight."

Caesar laughed, straining the injuries in his chest. "You wait and see. One day I'll be magnificent with this instrument."

"You may be right." He turned to walk away before stopping. "Just promise me one thing."

Caesar stared back blankly. "And what's that?" he asked, befuddled.

"Be sure to pass that flask to me when you start playing."

Caesar raised his eyebrows curiously. "And why should I do that?"

A sly grin pursed the corners of Big Jim's mouth. "I can only tolerate your playing when I'm drinking."

And then Big Jim walked to his tent for a much-needed rest.

Chapter 38

In Africa the natives appreciate a fine hunter for it is the hunter who feeds and protects the family.

Big Jim sat at a table on the veranda of *O'Malley's Bar & Restaurant* with Mary sitting across from him, watching his every move.

It had been a week since their return to Arusha and the excitement still buzzed throughout the town and local villages about his triumph over the demonic beast. His career had been elevated from a first-rate professional hunter to that of a volcanic folk hero.

To look at him one would have believed him to be overly humbled by all the attention, instead of overwhelmed. He sat there dressed in his hunting khakis with his shirt-sleeves rolled up to the elbow, pants tucked in his bush boots, and hat hanging on the empty chair next to them. His left arm was in a sling and he still walked with a slight limp from an injury he had received from the beast.

O'Malley came out with a fresh drink for them both. "Here you are, my friend," he said in his thunderous tone of voice. "Bourbon on ice, just how you like it."

Big Jim reached for the glass with his right hand. "Thanks, Sean. I know how difficult it is to keep a steady supply of ice on hand these days, so dry bourbon will do fine if need be."

O'Malley patted him on the left shoulder, oblivious of Big Jim's sling. "Nothing doing for the 'toast of Arusha,'" he said, grinning broadly. "Since your return my business has doubled with people who want a glimpse at the hunter who felled the beast."

There was no mistaking the number of by-passers tipping their hats to Big Jim while he sat on the veranda. It had been like this since their return.

When the gaming commissioner learned of the events in the bush they dropped all questions into the inquiry over his client Nigel Stewart's death. They even reinstated his hunting permits, and when news spread throughout the territory about the size of the buffalo he brought down the safari corporations received a record numbers of clients requesting to be hired for a shooting safari from enthusiasts from all over the world.

Big Jim winced from the shoulder tap O'Malley gave him. "Then ice will do fine," he said, lifting the glass to his lips. He took a long drink and sighed. "I've needed this all day," he said with relief.

Mary sipped her own glass. "They never found the buffalo's carcass where you left it in the long grass," she said, matter of factly.

This was true, Big Jim knew. He reported to Robert Forsythe, the chief commissioner, how he bagged the buffalo and left it in the long grass. Were it not for the ears and tail he provided as proof of his kill there might have been doubt to his story. No buffalo ever grew to the proportions he claimed.

However, there were so many reports of a giant buffalo on the rampage in the nearby territories and the size of the ears and tail trophy indicated this animal was in fact larger than most buffalo. The commissioner sent a team to retrieve the beast, but they returned empty handed.

"No one doubts your story though," Mary was quick to remind.

"Why should they?" Big Jim replied, sounding insulted that anyone would challenge his word.

Mary looked across the street and saw a number of professional hunters and clients staring at them. Among them were Bunny Allen, the actors Gregory Peck and Ava Gardner. The three pulled up in a land rover and climbed out.

Ava called out to Big Jim, "Hiya handsome!" Her confident, slightly scratchy voice was unmistakable among the throng of people walking past.

A fourth person followed them, walking close to her. Mary thought him to be familiar. "Say, isn't he...."

The four walked up to their table. Neither Big Jim nor Mary moved to rise from their seats. "I'd like to introduce my husband," Ava said, motioning to the man beside her. "This is Frank, and it's his first time to Africa."

Frank extended his hand. "Hello, pleased to make your acquaintance," he said, in a cheerful voice. He stood roughly the same height as Ava, which was not too tall, and looked painfully thin, yet somehow it suited his frame. His jet-black hair was slicked back in hair tonic and shined brightly even under the shade of the veranda. His teeth were sparkling white and his blue eyes piercing. "I've heard a lot about you," Frank said, still grinning broadly.

"I've heard a lot about you too," Big Jim replied, shaking hands with the gentleman.

"Frank came to join me while we film here for the next few months," Ava explained. "He's between shows on Broadway in New York so it works fine for both of us."

Not wanting to be left out, Bunny chimed in at the right moment. "He says word of your hunting expedition against the giant buffalo even reached the States." His tone reeked of doubt, the same as his expression.

"I suppose people like to gossip," Big Jim replied, unphased.

Bunny nodded. "They do at that."

Big Jim motioned to Mary sitting across from him. "This is Mary Watkins, an American journalist."

Frank and the others turned to face her. Frank took her hand gently and bowed at the waist. "Nice to meet you, dear. How do you like Africa?"

It was all Mary could do to keep from falling out of her chair. "I'm doing fine, thank you Mr. Sinatra," she said in a trembling voice.

"Please, call me Frank."

"Or why not Blue Eyes?" Big Jim suggested, with a slight grin.

"Only I can call him that," Ava quickly interjected.

Big Jim looked a bit uneasy with their attention and said, "I'd invite you to join us, but..."

Ava waved a flippant hand. "Thanks Handsome, but we have to be on our way. "Filming for *Mogambo* is about to begin and we're on a deadline. Gregory here is about to do some hunting with Bunny and perhaps you and Mary here will meet up with them?"

Gregory Peck stood behind Ava staring silently at Big Jim as though sizing him up. Big Jim recalled the sleight he received from the actor due to them sharing the same last name. "I don't think I'll be doing any hunting so long as I have this," he said, motioning to the sling on his left arm.

Frank shook his head. "Pity. I'd love the chance to go for a shooting with you."

Big Jim thought the singer sounded sincere.

Bunny decided it was time to speak up again. "They never did find the carcass to your buffalo, did they?" It sounded more of a challenge than a question.

Big Jim stiffened. "No," he replied, coldly. It did not do to challenge a professional hunter's word, so Bunny Allen was treading on dangerous water.

"But they sized up the ears and tail to verify his claim," Mary quickly interjected.

Bunny looked over at Mary as though insulted by her interference.

"I didn't think buffalo grow so large," Gregory Peck said, speaking up for the first time.

Big Jim held his stare for a moment before answering. It was his turn to appear as though sizing up the actor. "They don't."

The actor shuffled his feet and said, "Then how do you explain it?"

Big Jim shook his head. "I don't," he said, looking irritated. Then he seemed to relax and added, "We have a saying in Africa. It goes like this, 'In Africa there's always the unexpected in the Bush.'" He turned to the other hunter. "Right, Bunny?"

Bunny Allen did not answer right away. "You could say that," he said, nodding twice.

Ava could see how the men were not getting along. "Time to leave you two love-birds alone," she said, with a smile.

The group bade their farewells and walked inside O'Malley's for a spot of lunch. Mary remained star-struck at the sight of being so close to such famous people.

"Maybe you should write a column about them," Big Jim suggested.

She shook her head. "Enough journalists do that already. What about you? What do you and Caesar do now?"

Big Jim appeared confused by the question. "What do you mean?"

"You're not going to be able to hunt for a while, at least not while Caesar is laid up in hospice and your arm returns to normal. So what will you do?"

Big Jim looked out at the throng of people walking in the dirt streets of Arusha browsing through the shops and street vendors. He turned and stared out at the mountains in the distance and lush green plains, and then back to the glass of bourbon in his hand. Then he looked up at Mary.

"I'm going to take it one day at a time," he said with confidence. "And I'm going to pour myself another drink. Do you know why?"

Mary looked on, waiting anxiously for him to tell her.

A smile spread across Big Jim's face. Finally he said, "Because I've earned it!"

Mary laughed, and lifted her glass to toast with his when all of a sudden time froze. The people strolling along the sides of the street stopped too, as did the vehicles, horse-drawn carriages and wagons, and horseback riders. People walked outside from the shops too, for they heard the same thing.

Big Jim's eyes widened. The color of his skin went from sun-bronzed to pale white. Mary looked over to him and for the first time since they had met thought he appeared shaken, almost like he had seen a ghost. And this is precisely what Big Jim felt, like a ghost from his past had reappeared for a reckoning.

When the cry faded everyone on the streets turned to one another in utter bemusement. They looked like lost children in a park. Then one by one their heads turned in the direction of *O'Malley's Bar & Restaurant*. It did not take Big Jim long to realize they were staring at him sitting comfortably under the shade of the veranda.

Then the deep-throated cry sang out again.

Deep in the bush, somewhere far across the vast steppes and thick long-grassy plains, past the mountains of Kilimanjaro and Meru, a deep-throated guttural bellow shrieked long and steadfast. Its sound carried for an interminably long time before fading into oblivion.

Mwisho (The End)

Books the Author Recommends

White Hunter—The Golden Age of African Safaris
by Brian Herne

This book is a highly enjoyable and educating story about the history of professional hunters in Africa. Brian Herne has certainly done his research. He describes how the first white hunters discovered the wildlife on the Dark Continent and ventured into the unknown in search of game. I never knew how professional hunters played an important role in the preservation of wildlife until I read this book. Herne educates the reader about the unusual bond shared between hunter and prey.

King Solomon's Mines
by H. Rider Haggard

This classic story of treasure seekers still strikes a chord with readers who enjoy adventure and places on the far side of the world. I enjoyed the movie, but the book much more. Haggard describes characters in his story as if he experienced dangers himself.

Death in the Long Grass
by Peter Hathaway Capstick

This book informs the reader how a Wall Street man gave up his suit and tie to become a professional hunter in both South America and Africa. Capstick describes the adventure and danger one faces as a professional hunter with such clarity I was left feeling as though he stood before me describing it himself. He writes about the challenges one faces while on safari along with the excitement of a shooting safari. I found his book highly enjoyable.

Green Hills of Africa
by Ernest Hemingway

Not surprisingly, Hemingway was an avid hunter. In this book he describes his adventures in Africa while on safari, and one can see how this writer enjoyed going for a walk in the bush in search of game. I found his descriptions of the territory and challenges he faced very enjoyable.

Shout at the Devil
by Wilbur Smith

Smith's book takes place in Africa during World War 1 and he describes how poaching made some rich, but with a very deadly cost. It is an exciting tale of soldiers of fortune willing to risk everything for the chance of striking it rich, and I found this very helpful in getting into the mind of characters some may loathe, and others may cheer.

Mark of the Lion
by Suzanne Arruda

This was book one of six of 'The Jade Del Cameron' series by Suzanne Arruda. It takes place in Africa shortly after WWI and is about an American reporter who buys a farm and chooses to spend her life in Africa. She writes about life in Africa and ends up solving murder mysteries that seem to stumble upon her by chance. There is romance, action, adventure, and mystery all in one. Her series has been one of the best I've read about Africa.

Other Books by David Lucero

The Sandman

Who's Minding the Store?

About the Author

David Lucero lives in San Diego, CA with his family. He's a US Army veteran, and loves to travel, exercise, and write books. "Writing has been my passion since I was 14 years old. You could say it's an addiction, and in a highly fulfilling way." *Big Jim* is David Lucero's third published book. Learn more about the author on his website, www.lucerobooks.com

www.ingramcontent.com/pod-product-compliance
Lightning Source LLC
Chambersburg PA
CBHW071258250626
47159CB00004B/1232